the ghost of the past . . .

Already Victoria Steane had been cleared of one murder, not too long ago. The death had been ruled a suicide, the case closed.

Now she stood in a garden, with the scent of terror heavy in the air. Facing her was the man who once had done his best to hang her.

Unbelievingly she listened to his words:

"It was murder, you know."

And then the murderer struck again . . . .

"Intricately plotted and turbulent . . . romance and mystery adroitly mixed"

Time Magazine

"A treat right up to the last word . . . a real mystery novel . . . one of the tops"

Will Cuppy
New York Herald Tribune

Books by
MIGNON G. EBERHART

Another Man's Murder
Postmark Murder
Unidentified Woman

Published by
WARNER BOOKS

MIGNON G. EBERHART

UNIDENTIFIED WOMAN

WARNER BOOKS

A Warner Communications Company

All the persons and events in this book are entirely imaginary. Nothing in it derives from anything which ever happened.

WARNER BOOKS EDITION

Copyright © 1943 by Mignon G Eberhart
Copyright © renewed 1971 by Mignon G Eberhart
All rights reserved.

Published by CBS Inc. by arrangement with
Random House, Inc.,
201 East 50th Street,
New York, N.Y. 10021
Distributed by Warner Books

Warner Books, Inc.,
666 Fifth Avenue,
New York, N.Y. 10103

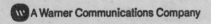 A Warner Communications Company

Printed in the United States of America

First Warner Books Printing: August, 1983

10 9 8 7 6 5 4 3 2 1

It was the last week in December that Henry Frame died.

He died under unpleasant circumstances. So unpleasant, in fact, that weeks later the memory of his death (and the manner of it) was still like a shadow hovering the house; like a figure skirting obscurely, but stubbornly, the edge of one's vision.

Not that anybody wanted to remember Henry, and not that anybody wasn't more than content to let bygones be bygones. Until, that is, an afternoon in March, over two months later. Monday, March the tenth, to be precise, a sunny day, unseasonably warm even in that semi-tropical climate: the day of the Colonel's tea party.

And it was Clistie who, that afternoon, first suggested the unpleasant memory of Henry's unpleasant death. Not that she mentioned Henry's name; for she didn't. But when the Colonel's car arrived to take them to the post, and Victoria went to tell Clistie that they were leaving, Clistie was doing a very odd thing.

It wasn't like her to do odd things. Clistie Forbes, fiftyish, thin, wiry, with observant eyes, and nubbly, devoted hands, had lived with old Mrs. Steane (Victoria's grandmother) for twenty-odd years, as housekeeper, secretary and confidante. She had run the house, the servants and the family for so long that she was a fixture, even now that old Mrs. Steane had been dead for five years and Victoria was twenty-three. And Clistie was practical and sensible. She didn't, as a rule, do the kind of thing she was doing just then.

She was sitting on a bench in a little niche made by a clump of pines quite close to the river edge and looking behind her. Looking very earnestly behind her into the clump of pines. Victoria could tell by the strained pose of her neck that she was listening.

Seconds passed and she did not move. She was as tense and still as a cat, stalking. Or, it struck Victoria unexpectedly, as some small, wary animal being stalked.

It was an extraordinary thought, although no more extraordinary than Clistie's pose. It caught and held Victoria for a moment, so that she too stood motionless on the terrace above, with the sun shining upon her bare, golden-brown hair. She was slender and erect; her small head was proudly set, so she looked taller, really, than she was. There was character in her face, with its short, straight nose and cleanly defined temple and cheek line; but just then, watching Clistie, her blue eyes looked dark and troubled, and her gay, soft, young mouth had an uncertain, worried curve. She wore a cream-colored, thin shantung dress and blue-linen sandals and carried a wide-brimmed straw hat. A light, warm breeze touched her cheeks and stirred the clump of pines. There was nothing there. Nothing to see and less to hear.

But Clistie did an even queerer thing. She got up and scuttled swiftly up the slope of green lawn and live oaks that lay between the river and the house, almost as if she were pursued. There was another bench, less sheltered, but very near the terrace, and she sat down there. She did not see Victoria; she stared down toward the river, or rather toward the pier—below which Henry Frame had died on a December night some ten weeks before.

But that was definitely in the past. Victoria took a quick breath and stepped down from the low, pillared porch, with its enchanting views of the river, through the arches made by the great liveoaks, laden and festooned with long ghostly wisps of Spanish moss.

"Clistie."

Clistie Forbes turned with a start. "Oh—Victoria! Haven't you gone to the Colonel's tea party yet?"

"We are just leaving. I came to tell you. Clistie, what were you looking at? Down there, I mean, in the pines."

"Nothing," said Clistie.

"But you—you looked as if you'd heard something. . . ."

"Did I?" said Clistie. She rose. Her greenish-brown eyes were perfectly blank. "You'd better hurry; your aunt doesn't like to be kept waiting." She led the way across the lawn, around the end of the house, toward the circle of driveway and the front entrance which were on the side opposite the river.

Victoria followed. When they reached the drive, Clistie said, "Run along, Victoria, don't keep them waiting." She gave Victoria a scrutinizing look—the kind of look she always gave her when she left the house. It all but took Victoria's chin and lifted her face to see if it was clean and if she had brushed her teeth, as Clistie had done, in fact, not so many years before. "You'll do," said Clistie, shortly and dryly, exactly as she had said it to a much younger Victoria, thin-legged and starry-eyed, in white organdy ruffles before her first dance.

6

And then Clistie added quite unexpectedly, "We ought to have some dogs."

"*Dogs!*"

"Oh, I know why we haven't. Your grandmother always hated them on account of the gardens. But it's—it's a big place," said Clistie. "On the river—in the country—with the pine woods . . ." She paused, her eyes thoughtful, then said, "Big dogs. Watch dogs."

"*Why?*"

"Oh, never mind. Only Victoria, I'm glad things are turning out as they are. For your sake. After Wednesday . . ." She paused again thoughtfully, looking at Victoria. "Yes, I'm very glad about that. Go on, now. Have a good time."

"But, Clistie . . ." began Victoria.

Aunt Bessie, sitting in the Colonel's car with Agnew and Thalia, had seen her. "Do hurry, Vicky," she called peremptorily.

Clistie turned toward the garden—a little promontory above the river, where there were chairs, a sundial and a Brittany millstone, sunk into the soil and originally level with it, but now almost hidden by the gradually encroaching soil and grass around it. Victoria waved at her and hurried to the waiting car.

By the time she reached the gates of Camp Blakoe, ten miles away, she had reassured herself. Clistie had been like that—nervous, not quite herself, really—since Henry's death. It meant, Victoria decided, exactly nothing.

Two hours later she was still sitting at one end of Colonel Bruce Galant's tea table, dispensing tea to those who wanted it, with Aunt Bessie at the other end of it, pouring coffee then unrationed. There were red roses in the middle of the lace-draped table, the flash of silver, the fragrance of coffee and cigarettes, flowers and perfumes. There were candles, though it was still daylight, and there were voices everywhere like the waves of a sea. Colonel Galant had been afraid they wouldn't talk.

Colonel Bruce Galant, tall, spare, gray-haired, born and bred in the old army tradition, was post commander at the big, new army camp. He had never married—which Bessie said was a mistake—and he was and had been for many years a close family friend of the Steanes. It was his first party and he had planned it to give the officers and their wives, pouring now into the big, new camp, a chance to get acquainted. "It shakes 'em down," he had said when he invited Victoria and Bessie. "Civilian life and army life are very different. Most of these people have been civilians all their lives; they've got to

7

blend now with the army. God knows when we'll get into the war; it may come any day. We've got to learn to work together. Maybe a few tea parties will help." "Esprit de corps," said Bessie warmly. "I see just what you mean. But it's too bad, Bruce, that you have no hostess."

The Colonel had looked briefly uneasy, as he always did when Bessie referred pointedly to his wifeless state. "But that's what I'm asking you and Victoria to do for me," he'd said quickly. "And Thalia, too, of course," he added hurriedly, lest it sound like an afterthought. They were all very careful of Thalia Frame's feelings since her father's, Henry Frame's, death.

Victoria, remembering the conversation now, glanced around the crowded little dining room. In a corner she caught a glimpse of Thalia's broad-brimmed straw hat and lovely little face, animated and smiling, between two stalwart and uniformed shoulders. Thalia was all right then.

The house was packed, and people were taking their tea or coffee out on the porch. Everyone was talking. Assiduous young lieutenants were supplying their majors' wives with cakes; the wives of the young lieutenants were exchanging confidences about living quarters; the older, more accustomed wives of the regular army officers were moving briskly about, chatting, seeing that the party "went," doing their full social duties adeptly. The party was a success, thought Victoria. Then someone moved, and she had an instant's glimpse of a face she knew too well. And for the second time that afternoon, but much more poignantly and forcefully, was reminded of Henry's death and the manner of it.

The man in the doorway, tall enough so she could see his shining black head, and brown face, and dark, hazel eyes over the heads of several people, was John Campbell. He was State's Attorney (and also, by an odd chance, the coroner) of Ponte Verde county. She knew his face too well because it was he who had been called when Henry Frame was found (drowned, below the pier, one arm caught around the willows with their leaves trailing in the muddy eddies of water over his face). John Campbell had been called because he was coroner. He had remained to investigate because he was State's Attorney, and had said Henry was murdered.

Someone was at her side. She poured tea automatically, inquired about lemon and sugar and rum, and offered the cup to a hand that came out of a uniformed sleeve and a voice that said "Thank you" and withdrew into the moving clusters of people around her.

So John Campbell was there, too! She had had only a glimpse of his face—hard and brown, with his hazel eyes

8

bright and intent—exactly as she remembered it against the gray, damp-stained walls of the little shabby courtroom—questioning her about murder.

Across the table, beyond the crimson lake of roses, Aunt Bessie was pouring coffee. Victoria absently watched her large, fleshy hands—dark and laden with rings. Bessie wasn't blonde, like the Steanes. She was dark, with masses of rather untidy hair, and large dark eyes which showed too much white. She was an emotional woman, changeable as the wind, and almost as violent. She could be unexpectedly charming and witty—and as unexpectedly would fall into fits of a brooding and melancholy silence which might last for days.

Her thick hand, with its winking diamonds, clutched the silver coffee-pot and stopped pouring. It was that that caught Victoria's attention: the silver coffee-pot held motionless in mid-air. She looked at Bessie, and Bessie was looking at someone near Victoria. Staring, really, her dark eyes showing white, startled rims. Victoria turned abruptly to follow Bessie's look.

John Campbell was standing beside her. He was wearing a uniform; there were the maple leaves of a major upon his shoulders. He was looking down at her, his eyes smiling but very bright and intent in his brown face, as she remembered them. He said, pleasantly, "How are you, Miss Steane? I see you don't remember me. I'm John Campbell."

She had not seen him since the investigation following Henry's death had ended; she remembered him altogether too well.

The brown stream started pouring again from the coffee-pot in Bessie's jeweled hand; but Bessie was nervous, thrusting the cup at the girl who stood waiting to receive it, pushing cream and sugar toward her, casting oblique watchful glances at John Campbell, at Victoria, trying to hear what was said. Rather oddly, too, in that moment, Victoria noted the girl who took the cup of coffee, helped herself to sandwiches and moved away. She was about Victoria's age, a thin, pretty blonde, with an efficient air that somehow gave an impression of officialdom, yet she was not in uniform so could not have been one of the hostesses. The girl, neat and thin in her gray, tailored silk dress, with a demure white collar and cuffs, moved away. Victoria said to John Campbell, "Tea?"

"No," he said. "That is—oh, well, yes. I'm afraid I startled you. Of course I realize that your recollection of me isn't a very pleasant one. But I—you see, I saw you from across the room. And I wonder if you could get away from this. There's something I want to talk to you about."

But there couldn't be anything he needed to say to her;

9

even if he meant to apologize, she didn't want to hear it. She said stiffly, "Sugar? Lemon?"

"I don't know. Neither. That is, yes, both. Look here, Miss Steane, I really would like to talk to you for a moment."

She dropped sugar in the cup and gave it to him without looking up. She said, "All that trouble about Henry's death is over. I suppose you were only doing what you thought was your duty. But now it is in the past and I hope will be forgotten."

He stirred the tea slowly, the silver spoon making a small tinkle against the cup. Around them voices and people and cigarette smoke and the little clatter of china, rose and fell in eddies. Aunt Bessie had been hailed by some friend and was carrying on a conversation with her; but she was still watching Victoria and John Campbell and trying to hear what they were saying, too. John Campbell said, "Yes, I understand. It was unfortunate, all of it. I . . ." He stopped and seemed to arrange what he wanted to say. "I wouldn't remind you of it," he said then, rather carefully, "if I didn't think it was necessary."

Necessary? Her head went up so she met his eyes directly.

"But that's all over," she said swiftly again. "The case is closed." She stopped abruptly because of the grave look in his face. He said, gravely too, "I hope so."

2

"*Hope so!*" Her voice sounded high and frightened. She caught it and her breath to a more normal level, and said, "What do you mean?"

There was an effect of hesitation in his reply, again, as if he waited to consider it. "Look here," he said. "Outside the door from the library there's a side path leading down to the lake. Will you meet me there, say, in about fifteen or twenty minutes? Or whenever you can get away from here?"

"But—but there's nothing," she began. He said abruptly, "Please. I'll wait for you there."

Someone behind him said, "Hi, John. So you're in the army now. . . ." He turned to reply and moved away. A voice at her other side said briskly, "More tea, Vicky, please. Lots of sugar and cake from the looks of her—it's for my major's wife." It was Hollis. His voice broke off, then he said, lower, "Vicky, who was that tall, black-haired fellow talking to you? It looked like the fellow that accused you of pushing Henry into the river."

"Yes. That's who it was. John Campbell."

"I thought so. That's right, his name was Campbell. All done up in uniform now! Well, did you put a pinch of cyanide in his tea?"

"No," she said shortly, lifting the tea-pot.

"An opportunity wasted," said Hollis. "God, it's hot. So this is army life! Wonder what it'll be like if and when we get into the war! How do you like the Colonel's little pep meeting?"

Hollis Isham was, unlike his mother, very fair—a hard blond, with a long face that flushed easily, and cold, light-blue eyes. He had, however, his mother's gift of unexpected charm. He and Agnew were actually Victoria's second cousins. Bessie Steane Isham (widowed many years before) had been a first cousin to Victoria's father. The family was small, however, and Bessie and Victor Steane had been more like brother and sister than cousins. After Victor, and then old Mrs. Steane, died, Bessie had taken Victoria under her own somewhat tempestuous wing, along with her two sons. Since Victoria's house was big—too big, Victoria often felt—Bessie and Agnew and Hollis lived with her. Bessie liked Victoria, quarreled with Clistie, bore with Agnew (barely eighteen) and adored Hollis.

Now Hollis' slender, handsome face was a little flushed; his blond hair lay in tight, damp-looking ringlets. He looked very slim and very elegant in his uniform. Victoria said, "Don't talk like that, Hollis."

"Afraid somebody will hear me? Suppose they do! Where's the cake? Oh, I see. I've got a leave tonight. I'm coming home with you to the festive dinner party. See you later, darling."

He waved gracefully at Bessie, whose dark eyes had lighted instantly and who was watching him with an adoring smile, and went into the living room.

The clusters of people around the table were thinning out. Thalia had disappeared. At the door of the little hall Colonel Galant was shaking hands with a few people who were leaving. Victoria glanced around the almost empty room and got up.

Bessie was talking to a corpulent medical-corps officer, or rather listening to him. Phrases floated to Victoria's ears. " . . the good old days of cavalry. Lots of broken bones in those days. Oh, well, no war is ever like another war. . . . And when we once actually get into this war, as we're going to do, we'll be all set to move quickly."

Bessie lifted her eyebrows inquiringly at Victoria, who said, "No more customers, darling. I'm resigning. . . ."

"We weren't given tea in the old days, either," said the Colonel, and lifted his cup with a look of intense dislike. Victoria went into the little library adjoining the dining room.

Agnew was there, tall and lanky, blinking nearsightedly because he wasn't wearing his spectacles and munching sandwiches rather morosely from a large heap on his plate. Victoria sidled through clusters of uniforms, of print silk dresses and wide straw hats, reached his side and put predatory fingers on the sandwiches.

He peered at her. "Hey, don't take all the pâté ones; the chicken are as good. Or almost," said Agnew, and watched her brown fingers anxiously. "Oh, Vicky, you are a pig."

"Pig, yourself," she said, eyeing the remaining heap. "Where is Thalia?"

"I don't know, but I can tell you just the same. In the center of the largest circle of uniforms."

"I'm glad she's having a good time," said Victoria absently. They munched in silence for a moment, and Victoria thought again of Henry Frame.

In its essentials, it was a simple enough story: a trusted employee, Henry Frame, embezzled over a long period of years. When he was threatened with exposure, he committed suicide.

Those were the facts. It was the circumstances that had made it so difficult for all of them. John Campbell, thought Victoria, had been largely responsible for the significance those circumstances took on—as if he'd painted them, adroitly, with sinister colors. Yet in their true colors the circumstances were altogether comprehensible.

Victor Steane, Victoria's father, dying and knowing he was dying, had sent for Henry Frame. That was over fifteen years before; Victoria was a child of eight or so, and old Mrs. Steane, her grandmother, was still alive. The Steane Mills, at the time of Victor Steane's death, had been flourishing. It was an era of building and prosperity, and the mills—lumber mills—under Victor Steane's control and ownership had been at the time of his death at a peak of production. And there was no one in his family to take over the management of the mills. His mother was old; his wife had died several years before; Victoria was almost a baby. Bessie Isham knew nothing of the business, and, at the time of Victor Steane's death, Hollis was twelve and Agnew three. Some time, it was the tacit understanding, a place would be made for each of them, if he wanted it, in the mills. But then there was literally no one to take over the management of the business; no one, that is, but Henry Frame. Henry Frame knew the business; he was Victor Steane's trusted employee and closest friend.

In order further to protect his mother and his daughter, and having, as all of them had always had, the fullest confidence in Henry Frame, Victor had also provided against

12

his removal from the management of the business. Henry himself could resign and still retain his block of Steane Mills stock, but no one could force him to resign without proof of what Victor Steane called, in what he must have considered an ironic little phrase, "flagrant dereliction of duty."

In the end, of course, the arrangement worked out so that Henry Frame was actually accountable to no one. He was not only the manager of the business; he was its unquestioned czar. It would take months for the accountants to disentangle the past records. It was all coming out slowly. The important fact was that Henry Frame, that gray, dry, tight-lipped little man with winking, serious eyeglasses had, over a long period of years, systematically and simply, stolen from the business placed in his care and from, naturally, Victoria and Bessie, and Bessie's children.

It wouldn't have come out when it did; it wouldn't have come out for years, perhaps, if Victoria hadn't asked for more money that winter. She was given, of course, enough to live on; by pinching pennies she could keep up the house which Victor Steane, having nothing else to do with his money, had built on the beautiful banks of the St. Sebastian shortly before his wife's death. It was the house that was expensive and a drain on the money Henry sent her. Her other expenses could be and were simplified—ridiculously simplified, Bessie had often said, for a young woman in her position. But none of them, ever, had questioned Henry's integrity, or his wisdom.

Until that winter—when for the first time Victoria began to inquire into the business. It was a war year in Europe; and war was coming—sooner than anyone then realized—to America. She was supposed to be a very rich young woman. Yet she had no money in her own hands. Up to then there hadn't been anything that she wanted to do with money passionately enough, to induce her to make a stand against Henry. But that winter every mail brought legitimate and heartbreaking appeals for help and the next winter was to bring more.

It takes money to buy and equip ambulances or to clothe and feed the homeless. Victoria asked for more money.

In the end, Henry Frame had come from New York to see her. He'd brought Thalia, his daughter. He'd been fatherly, kind, indulgent with Victoria, until that last dreadful interview when Victoria, not suspecting Henry's dishonesty, had insisted. She had told him that it was time she took a more direct interest in the business of which she owned so large a share, and that she intended to do so.

That was at night, after dinner—a cold, chill night just after Christmas with a fog heavy upon the river and upon the house. It was the next morning when Henry had been found drowned.

But they didn't know, then, that he had such a motive for suicide. So John Campbell had said it was murder; had said it *must* be murder—and had investigated.

Of them all Clistie had had no motive—unless devotion to Victoria might provide one. The servants had no discernible motives, although they were investigated. Michael Bayne could conceivably have had a motive; he was manager of the small and relatively unimportant West-Coast office of the Steane Mills and had come on only a few days before to meet Henry. Michael was investigated, too. Bessie (and Hollis and Agnew) and Victoria, however, had solid, hard and fast motives. Not one of them could get control of the business or of any more money than Henry chose to give them as long as he held the purse strings, and as long as he was sane, as he undoubtedly was, and not guilty (as far as any of them knew or guessed) of any "flagrant dereliction of duty." And as long as he was alive. Naturally, Victoria who had rebelled against Henry; who had quarreled with him (a quarrel, which, unluckily, was overheard by one of the maids and extracted from her by John Campbell); Victoria, who owned by far the largest single block of Steane Mills stock, had the strongest motive of them all for killing Henry.

There followed about three weeks of horror. It was nothing else. The coroner's inquest—adjourned. The newspapers. The columns of print. The pictures. The inquiry. The nine-days' wonder of it.

And then the fact of Henry's long embezzlement had been uncovered. The decision of the coroner's jury had been suicide.

Thalia, a victim of Henry's death in spite of anything they could do, stayed on with them. Henry had not only embezzled money; he had made a series of fantastically unsound investments with it. There was no question of restitution. Luckily, however, he had been cautious enough not to kill the goose that laid golden eggs for him, and the business itself was in good shape. Henry had stolen only from its profits. Thus Victoria could easily provide for Thalia, and would; it was the least she could do. All of them, even Agnew, who didn't much like Thalia, had done what they could to make her forget the bitterness and tragedy of Henry's death.

Agnew polished off the last sandwich and reached for a plate of little cakes he had cached on top of some bookshelves. Victoria glanced at her watch.

"What's the matter with you?" said Agnew. "Got a date?"

"Yes," said Victoria, making up her mind.

14

"Good," said Agnew, heartily. "I approve. After all, day after tomorrow is Wednesday." His face sharpened. "Who?"

"Nobody I like," said Victoria a little grimly. "See you later."

She took a small chocolate cake, ignored a sharp and protesting cry from Agnew, and edged toward the door at the other side of the room.

Probably it hadn't been twenty minutes; probably it was a mistake to meet John Campbell; but certainly, she was not afraid to talk to him. The case, however, was over and closed; that was a hard and solid fact, no matter what John Campbell thought of it.

She let herself quietly out the door. There was a small, newly graveled path leading down to the lake, which lay in a long half-moon and sparkled now with gold from the low western sun. There were clusters of palms along the strip of sandy beach, which were outlined sharply and gracefully against the clear sky and gold-dappled water, and gave the scene a tropical note. There were pines, too, feathery and green, bending to the light breeze.

The great, not yet completed army camp lay behind her, far-flung and shimmering in the sun. It was an enormous camp, with acres and acres of long, low buildings that were offices or mess halls, or hospitals, and acres and acres of tents, built up sturdily with sidewalls of lumber and screens inside the brown canvas. Scattered groups of bungalows, new and bright with paint, were officers' houses.

A few months before there had been nothing there but sand and palmetto and pines; now, miraculously, it was a city—an unfinished as yet but already a strangely military city with sentries, gun parks, magazines and great areas of storehouses, now heavily guarded. Armies of workmen and construction engineers had come; and many of them were still there, although now the first waves of America's new army were beginning to pour into camp. During the early weeks of construction visitors were permitted to come in and out of the camp; now that troops were actually arriving, more and more of them every day, the discipline of a great army camp was being rapidly tightened. War was still in the future; yet preparations were already being made in case of war, on a vast scale and with great wisdom and foresight.

It was Colonel Galant's task to head and establish that organization down to the most minute detail, and in the shortest possible time. It was a big and important task; one that required untiring energy, knowledge and experience. A month before the camp had been an unwieldy and, to the eye of an outsider, a hopelessly confusing area of half-finished roads,

15

and buildings; a month from then it was to be a perfectly organized, smoothly functioning military post, geared to top notch efficiency. It lay now, as if momentarily caught and photographed in that swift process of change and development sprawling in the sun, alive with troops, and guns and great fleets of army trucks waiting for America's entrance into the war, which even then was felt to be inevitable. Looking back, Victoria could see the flag above the parade ground lifted a little in the breeze, so its colors were bold and clear and beautiful against the quiet sky.

It was almost sunset; in a few more minutes it would be taken down. She strolled on toward the lake.

To Victoria, the swift building of the great camp, and the speed and efficiency with which a huge military machine was blossoming into operation had been exciting and awe-inspiring. She had watched it from the beginning; everyone who lived in the vicinity of the camp had watched it burgeon and spread like a tremendous plant. She wasn't really of the army, no more, that is, than thousands of other women whose lives were then, and later to be caught up and enmeshed in a national need. Colonel Galant had been sent there as post-commander and had, naturally, made her house what Agnew called his "home from home." Hollis, leaving his not very important position in the New York office of the Steane Mills when he was conscripted, had had the good luck to be sent to Camp Blakoe. Friends at a distance were constantly writing to Bessie or to Victoria: little introductory notes asking them to look up this or that friend who was coming to stay near her husband who was at camp.

Bessie always did so and had little dinner parties. Hollis brought his friends home. Agnew adored anything in uniform —except Hollis, who to Agnew was no different in uniform than Hollis in mufti, although to Bessie, obviously, Hollis was the whole United States Army; and even Clistie, who had never got on too well with Hollis, softened and saw to it that the cookie box was full. Pine Beach, the nearest city of any size, was almost a hundred miles away; there were a few very small towns dotted here and there in the vicinity of Camp Blakoe—lazy, little Southern towns, jogging along their quiet way, were already all but overwhelmed with the sudden tide of men and business which rolled upon them in the wake of the great army camp, crowding their streets and stores and hotels, packing the motion-picture theatres, snatching up every house and every room that could be lived in until a town of, say, fifteen hundred persons was suddenly augmented in population to ten times that. Dotted along the lovely, tranquil banks of the St. Sebastian River, there was a

16

sprinkling, but only a sprinkling, of country houses, and to these inevitably much of the social life of the camp drifted. Victoria's house was one of them, and Bessie, a born hostess, frankly enjoyed it. All in all, Camp Blakoe was an integral part of their lives.

After, that is, the rather dreadful interlude following Henry Frame's death, during which they avoided seeing anyone— although it had occurred during the time when the camp was being built and before it was actually occupied.

She stopped at the edge of the lake, took off her hat, and let the light breeze touch her face and her smooth, high pompadour, while she looked thoughtfully across the lake to where a village, swollen far beyond its normal size, lay snugly on the farther shore. There were already a few lights.

What was John Campbell going to say to her?

The case is ended, she'd said. And he'd said, quietly, "I hope so."

She turned at the crisp sound of footsteps, and John Campbell was coming toward her along the path.

Probably, all her life, she would shrink from anything that reminded her of the weeks following Henry's death. That, of course, included John Campbell.

She didn't feel any particular grudge; she didn't hate him. She had been, she supposed, afraid of him; all of them had been afraid of him, except, perhaps, Thalia, whose gentle poise had never wavered for an instant under his inquiry. But then Thalia had not been suspected of murder.

He looked well in uniform, she thought; the trim lines suited the swinging, graceful way he walked, and the way he carried his black head. He, too, she admitted rather grudgingly to herself, had charm—the kind that is as elusive as the rain and as unconscious. It was in his rare smile; in the way his brown face lighted; in his bright, discerning hazel eyes. But he had force, too, a suggestion of latent strength below that pleasantly impersonal manner.

But he looked different in uniform. She remembered him in tweeds, browns and grays—well-tailored, perhaps, but loose and likely to sag at the pockets, owing, she'd discovered, to a habit of carrying a supply of dog biscuits for his setters. Several times he had turned up with rather startling informality in riding habit—well enough tailored, too, but shabby and worn. There had been nothing informal, however, about his inquiry.

As he approached her, indeed, she remembered everything about him, even quite small things, such as the touch of gray above one temple, and the little laugh lines around his eyes. She even remembered his hands, long and brown, too, and the

17

way he wore a seal ring, so the seal, to her, looked upside down.

It was really disconcerting to remember anybody like that, so well and so familiarly that she and John Campbell might have been friends all their lives; as if indeed some very close relationship had existed between them, so every line and every look was inexpressibly familiar to the other. Lovers would remember each other like that.

. She thought that unexpectedly and caught it back as if it had wings and might escape her. It was, of course, the reverse of their relationship. They had been enemies, rather—a hunter and his quarry. A State's Attorney and his principal suspect. A policeman and his prisoner.

Well, in any case, all that was over.

Nevertheless, as 'he neared her, her hands tightened around the brim of her hat. She didn't know that she had taken almost exactly the pose with which she had many times answered the steady pound of his questions—head up, eyes direct and blue and defiant—and frightened below that defiance.

He came to her and stopped. Suddenly, with an impulsive quickness that she had never heard in his voice before, he said, "Victoria, I am sorry; I didn't mean to frighten you."

She had braced herself for that meeting. She saw the different, less-guarded look in his eyes without, actually, seeing it. She heard her first name—he'd always called her Miss Steane, pleasantly; never anything else—without actually hearing it. Later she remembered both. Then she said, stiffly, "I'm not frightened. What do you want to tell me?"

There was an instant of silence. As if waiting for a signal, the sun seemed to drop down in that instant, below the rim of the lake, leaving only a rosy afterglow.

The look in his face imperceptibly changed; his voice, when he spoke was not impulsive and quick; it was as she remembered it, pleasantly impersonal and cool.

He looked away from her, out across the lake. "I'm sorry. But I . . . The fact is, Miss Steane . . ." He paused so long then that it was as if she paused too, her heart and her breath and her thought. Finally he said, abruptly, as if he hadn't been able to think of a better way to say it, "The fact is, the coroner's inquest was wrong—about Henry Frame, I mean. It *was* murder, you know."

3

It was suddenly darker. All the brave color had left the sky, for the flag was gone too, with the sun. The lake took on a

18

slate color and looked secretive and sullen. Lights in the village across the lake gleamed now very distantly from blue haze. All at once, instinctively, Victoria was aware of the land, a dark, semi-tropical land; sand and swamp and ragged, stark, pine forests surrounding the camp, threatening it, resenting this man-made intrusion upon its age-old silence and mysterious, un-empty emptiness. Certain land has that quality at night; as if its own being and strength and primeval entity emerge then, intangibly but strongly—threateningly.

She had to say something. *But it wasn't true. Henry hadn't been murdered. There was nobody to murder him.*

The tall man beside her turned quickly toward her again. "I really am sorry. But, don't you see, I had to tell you."

There was another instant of silence; his eyes were as dark as the slate-gray lake below them. He said, rather gently, "Let's walk for a bit. The path goes along the lake for half a mile or so." He put his hand lightly on her arm and she walked slowly along the graveled path beside him. Above them, people were leaving the Colonel's little white house; there were cars and voices and lights. Ahead on the long slope above the lake, a newly arrived regiment was parking its equipment wearily, but with hair's breadth precision, so that the long lines of dun-colored, high-wheeled army trucks were in close, orderly rows, and the great, mounted guns pointed across the lake, a solid, brooding rank against the darkening sky.

War and rumors of war, and the heavy distant tread of the Four Horsemen.

Victoria thought that, too, as if thought of the immediate present—of John Campbell and the thing he had said—was blocked off completely, switched to some other track than one that entered her own mind.

But that was nonsense. She must think and talk and tell him he was wrong. That there was all that proof.

John Campbell said quietly, "I'd better explain. You see, the whole thing is, I'm in the army now. I'm not State's Attorney now; and I'm not the coroner. I never wanted to be coroner anyway, but there wasn't anybody else who'd take the job for the small pay, and I had the time for it. It's a very sparsely populated county—or was before the camp was built —and taxes were low and salaries for county officials low, too; we were all very poor here, you know. Somebody had to be coroner, and the job was wished on me. But that's not the point. The point is that, now, I'm not State's Attorney and coroner. I'm not official in that sense at all. Anything I say now is just—just as a citizen. Anybody."

She said, "Why . . . ?" falteringly, and stopped.

"Why am I telling you this? Because I think I have to. At the time I had to go along with the decision of the coroner's jury; I couldn't . . ." He paused there rather oddly, as if he'd checked himself, and changed it. "I didn't combat the jury's decision. I had given them all the evidence, all my reasons . . ." Again he seemed to scrutinize his own word and change it. "Most of my reasons for believing it to be murder. Their decision, in view of the evidence Bayne turned up, was suicide. So I—in the end I let it ride."

"Henry knew he was faced with disclosure! He knew that this time I wouldn't give up. He knew I intended to learn about the business. He knew . . ."

"Do you think you would have found evidence of his stealing? Evidences he had successfully kept covered for years?"

"Yes. I . . ." She stopped and said more honestly, "Not right away. I knew nothing about the business. But nevertheless he was frightened. It meant disclosure in the end."

There was a little pause. Then John Campbell said pleasantly, "Perhaps. But he would have had time—time to hide any traces, time to think, time to rearrange affairs. He wasn't threatened with disclosure immediately, the next day."

"But why are you telling me this now? Why do you say he was murdered?"

An airplane, faintly yellow in the gathering dusk, swooped out of it away above, its engine very loud and staccato. It whirled slowly around the camp and away again toward the naval base, before John Campbell replied, and then it was not a reply. He said, obliquely, as the sound of the engine drew away, "You know all the evidence as well as I know it."

"I know that he was found drowned. But he couldn't swim and never had been able to swim, so he wouldn't have gone into the river without intending to. Therefore I think it *was* intentional—suicide. You said somebody saw to it that he drowned. I know I had had a quarrel with him and a silly little maid heard part of it and repeated what she heard, and you believed her. . . ."

"You admitted it," he said. "You admitted that you'd told him you were helpless as long as he lived; that you couldn't remove him from his position as manager, that you couldn't make him give you more money. You admitted his anger."

"But I didn't murder him! There was no evidence of murder, except—except a scratch on the pier, and you said it was made by the heel of his shoe, as if somebody had struggled with him there. And there was a bruise on his head, and you said somebody could have struck him—not enough to kill him but to make him unconscious. So when he was pushed into the river, even if he recovered consciousness, there was noth-

20

ing he could do but drown. That's the evidence—all of it."

"No, that isn't all," said John Campbell. There was a sudden surge of harshness in his voice. He said, staring straight ahead of him, his brown jaw hard, "You've forgotten the most important thing. That's the fact that he was the kind of man someone might want to murder."

It sounded almost as if he'd known Henry. Victoria cried, "But you didn't know him! You knew nothing of him, or of me. Yet you accused me of murder!"

"You had the strongest motive," he said shortly, looking straight ahead. "But, as you say, that's in the past. I only meant to tell you—now—that while I was an official my hands were tied. I had to accept the coroner's jury's verdict and call the case closed. And, besides, we really were up against a stone wall of no evidence. Motive, yes; but real and concrete evidence, no. We explored every possibility. I was, at least, convinced that there was nothing more to be done. I wanted to keep the case open, but the verdict was suicide. I couldn't argue with it. But then, today, seeing you here, it seemed to me that I had a kind of—duty. I still believe he was murdered. Therefore—well, murder is not a nice thing, you know. It's like a tiger lying in wait. Like a madman in ambush, hidden."

She said, in a stifled way, "You are trying to frighten me."

"No, I . . ." He broke off, and turned to face her, putting his hands hard around her wrists as if to compel her to listen. "*Yes*," he said. "Yes, I suppose that's exactly what I'm trying to do. Murder is what I said it was. And there's so much money—your money now, altogether your own. It's so important to so many people. So horribly important. Do you understand?"

"No. You are warning me! As if someone murdered Henry and my money was the cause!"

"I only want you to understand that—that might be the cause of it. If I knew the truth . . ."

"You mean if you knew who murdered him?" she cried sharply. "But no one murdered him! He couldn't have been . . ." She paused, checked by a sudden thought. She said slowly, "You don't believe, now, that *I* murdered him?"

"No. I don't believe that you murdered him."

"Did you ever really believe it?"

He didn't draw away from her, but there was a sense of withdrawal. His eyes didn't waver but still, in their depths, were suddenly remote and inscrutable.

"The evidence—the motive, rather, pointed toward you."

As if someone else were putting words into her mouth, Victoria went on, "Would you have sent me to the Grand

21

Jury with a request for an indictment?"

He started to speak and stopped, his mouth so tight that the hesitation was incongruous. Then he said rather heavily, "Yes."

For a long moment neither spoke. An automobile door slammed above them, on the slope toward the Colonel's house —loud in the stillness. The sound of the airplane had died away long ago, so there was only silence in the sky and on the lake. Lights were all over the camp now, outlining tent walls, and shining bright and clear from mess-hall windows. It was much darker. Even the crimson afterglow had left the sky, and a white-feather moon rode high and soft. Victoria could see it over the shoulder of the tall man in uniform before her —serene and quiet in the twilight sky.

She knew he was looking fixedly down at her, and, as if he'd spoken, but rather slowly, she turned and met his intent, hazel eyes. His clasp on her wrists relaxed; he took both her hands in his own.

Another door slammed sharply somewhere. It was the side door into the Colonel's house, thought Victoria in a rather remote way; as if the Colonel's house and the camp and the car—waiting for her now—were very far away.

"Why?" she said. "*Why* have you—told me this? Don't you see that you've said too much not to say more?"

It broke the curiously quiet moment. He looked away from her eyes and down at his hands holding her own. His peaked, slender black eyebrows gave a small, rather surprised lift; he released her hands gently.

"I was wrong to do it. I thought I had to tell you, to—to warn you, I suppose. I've only alarmed you, needlessly."

Agnew was coming down the path from the Colonel's brightly lighted little house. It was Agnew, she thought, who had slammed the door. She could hear his footsteps plunging along the sloping gravel path toward them. Halfway he stopped, picked up a stone and shied it toward the lake, where it splashed loudly. As Agnew waited to watch the widening circles, she said, *"Warn me against what?"*

Agnew's tall, lanky figure started toward them again. John Campbell said, "I don't know. If I knew—but I don't. It's only the fact of murder, unsolved; unsettled. Perhaps—unfinished. But I've no proof. I'm sorry I spoke to you. It was an impulse, seeing you here. I was wrong."

Agnew, scuffling gravel loudly, came up to them. "Vicky, for gosh' sake, come on. Everybody's waiting. You'll be late to your own wedding." He saw the maple leaf on John Campbell's shoulder and stopped abruptly. A major, in Agnew's opinion, was not to be hustled out of the way. "But it's all right," he said quickly, admiring the maple leaf. "We can wait. Don't hurry, Vicky."

He hadn't recognized John Campbell; he had eyes only for the uniform. John Campbell said to Victoria, "Wedding! *Your* wedding?"

"Yes." She put her hand on Agnew's bony wrist. "Agnew, you remember Mr. Campbell. Major Campbell."

"Major . . ." Agnew peered more closely at Major Campbell's face. He stiffened. "Oh," he said. "Yes, I remember." He added reluctantly, coldly polite, "How are you, sir?"

Major Campbell spoke pleasantly but rather quickly to Agnew and turned to Victoria again. "Your wedding! When is it to be?"

"Wednesday."

"They're waiting, Vick," said Agnew, face sulky, pale-blue eyes watching John Campbell.

"Wednesday! But—that's day after tomorrow! Who is the man? Isham?"

Agnew had put his hand on her arm. She said quickly, "No, not Hollis! It's Michael Bayne I'm going to marry. You remember him."

"Oh," said Major Campbell. "Yes, I remember him. I ought to have said, 'Who's the lucky man?' Well, good wishes. You'll be leaving here, then, very soon?"

Agnew uttered an impatient puff and tugged covertly at her arm. "Very soon," said Victoria, and added, unexpectedly, "Thank you."

"Don't thank me. Tell Bayne what I've just told you," said Major Campbell, and put out his hand. She put her own hand in it; he gave it a brief, hard pressure, and said rather perfunctorily, "I hope you'll be very happy," and turned away.

"Do hurry along, Vicky," said Agnew impatiently. She had a last quick glimpse of John Campbell's tall, uniformed figure swinging down the path into the dusk, the white gravel crunching briskly. Agnew's thin hand at her elbow pushed her toward the house while he muttered crossly in her ear. "What do you want to talk to a guy like that for! My God, Victoria, he'd have had you in jail last winter, if he'd had his way! My God!"

"Don't swear," said Victoria automatically.

"Yes, but—oh, come along. Mike's probably at home waiting, while you moon about with an ex-policeman!"

"He was State's Attorney."

"It doesn't matter what he was," snapped Agnew, sounding like his mother. "What'd he mean, to tell Mike what he'd just told you? What'd he tell you?"

23

"Oh—nothing really."

"You mean nothing you want to tell me. My gosh," said Agnew peevishly, "when will you stop treating me like a baby? What'd he talk to you about? Come on, tell me. I'll not tell anybody."

"Nothing, I tell you," said Victoria suddenly impatient. "He just—talked about Henry's death. . . ."

"Well, I could have guessed that. What'd he say exactly? Did he apologize for the way he treated you?"

"Well, yes, in a way," said Victoria, grasping at it. Agnew was as curious as a cat and as quietly tenacious.

Agnew said, "I suppose if you won't tell me, you won't. Never mind. I'll find out."

"Find out what?" asked Hollis, lounging into the little library. "Everybody's waiting for you two. What are you so busy talking about?"

"We're coming now," said Victoria, and walked past him into the living room. Agnew and Hollis followed, Agnew saying nothing so ostentatiously that Hollis gave him a sharp and inquisitive glance. But he said pleasantly, "Colonel's coming to the house to dinner too. All in honor of your precious Michael, darling. Though why you want to marry him when . . ."

Agnew interrupted, "When she could have had you," he said, with a cackle of laughter.

"Right for once," said Hollis, his fine, slender face unmoved and his light eyes very blank and still. "Some time your tongue's going to get too clever for you, little brother."

Bessie and Colonel Galant were at the front door. Thalia was strolling toward the driveway, escorted by three obsequious, elegantly uniformed young officers. Bessie glanced at her two sons, and said quickly, "Now boys, don't quarrel. Where on earth have you been, Victoria?"

"She's been with me," said Agnew, his thin face so expressionless that Victoria wondered, not for the first time, at his powers of concealment.

The Colonel's car was waiting for them—a dun-colored army car with a respectful boy in uniform at the wheel. The three officers bowed with much style as it moved away, and Hollis, sitting beside the driver, laughed. "I'm in august company," he said over his shoulder. "It isn't often I get bowed to by my superiors."

"I think it was Thalia who got the bows," said the Colonel. "Vicky, my dear, you should be sitting here, and not on the jump seat. Am I so old my bones have to be deferred to?"

"It isn't your bones," said Victoria; "it's your position."

Agnew chanted, "It's in the book. Ranking officer sits in

24

the right-hand corner of the rear seat. Here's a sentry, Colonel."

The Colonel chuckled, then gravely returned the sentry's salute.

Thalia, in the back seat, held her hat against the breeze. She was looking, as always, very pretty: pale-pink crepe outlined her beautiful little figure; her wide pink hat shaded her small face and gave it and her soft dark eyes, and her full, pretty red mouth an extra touch of mystery and loveliness. She said softly, "Vicky, wasn't that John Campbell? I mean the tall dark man in a major's uniform that talked to you—so long—at the tea table."

"Tall, dark and handsome," said Agnew in a disapproving mutter.

"Yes," said Victoria briefly. "That was Major Campbell."

"That's what I thought," said Thalia. Her voice was perfectly even and gentle; yet, oddly, it seemed to Victoria to have an undertone of a kind of amusement.

But that was wrong, she decided swiftly. John Campbell could arouse only tragic and sad memories for Thalia Frame.

They went on smoothly, past acres of tents, lighted now, and long, low buildings that loomed up ghostly in the gathering twilight. They passed gun parks and commissaries and at last the gate where another sentry saluted smartly. There the car turned into the public highway. Victoria, however, sat in silence, thinking, not even hearing the desultory conversation going on in the car.

Suppose John Campbell was right! Suppose Henry Frame had been murdered! Suppose the case was not really ended at all!

4

It was an unwelcome and a horrible thought; it leaped into her mind and fastened itself there as if it had claws.

For people are not murdered by accident and people are not murdered by strangers.

During the time of the investigation Victoria had never, even for an instant, believed it was murder. She had never even briefly given credence to such a theory about Henry's death. It had to be accident or suicide, for there was no one to murder Henry. She, the entire family, had taken the instantaneous and unwavering stand that there was no question of murder. John Campbell—on the most charitable basis of explanation—was mistaken; young, zealous, determined, and mistaken. It had been simply and sheerly impossible to entertain for an instant the notion that one of them had killed a man.

It was still impossible to do so. John Campbell was wrong.

Yet she could not stop thinking of her talk with him and the things he had said—although to permit herself to do so was like looking over a precipice, up to now veiled in clouds, which opened to reveal ugly and dangerous depths at her feet.

She was so engrossed in thought that she was surprised when they turned in at the gates of the house, passed the gate cottage (occupied by the gardener, who never paid any attention to the cars that came and went), and the scent of orange blossoms from the grove north of the house came into the car. Orange blossoms—Clistie intended her to wear them on her rose-point cap, on Wednesday. With the wedding lunch in the garden where the azaleas were blooming in pink and crimson masses.

"The bridegroom's here," said Agnew, and nudged her with his sharp elbow. "Wake up, Victoria. We're home, and there's Mike's car."

"She hasn't said a word for ten miles," said Hollis, and helped her out of the car. The moon was white and shining now; touching the roofs and gables of the long house with silver; there were lights in it, everywhere. Michael's long gray coupe in the driveway glistened whitely. He had flown from Seattle, but had sent his car on, a week before, to Pine Beach, where there was an airport. The door was open, and Clistie (already dressed for dinner, in the new brown lace and chiffon dress she'd made for the wedding) was standing there beside the smiling Negro butler, waiting for them.

Michael was upstairs, changing, she said, and in another few minutes they would have been late for dinner. "Dinner's at eight and you'll want cocktails first," said Clistie. "You want a drink right now, don't you, Colonel?"

She led him toward the drawing room. Victoria lingered a little, as the other went upstairs, in front of the long mirror in the hall. How long had it been since she'd seen Michael—five weeks, was it? That was half the time of their entire acquaintance; when they'd told the family of their engagement everybody had exclaimed. But you've only known each other since Christmas, they'd said, particularly Aunt Bessie.

Yet the way she and Michael had known each other, the peculiar situation they'd been plunged into had counted far more than years of a desultory social acquaintance. Time alone didn't matter.

She hesitated, looking at herself rather doubtfully. Brides were supposed to look beautiful. She took lipstick from her bag and touched it to her mouth, sleeked her shining pompa-

26

dour up another fraction of an inch, and turned toward the stairway.

Michael, she knew, was in the green guestroom, midway in the hall. Clistie had put flowers in it that morning. Victoria stopped at the door, intending to knock, and then didn't. Michael had just arrived; he was probably in the bathtub or shaving. She went on to her own room where the lights were on, the curtains drawn and her dress laid out. It was a new dress too, pale yellow chiffon with a full skirt. There were slippers to match and fresh violets in a vase on the dressing table to be worn at the v at her throat.

She took up the little gold clock beside the violets on the dressing table. Everyone, some time, had been struck with the relentlessness of time and Victoria was then. What *was* time, she thought, ticking away like that in the hollow of her hand? Measured and weighed, yet wholly mysterious, imponderable, and forever escaping. Forty-two hours made Wednesday noon.

She put down the clock abruptly, and opened the wall of mirrored cupboards.

Thinking of time, though, and thinking, in spite of herself, of Major John Campbell and what he had said, she forgot to put on the violets and selected the wrong slippers. Descending the stairway, she discovered her mistake; the gilded narrow straps that made the toes of gold sandals showed as she went down the steps, instead of the pale yellow slippers that had been matched to her dress. It was too late to change, however: there were voices in the drawing room, and she went on down the stairs.

So it was that she and Michael met for the first time in five weeks more or less publicly. They met in the long drawing room, in fact, with everyone in a group in front of the great fireplace and around a table where there was a tray of cocktails and a low green bowl of scarlet camellias. Michael saw her stop in the doorway and put down his glass and came to her smiling, his hands out.

Michael Bayne, just under thirty, was manager of the branch office of the Steane Mills in Seattle, and had been manager there for several years. It was a small office, controlling very little business but existing for the convenience of an office located near certain timber supplies. It had been established for that purpose a few years previous to Henry's death. That was why Michael Bayne was put in charge of it. He had been a buying agent for the Steane Mills, and he was on the West Coast at the time. He was young but very capable, and he had had quite enough business experience to take over so small a portion of it. The Seattle office had emerged entirely

27

clear from the debacle of Henry's embezzlements, which had been confined altogether to the New York office, where by far the bulk of the business went through Henry's small, pink, dishonest hands. The occasional order that went directly through Michael's office was too small to balance the risk of trying to steal part of it; besides, Michael would have caught any unaccountable discrepancies. Henry had consequently let Michael's office strictly alone, except for periodic reports.

Victoria, indeed, wouldn't have known Michael if, at the time Henry came south, Michael had not already been on the way to New York to give Henry one of those reports. Henry's trip south, to discourage Victoria's request for more money, was unscheduled; consequently, since Michael was already on his way east, he had wired Michael to change his reservation at Chicago and come south instead. Michael had done so and thus had seen Victoria for the first time.

Victoria and Bessie, and Hollis and Agnew. And naturally, Clistie. Thalia had already known Michael. They'd met in New York on his occasional visits to see her father. They'd been, in fact, rather friendly, doing an occasional night club or theatre together; but to the others Michael was a stranger.

He did not remain a stranger long.

For it was only a few days after his arrival that Henry drowned himself, and John Campbell had called it murder. So that, all at once, in the sudden intimacy of shared anxiety, Michael had stopped being a stranger. He had been, in fact, like a rock of refuge, like a bulwark, like a fortress. He had stood between Victoria and the newspapers. He had tried and frequently succeeded in standing between her and John Campbell. Bessie had taken to her bed, hysterically. Hollis had got himself moderately tight and managed to remain in that condition the whole time. Agnew had been frightened and nervily quarrelsome and, besides, he was only a boy. Even Clistie had had an attack of nerves and crept around the house like a shadow, but—what was rather unusual of Clistie—said very little about Henry and his death.

So it was actually Michael who was Victoria's refuge and defense.

And in the end it was Michael who knew enough of Henry's high-handed and autocratic methods to suggest an investigation that went farther than a glance at books (dummy books) already checked on by accountants. It was Michael who went himself to carry through the investigation and got back with proof that Henry Frame had had a motive for suicide barely in time to prevent John Campbell's request for a Grand Jury indictment.

After the case was closed, Michael had stayed on for a

week or two, and the night before he went away he'd asked Victoria to marry him. He took her in his arms as he had done once before, after a particularly long bout of questioning—when, after John Campbell had gone, Michael had held her and told her not to be frightened, that he'd do something—he didn't know what—but something. That he'd not let them try her for murder.

And he hadn't let them; he had done something to stop it.

They set the wedding date that night; the azaleas and orange blossoms would be out when he returned to marry Victoria.

The azaleas were blooming now, and the orange blossoms; the little interlude of waiting was over. And Victoria stood in the arched doorway, yellow chiffon clinging to her waist and falling in a swirl around her feet, her shoulders bare and her golden-brown hair swept up high, her face a little white under its soft tan and her eyes very large and dark. Waiting for Michael as he crossed the long room toward her.

The great boughs of crimson azaleas on the tables, Bessie's white and green gown, the sparkle of glasses all looked bright and very gay. Colonel Galant had risen, gray-haired, erect and spare in his uniform, smiling toward Victoria, glass in his hand. Hollis was standing at the piano, and he looked over his shoulder, and did not smile. Thalia beside him, in a misty blue gown, her white arms outstretched as she leaned against the piano, turned her wistful, lovely little face with its soft dark eyes toward Victoria, too. Agnew, incredibly lanky in dinner clothes, looked sulky. Clistie, sitting in a corner of the Burgundy red sofa—very fine in her new brown lace with its turquoise ribbon—was quiet too, but was not looking at Victoria. She was staring thoughtfully at the toe of her turquoise slipper.

Against this vividly patterned background, Michael approached Victoria.

The severe black and white of dinner clothes was always becoming to Michael. He was not trim and elegant like Hollis, but there was something substantial and solid about his compact figure and the strong sharp curves of his nose and chin.

His clear gray eyes were smiling.

"Hello, Victoria," he said.

The sharp, bright picture behind him broke up, moved, shifted, became only a group of people, drinking cocktails before dinner.

Michael took her in his arms; he kissed her and looked down at her, smiling.

Michael hadn't changed. Neither had she.

But she couldn't marry Michael on Wednesday.

29

5

Why?

And what was she to do about it?

Michael linked his arm through hers and led her toward the others. "Cocktail, dear?" he said, and put a glass in her hand. Colonel Galant was beaming. "You look as sweet as a bride tonight, Vicky," he said, and lifted his glass. Thalia turned and murmured something low to Hollis. Bessie's dark face, so unlike the Steanes, looked heavy and weary with the sagging lines under her chin and the brown circles around her great dark eyes; but she was smiling, and jewels were glittering at her swarthy throat and on her fingers. She always had a certain charm; a warmth in her dark eyes, something contagious in her smile. Bessie had made the arrangements for the wedding. Clistie had done the work. What would Bessie say when Victoria told her there was to be no wedding?

No wedding? Could she hurt Michael like that? Two days —not quite two days actually—before their marriage?

But she couldn't marry him, either.

She set down her glass with suddenly clumsy fingers. The big sapphire on her left hand shone coldly; Michael had given her that. She'd give it back to him; but no—she must keep her promise. She couldn't be like—well, like Aunt Bessie, swayed frantically by the lightest wind. Not that Aunt Bessie, not that anybody with a scrap of decency would jilt a man, out of hand, just before the wedding.

Yet marriage was irrevocable.

She had to think, really think. Pay no attention to all those scattered, incoherent, desperate little voices in her mind, as if a dozen Victorias were all arguing in emphatic whispers. A dozen Victorias, except all of them knew that she'd been wrong to promise to marry Michael.

Why had she promised, then?

"Dinner is served, Madam," said Jody, in the doorway, extra stately and extra suave because it was almost a wedding dinner.

Bessie acted as hostess "Michael, will you take Victoria in? Hollis . . ." She nodded at Thalia, and stretched out her jeweled, swarthy hand toward Colonel Galant. "Bruce, dear, you'll have to put up with me. Agnew, will you take Clistie?"

Agnew, who liked Clistie, pranced up to her with the gayety of a young colt and one unaccustomed cocktail, and offered her his arm. Michael's arm felt warm and hard through the black coat sleeve, below Victoria's fingertips. The candles on the tables were in tall silver candelabra, the best and oldest, got out for the occasion. There was a low silver bowl of scarlet camellias.

"Michael sits beside you, Vicky, dear," said Bessie. "After Wednesday, you know, you'll always be separated at dinner parties."

Michael, holding her chair, leaned over to say in her ear, "But together at home. Vicky, darling. . . ."

Thalia sitting opposite, beside Hollis, lifted her soft, dark eyes to Michael as if she'd heard. Hollis had been drinking a little too much; his fair face was flushed, and he was exaggeratedly devoted to Thalia. Agnew was uncomfortable in this stiff collar and pulled it down with an uneasy jerk of his prominent Adam's-apple. When Jody brought wine around, pouring with great style and flourish, Colonel Galant got to his feet and in gracious, old-fashioned phrases made a toast to Victoria and to Michael. Michael put his hand upon Victoria's. He didn't seem to notice how cold her fingers were; nobody noticed anything. Why had she promised to marry Michael?

Because she loved him, of course; because she wanted to be his wife. Because he had been so terribly kind to her when she needed a friend; because he had actually, literally, rescued her from, to say the least, a very unpleasant threat—and from, conceivably, trial for murder.

Was *that* why she felt now that she couldn't marry him?

Somebody spoke to her and she replied, and didn't know what she said. She felt as shocked and numbed as if she'd been plunged into an icy stream.

She couldn't marry Michael—and she knew why.

She would scarcely have known him if it hadn't been for Henry's death. He would have stayed a few days at the house and left. They wouldn't have been plunged together into horror—into anxiety and apprehension, yes, and fear; they wouldn't have been thrown into each other's arms, seeking each other's support in time of need. He wouldn't have acted, really, a hero's role, with herself a heroine.

Thus the whole circumstance of their engagement was artificial, fictional, unreal; marriage needed something real for a basis.

Need of each other's courage wasn't love. Gratitude wasn't love.

If she had only perceived what was now so clear to her, before Michael came and before it was too late to draw back! But she hadn't known it until Michael came and she saw him.

The dinner was very long; it seemed to Victoria it would never end. She must have eaten and smiled and said what was expected of her, for no one looked at her with a question in their eyes.

31

Jody, the old Negro butler, and his wife, had taken special pains with the dinner. Even now fat old Ernestine was peering in through the tiny glass slide in the door to the butler's pantry, watching to see how they liked her dessert. An imposing dessert, all meringues and cream with two meringue birds hovering miraculously above it; as Jody bore it around the table with modest pride, she saw her own name, "Victoria" on one side of the mound, and "Michael" on the other. She caught Ernestine's eye and, as the eye regarded her proudly but sharply, had to take a very large portion of dessert.

At any rate, dinner was nearly over. What was she going to do?

Well, that was obvious, wasn't it? She'd have to marry Michael. It was too late to do anything else.

Bessie said, rising, "You men needn't think you're going to sit around the table tonight. We'll have coffee together in the library. Unless . . . Oh, Michael, you and Vicky haven't had a chance for a word alone. Run along outside if you want to; there's a moon. Bruce, my dear . . " She slipped her hand through his arm again.

The others, talking, were moving toward the library. There were French doors on the river side of the dining room, leading upon the long open terrace, and she and Michael went that way. Yes, she'd have to marry Michael. A girl couldn't change her mind like that, suddenly, unreasonably, at the last moment.

The warm, bright moonlight fell upon them as they walked along the terrace. The river shone like fluid silver beyond the great arches of the liveoaks and the long wisps of Spanish moss. It had the exaggeration of a stage setting: the moonlight, the distant river, herself and Michael entering upon the silvery terrace from the lighted windows behind them. Only Victoria didn't know what her lines were.

Rather she did know. The whole thing was awry; they'd been thrust into each other's arms by circumstance; it was all very romantic, very apt, and altogether false; but she couldn't tell Michael now.

At the end of the terrace Michael stopped and took her in his arms and kissed her. He lifted his head, looked down at her face in the moonlight with a kind of question and then slowly released her. He got out cigarettes and said, matter-of-factly, "Well, everything's in shape for our trip. I can be away from the office for a month. Cigarette?"

They had planned to drive, slowly, through the Canadian Rockies. That too seemed altogether unreal. She shook her head as he held cigarettes toward her. He took one himself and lighted a match. The little flame made a golden, softening glow upon his face, with its broad, generous cheekbones, its strongly marked nose and chin, and straight mouth; his gray eyes were narrowed just then, watching the little flame. His expression was rather thoughtful.

"How nice," she said, and stopped, inwardly appalled at her own absurd, polite words. Yet, what could she say? she asked herself rather desperately.

Michael tossed the burnt match over the wide balustrade. Beyond him, away down the silver slope she could see the end of the pier thrusting out into the water from the mass of willows, and making a sharp black shadow on the water below it. The pier beneath which Henry Frame had been found. Murdered, John Campbell said that afternoon.

Michael said abruptly, "Look here, darling, what's wrong? I think you're cold. Romance is all right, but I don't want my bride to have the sniffles. Let's go in."

"Michael . . ." She didn't intend to say it; she hadn't planned the words; they came out quickly, breathlessly, in spite of herself. "Michael, I didn't know until tonight when I saw you again. You see, it's all wrong. Marriage is different; it's real. I—I'm terribly sorry."

There was a silence. She glanced at him and quickly away. His face looked pale in the white moonlight; his eyes shadowed, his cigarette poised in one hand, halfway to his lips.

Wasn't he ever going to say anything? she thought desperately, as the silence lengthened. And then he said slowly, "What *do* you mean?"

She was launched upon it now; she had to go on. She locked her hands together and tried, reasonably and quietly, to make him see it, too. "Our marriage would be a mistake, Michael. You see, it was all unreal. It was artificial. We weren't really in love with each other. It—it was like a story, or a moving picture. We were carried into it, in spite of ourselves. It was only the—the happy ending. Do you see, Michael?"

There was another long silence. Then he lifted his cigarette to his lips. "Are you trying to tell me, Victoria, that you don't want to marry me?"

"Oh, Michael, yes. I can't help it, believe me. I didn't know. Marriage is . . ." She stopped and again tried to explain something that was clear and articulate only in her mind and extraordinarily slippery and tenuous when she tried to tell Michael. "Marriage is real, Michael. The other wasn't."

"Let me get this straight, Victoria. All this talk of stories and moving pictures and happy endings . . . The thing that's important is that I love you. And you love me."

"That's it," she said miserably, not looking at him. "I don't
33

love you, Michael. That's what I'm trying to explain. . . ."

"Why did you promise to marry me if you didn't love me? Gratitude?"

"No, no."

"Then why?"

"But I've tried to tell you, Michael."

He laughed a little and passed one hand over his eyes and turned again to look down at the river. "You've not been very clear. And it's—well, it's a little late to break our engagement Remember, everybody gets a moment of uncertainty before they're married."

"Michael, it's not that."

"Vicky . . ."

"Michael, please understand."

They faced each other again in the warm moonlight. Someone in the house touched the piano; its clear notes fell light and mellow through the night air and then ceased abruptly.

"I love you, Vicky, and you love me," said Michael suddenly again, and took her in his arms.

A door opened down at the other end of the terrace.

"Michael—it's Jody!"

"Suppose it is—oh, all right." He let her go. Jody had seen the embrace and was chuckling a little as he trotted up to them. He put down the silver waiter he carried on the wide balustrade. "Your coffee, Miss."

"Thank you, Jody."

"Nice, pretty moon, Miss. Honeymoon."

"Yes, Jody."

Grinning and pleased, the old Negro trotted back along the terrace to the dining-room doors. Michael said, "Look here Vicky. Are you serious about all this?" She met his eyes, and he stopped. After a moment, he said slowly, under his breath, "I believe you *are* serious. Vicky . . ."

"I'm sorry, Michael," she said unevenly.

He stood again in silence, looking down at her. The cigarette burned down in his fingers and he tossed it over the balustrade. At last, he said, "Well. All right. But—here, I'll pour the coffee. Then let's walk a little and talk things over. We'll have to tell them, you know. Call off the wedding. It's going to be a little upsetting."

They drank in silence, watching the silvery river.

But Michael hadn't really accepted it. He put down his cup and slipped her arm through his. "Let's walk," he said again. "And talk this out. I'm a—kind of plodding, earnest soul, you know. I want to get it all straight in my mind."

They strolled for a long time through the garden. The worn, grass-grown brick paths felt damp and warm through

34

Victoria's thin slippers. They passed the formal patterns of the rose plot, and at the end of the garden the clipped, high yew hedge made a deep black line of shadow. They came out at last, as Clistie had done that afternoon, at the little promontory overlooking the river. There was a sundial, stone chairs, a millstone sunk into the soil with the turf grown over it. Off to the south, visible above the black line of the yew hedge, lay the pine woods, extending for a mile or so along the river—mysterious, now, and black below the fringe of silver moonlight—deserted, except for one or two forgotten Negro shacks.

It seemed to Victoria that they said the same things over and over. But at last Michael, breaking a long silence, said, "It's all right, Vicky. I think I understand you. I hadn't thought of it just that way. But maybe you're right. Big hero saves girl, asks her to marry him, clinch. As you say, the happy ending. But false."

"I'm afraid so, Michael. But I didn't know until . . ."

"Until tonight, when I came," said Michael. "Well, that's natural, Vicky. In any case I don't want you to marry me unless you want to, and are sure you want to. Well—there's no use in telling anyone till tomorrow. We'll give ourselves tonight to think about it, Victoria."

"Michael, I'm sure now. I hate myself . . ."

"Don't hate yourself," he said cheerfully. "There was nothing else for you to do. It's only fair to yourself, and to me." He slipped her arm through his own again and they turned away from the river, back along the shadowed paths toward the lighted house. This time they crossed the porch toward the door that opened directly into the drawing room. Michael, however, stopped at the door, and leaned over and kissed her lightly.

"I'm going to walk a bit. Good night, Vicky. Don't worry." He held the door open for her and then walked quickly away. She could hear his footsteps along the porch.

She'd have felt better if he had reproached her; it might have lightened the weight in her heart.

The long drawing room was empty except for Agnew hunched under a lamp with a book. He looked up. Agnew so sunk himself into a book that it was always an effort for him to come back from the world of fancy into the everyday world of reality. He knew, however, when she asked him, exactly where everybody was. He rubbed his eyes and said that Colonel Galant had had to go back to the post early, and his mother had gone to bed. Thalia and Hollis had gone to Ponte Verde. "They went to the movies and they wouldn't take me. Mom said my eyes wouldn't stand it. What Thalia sees in Hollis . . ." He yawned and said reflectively, "You

35

know what? I think she's a dark horse. Thalia, I mean. Besides, she's got such funny thumbs."

"*Thalia*—well, really, Agnew! Where's your chivalry! And your glasses," said Victoria mechanically. "Has Clistie gone upstairs?"

He had gone back to his book and looked up again reluctantly. "Clistie? She's around, somewhere . . ." He peered vaguely along the hall. "She's still busy as a bee. Saw her coming from the pantry a while ago—maybe an hour or so. She's in the library, I think. No, that was right after dinner when she got Hollis in there and gave him hell for drinking too much. Then Thalia came down with her coat and Hollis came out of the library and they left."

"Hollis wasn't tight, was he?"

"No, not really. If he was, Clistie sobered him up." Agnew chuckled. "Mom was too busy talking to Colonel Bruce to notice her pet lamb was getting a shearing."

"But you noticed," said Victoria rather dryly.

"Well, you know how Clistie's eyes snap when she's mad. Hollis was mad, too, when he came out. White as a sheet." Agnew blinked, and said, "And you look a little stricken yourself, baby. Where's the boy friend? You haven't had a row, have you?"

She wanted suddenly to tell him—to tell him not only about Michael, but about her talk with John Campbell that afternoon. It would have been a relief; and Agnew had a certain dependable commonsense.

Yet, just then, she couldn't talk of Michael. And to tell Agnew what John Campbell had said would be to give his words—his warning, really—more significance than it deserved.

She said evasively, "Michael's coming in soon," and turned toward the hall.

"Okay," said Agnew. "Keep your little secret. But you look like a girl going to her room for a good cry."

"Well, I'm not," she said, and started quickly upstairs. She glanced back from the landing. She could see Agnew already immersed in his book again as if it were a bath. Even now that he was eighteen if one didn't send Agnew to bed he was likely to read till dawn. As mechanically as she had inquired about his glasses, she looked at the big grandfather's clock that stood in the hall below. It was only a little after eleven.

Her own room was on the south and east, above the drawing room and porch and at the very end of the long hall. It was unexpectedly dark when she reached it, except for the white moonlight pouring through the windows. As a rule, Lilibelle turned on the light when she turned down the bed

That night, excitedly, Victoria thought, she'd forgotten it.

The unearthly white moonlight made the room look different, unfamiliar. Her wedding dress, its train too long for the cupboards in the dressing room, hung from a padded hanger on a thin wire•Clistie had had stretched from one window casing to another. The veil was there, too, with its rose-point cap made from her grandmother's wedding veil; both veil and wedding gown were covered with a thin sheet of white muslin. It looked rather ghostly, hanging there in the moonlight. Her wedding gown that wasn't going to be a wedding gown.

There was no use trying to sleep. Without turning on the light, Victoria crossed the room toward the balcony which, however, was not really a balcony. It was merely a part of the roof of the porch below, railed, and circled with vines, and accessible from Victoria's room by French doors.

As she passed the corner where the wedding dress hung in its white cover, her foot struck something hard and metallic. She glanced down and caught a hard, steely gleam against the rug; scissors, probably. She thought that Clistie must have been adding a last stitch to the dress and didn't stop to look closely. She went onto the balcony, closing the French doors behind her. There was a chaise longue there and a chair or two.

The shadow on the little balcony was deep, for there was a canvas awning above and trellises on either side which supported thick vines of bougainvillaea. She settled down on the deep chaise longue and pulled the light woolen rug around her bare shoulders.

It was very quiet. The lawns were white where the moonlight fell upon them, and sharply black in the shadow of trees and shrubs, and along the hedged paths where she and Michael had walked. The river flowed in silvery patches beyond the trees. It was a beautiful but rather strange night—as still as a painted scene in black and white.

Michael, she realized presently, was on the porch below; a little floating fragrance of cigarette smoke drifted upward to her, and once she heard the creak of one of the long rattan chairs which, with their bright cushions, made the porch gay with color.

So Michael couldn't sleep either.

She pulled the light rug closer around her. Agnew had been right, as he often was, but crying wouldn't mend the thing she had done to Michael.

Bessie would be secretly pleased when she knew of their decision not to marry—in spite of the eleventh hour abruptness of it. Clistie wouldn't like it; Clistie had wanted her to marry Michael.

A night bird rustled somewhere near. The moon was higher and the shadows had shifted a little. Once she thought she heard someone or something moving, or talking perhaps, distantly, and concluded she was wrong, for when she listened there was only the murmur of the river.

It was shortly after eleven when she went out onto the balcony; it must have been nearly twelve when she heard Michael get up from the creaking rattan chair on the porch and begin to pace up and down on the strip of lawn between the house and the garden. She could hear him cross the porch and could hear his footsteps on the turf. Presently she went to the balcony railing and looked over. The moonlight was clear upon his tall figure. He was smoking, head bent, pacing along slowly. She said softly, "Michael . . ."

He looked up with a start and came nearer the balcony. The moonlight was clear and white upon his face. "Why, Vicky! I thought you were in bed and asleep hours ago." He paused and said, looking up at her, "You're worrying, aren't you?"

"Well, my self-esteem is not at its highest point," she said. The words were light enough, but in her voice lay a plea for forgiveness.

He laughed gently. "My Victoria-esteem is exactly where it always was. Now don't be a dope. Everything's all right. Go on to sleep. I'm going to, as soon as I finish my cigarette. Good night, Vicky."

There was a moment of silence. Then Victoria said, "Good night, Michael."

She went back to the chaise longue. He resumed his pacing up and down, slowly, on the grass, and presently went into the house, for she heard the door close.

Again the night fell into that spell of moonlit silence.

Some time afterward a car drove up to the front entrance, apparently, at the other side of the house. Its engine woke the still night, and then was turned off. Hollis and Thalia, thought Victoria, returning from the movies. Hollis must be intending to spend the night at home, for the car did not drive away again.

It was perhaps ten or fifteen minutes after that, that Victoria heard another sound—an odd sound, really, for it came from, she thought, her own bedroom and sounded like a door closing. She lifted her head and listened. The night was perfectly silent again; nothing moved across the bright patches of moonlight; no shadow altered its shape. But the impression of movement in the room behind was so clear that after a moment or two she got up, opened the French doors, went to a table lamp and turned it on. No one was there; the door into the hall was closed. It had been, obviously, nothing. Still feeling too wide awake for sleep, she turned off the light and returned to the balcony.

She had barely settled herself in the chaise longue, with the silvery, secretive river far below, when it happened.

That was a scream.

A long, sharp scream of agony and of horror. A scream that tore into the waiting silence of that black and white world and ripped it apart. A scream that sobbed at its height and broke off.

It came from the pine woods beyond the gardens, along the river, and it was a woman's scream.

Oddly enough, Victoria's first thought was like Clistie's that afternoon. We ought to have dogs, she thought numbly. Then she got to her feet, stumbling, entangled in the rug.

By the time she got to the balcony railing, the night was silent again—but waiting now, shocked and listening.

So the black, sharp shadows and the wide, white river and Victoria, frozen on the balcony, heard it when it came. That was a deep, faraway splash in the river—a distant splash, heavy.

6

It seemed to Victoria that everything in the night, every living thing under that white moon, must have heard the scream and the deep splash that followed it. As if even the hedges and the river had ears to hear and hearts to stand still with horror.

Yet no one did hear, apparently, for nothing moved and there was no sound. There was only that dead silence, still shocked, still motionless.

Then she moved, stumbling again in the folds of woolen rug, groping for the handle of the French door she had closed, stumbling again through her bedroom. She found the door into the hall and flung it open. There was a small night light above the stairway. The great tapestry on the wall above it hung motionless; the hall was empty except for those long-ago woven figures in the tapestry. She ran to Clistie's door and knocked, opened it, and Clistie wasn't there.

A light was on beside the bed. The bed was untouched. Clistie's nightdress and shabby green dressing-gown lay neatly across it with scuffed brown bedroom slippers set on the floor below, toeing out in old-fashioned dancing position. Somebody had screamed—horribly, as if in agony, and then stopped with more horrible abruptness, down there in the pine woods. Who was it? A woman—then was it Clistie?

Her heart rocked. Literally, so it hurt.

She must do something, find somebody, tell them, go to the pine woods. Why hadn't someone else heard that scream? It couldn't have been much more than a quarter of an hour since Hollis and Thalia had returned. Hollis! She would tell him. She turned back into the hall. A line of closed bedroom doors met her eyes. It was incredibly hushed and quiet; the blank doors forbade her entrance. Where was Hollis sleeping? In his own room, naturally, just beyond Agnew's room. She knocked and, again, opened the door. The room was dark and she felt for the electric-light switch. "Hollis—Hollis—wake up!"

The light flashed on, but she'd made a mistake. It was Agnew's room instead of Hollis'. Agnew was sitting up in bed, blinking and rubbing his eyes; his hair was tousled, his pajamas shrunken over his long wrists.

"For gosh' sake, Vicky!"

"Agnew, did you hear it?"

"Hear what? Gosh . . ."

"Hear that scream! In the pine woods. Agnew, wake up . . ."

He was slipping down in bed again, and she ran across to him and put her hand on his shoulder. "Agnew, listen! It was a scream. A scream in the pine woods. And then a—a splash. Horrible and heavy in the river. Oh, Agnew, listen to me . . ."

"I am listening. Vicky you're crazy. You've had a nightmare," said Agnew severely. "Pull yourself together. Nobody screamed."

"You were asleep. You didn't hear it. Agnew, we've got to go down there and look. Somebody screamed. . . ."

"Stop saying that," snapped Agnew. "Don't be hysterical!"

"Oh, *hurry*. Get up—here's your dressing-gown. Agnew, you've got to come with me." She snatched his flannel dressing-gown from the floor and thrust it at him. "Please Agnew, *wake up*."

"I *am* awake," he said peevishly, yawning. "I just went to bed a few minutes ago. I think you've been dreaming. What exactly happened?"

"I tell you I don't know." She was nearly sobbing. "I was on the balcony and I heard it—oh—I'll call Hollis." She whirled around and started toward Hollis' room, but Agnew scrambled sleepily out of bed, slung the dressing-gown over one shoulder and caught her by the time she reached the door.

"Okay," he said soothingly, clutching her arm. "I'll call Hollis. And Clistie. I'll call Clistie."

40

"But she's not here. She's not been to bed. I'm—I'm afraid it's Clistie that screamed. . . ."

Agnew's sleepy face looked abruptly white; his eyes snapped so they were bright and wide awake. After an instant, he said, rapidly, "Vicky, you're afraid. You're thinking about Henry. Nothing's happened. You heard only a—a rabbit, or a bird or . . ."

She pulled away from his clutch on her arm and he followed her into the hall.

And Clistie stood there. Clistie in the green dressing-gown, clutching it up tight around her throat; she still wore her turquoise slippers because Victoria could see them, below the tailored ankle-length dressing-gown.

"Clistie, where have you been? You weren't in your room a minute ago. Did you hear it?"

"Sh—sh— You'll wake the house. I was—was downstairs, making sure the gas was turned off. Ernestine is so careless."

"But your dressing-gown was on the bed. . . ."

"I just now put it on. Victoria, what's wrong? Did I hear what?" She put her thin, strong hand on Victoria's arm and shook it. "What *is* the matter?"

"She's had a nightmare," said Agnew in a husky whisper.

"It wasn't a nightmare," protested Victoria, whispering, too. "Clistie, somebody down in the pine woods . . ."

"She says somebody screamed," cut in Agnew. "She's been dreaming."

"There was a horrible scream and then—then a kind of splash. As if somebody . . ." Victoria caught her breath sharply, and said, "I mean something had been let down in the river."

Clistie's narrow, long face was always sallow. There, in that night-lighted hall, though, with the closed, dark panels of the line of bedroom doors beyond her, it looked suddenly waxen. *"Screamed?"*

"Yes. Yes, Clistie, I'm sure!"

"She's thinking about Henry; dreaming about it, I mean," said Agnew. "I've had some nightmares myself since that happened. I'd say give her some hot milk and put her to bed." He peered at Victoria and exclaimed, "For gosh' sake, Vicky, you've not even undressed! You came up to bed ages ago. Where have you been?"

"On the balcony," said Victoria shortly. They were all whispering, their words making vehement, rustling little echoes along the empty walls and down the stairwell. "That's why I heard it. It was loud and high and it—it stopped . . ." said Victoria, and tried to tell them how it stopped and couldn't. "Didn't you hear it?"

"I certainly didn't hear anybody scream," said Clistie. "You go to bed, Victoria. It's late. You go to bed, too, Agnew."

"But, Clistie, we've got to go down to the pine woods. I . . . Oh, *won't* you understand, both of you! Somebody was being"—she swallowed hard—"being hurt."

Clistie's dark eyes flickered. Agnew looked uneasy, and rubbed one bare ankle over the other. Clistie said, "Look here, Vicky. Will you go to bed if I send somebody down to the pine woods with lights? You're—" she hesitated and said —"you're sure it *was* in the pine woods?"

"Oh, yes. Nothing moved in the garden. It's so moonlit I would have seen it. We must hurry, Clistie. . . ."

"I'll call somebody. I'll see to it."

"I'm going with you," said Agnew.

Clistie shook her head authoritatively. But Clistie did believe her story now, thought Victoria, for she too looked frightened and the thin, hard hand that clutched her dressing-gown together at her throat was white-knuckled and tense. "No, you can't go," said Clistie to Agnew. "I'll call Judson on the house phone and tell him to take a light and look. That is, I'll do it, if you'll both go back to bed."

"But . . ." began Agnew rebelliously. Clistie cut him off short.

"I won't do a thing unless you both go to bed. Go on, now, Agnew, you mind me." Agnew scuffled his bare feet, looked sulky, but was routed by Clistie's habitual authority and vehemence. Victoria said, "No, I'm going. . . ." But she too was defeated by Clistie, who shot an imperative glance at Agnew which sent him reluctantly backward into his bedroom. She took Victoria by the arm. "Now you come along with me. You can't go any place dressed like that. If anybody really was down there in the pine woods . . ." Clistie's throat seemed to choke a little, but she said, "Screaming—we'd better get Judson right away and no time wasted. I'll ring him as soon as you go to your room and go to bed. . . ."

Everybody minded Clistie. "Wake up Hollis, too," said Victoria.

"All right, all right," whispered Clistie. "I'll see to it. I always do see to things, don't I? Now be a good girl and go to bed. I promise you there'll be a thorough search. I'll bring you some hot milk and tell you about it. Go on, now. . . ." She gave Victoria a little shove toward her bedroom and, turning, pattered quickly away. The telephone that connected with Judson's cottage was in the hall, downstairs.

Everybody obeyed Clistie. She was utterly resourceful and efficient. Nobody ever questioned her ability or her methods or her decisions. To Clistie, naturally, Hollis and Agnew and

42

Victoria were still children and would always remain children. But even Bessie yielded to Clistie.

Victoria went reluctantly into her room. Clistie was right, of course. Victoria couldn't do much in the way of searching the pine woods—in a yellow chiffon dinner gown and gold sandals. She went out on the balcony again. There was no sound anywhere; the garden, the paths, the silvered river were empty and utterly silent. The black blotch that was the pine woods was silent too.

Had she fallen suddenly asleep and dreamed?

But she knew she hadn't. Presently there would be lights going toward the pine woods. And presently Clistie would come back. She'd better change.

She went back into her room, turned on lights, took off her slippers and dress, and went to the windows and looked again and could see nothing. But Judson would take the path from the cottage, behind the black yew hedge. She returned to her dressing room and put on slacks and a sweater and tennis shoes. And then, after awhile, took them off again, and went to bed and couldn't stay there. She wandered to the windows and stared down at the black and white world, hushed and still—with no lights showing anywhere. She went back to bed. She wrapped herself in the dressing-gown again and went out on the balcony. Still there was no motion anywhere that she could see; no glancing lights; no voices; no sound at all.

It probably hadn't been as long as it suddenly seemed, since she'd watched Clistie go toward the stairs. She wished she'd looked at the clock. She did so then, wandering into the little dressing room, stopping to light a cigarette, nervously. She ought to have insisted; she ought to have gone herself. She ought to have done anything that was decisive—instead of prowling like a nervous cat from window to balcony and back again! *What was happening in the pine woods?*

She had been sitting with the little gold clock in her hand, at the dressing table; she hadn't looked at the clock at all. She looked then and it was almost two.

How long had it been since Clistie went downstairs and why didn't she come back?

She couldn't wait any longer. She got up, put out her cigarette with jerky fingers and reached again for the slacks and sweater. As she did so Agnew opened the door and called, low-voiced, "Vicky. Vicky, are you still awake?"

She went to the dressing-room door. "Is Clistie back?"

Agnew said, "Oh, there you are," and came in. He was still in pajamas. His face was so pale that the freckles stood out, and he'd put on his spectacles so he looked very odd with his blond, straight hair lanky and rumpled, and his bare, bony

43

feet and pajamas. "Where's Clistie?"

"I don't know. I've been waiting. I'm going down there."

"She didn't call Hollis," said Agnew. "I waited and waited. Then I got up, just now, and went to Hollis' room, and she hadn't called him. He's in bed and asleep; he didn't hear me open the door, but I could see him there in bed, the moonlight is so bright. She didn't call Michael either. I looked in his room, too. Vicky, she ought to have come back by now. It's been over an hour."

"Oh, no, it can't have been so long!"

"It is, though. Vicky, what do you suppose . . . ?"

"Go and dress. Hurry. I'll telephone Judson's house."

"No, I will," said Agnew. "While you dress." He slid out the door again.

Nothing, of course, had happened. Nothing could have happened. Victoria's hands fastening the slacks and shoelaces were clumsy and fumbling. She pulled the sweater over her head and was in the hall when Agnew came running up the stairs. His face was whiter than ever. "Judson says she didn't telephone at all. He was asleep. She's not in her room and she's not downstairs. Vicky, where do you think she is? Vicky, did you really hear something in the pine woods?"

"Call Hollis and Michael. I'll tell Judson to come."

"I already told him to come to the house," said Agnew, and gave her a queer unsteady look as if he were on the verge of tears and then wheeled around to run to Hollis' room.

Victoria followed him. Clistie would be furious if they roused the house to look for her. But Clistie ought to have returned before now. Clistie—and that scream down in the pine woods.

She reached the door of Hollis' room and he was awake, trying to understand Agnew, sitting up abruptly. "Scream!" he cried, and saw Victoria. "For God's sake, Victoria, what does he mean?"

They tried to tell him, both speaking at once. "How long ago?" he said, getting out of bed.

"Almost an hour," said Agnew. "Here's your pants."

"Are you sure she's not in the house?"

"I looked downstairs. And she's not in her room."

Hollis reached for a sweater. "We'd better take a look. If she went alone down to the pine woods . . ." He gave Victoria a swift glance. His hard, light-blue eyes had bright black pupils. "That's funny about the scream. When did you hear it? What was it?"

She told him again. As she finished, they heard the distant, muffled peal of a bell.

"There's Judson now," said Hollis. "Vicky, you and Agnew

search the house again. Better wake Mother and tell her. And wake Michael."

He ran downstairs to open the front door for the gardener, Judson, a heavy, slow Scotchman, fifty or thereabouts, with a light hand for seedlings and a heavy hand for subordinates.

Suppose Clistie came walking in from, say, the south porch, unperturbed, angry because of the fuss they were making, thought Victoria. But she'd call Michael anyway.

Michael, too, was asleep. Agnew knocked and shouted and opened the door as Michael awoke and turned on the bedlight and sat up, blinking. "What's the matter? Victoria, what's wrong?"

"Oh, Michael, it's Clistie . . ."

Again, both talking at once, they told him.

Michael saw that she was terrified. He was out of bed and in bathrobe and slippers before they had finished. "Have they got lights? Don't be frightened, Vicky. Nothing could have happened to her. . . ."

"Happened to whom?" cried Bessie from the doorway. "What's everybody running around and shouting about? Agnew, put your slippers on. Really, Victoria . . ."

They told her, too, rapidly. Bessie cried brokenly, "Like Henry! Like—oh, what am I saying!" She caught herself quickly, her face and lips like ashes, her dark eyes showing frightened white rims. Her hair was streaming over her shoulders and she wore a pink chiffon negligee, a little draggled. She seldom removed her jewelry at night and a small diamond necklace glittered at her throat, and bracelets were on her wrists and rings on her fingers. "I'll get you a flashlight, Michael," she said. "But nothing could have happened."

Michael, running toward the stairs, called back to Victoria reassuringly. "Don't worry. We'll find her. It'll be all right." Bessie hurried to her own room, snatched up a flashlight, and ran to hand it to Michael, over the stair railing. Thalia had been awakened too, and câme hurriedly from her room. Even then she was lovely—soft dark hair smooth, heavy blue taffeta dressing-gown fresh and uncrumpled and tied neatly at her slender little waist with purple velvet ribbons.

"What *is* the matter?" Thalia cried, staring at them. "Is the house burning down?"

"He said to search the house," said Agnew. "Come on. . . ."

Search the house, of course. Clistie must be there—fallen asleep somewhere.

But she was not.

She wasn't on the porch either. Or in the gardens.

She wasn't in the garage and none of the cars was gone.

She wasn't in the greenhouse; certainly she wasn't in the little lodge house at the gate.

And if she was in the pine woods, she didn't answer to voices calling her, and the men, looking now in earnest, found no trace of her having been there. By that time the servants were roused and it was beginning to be light.

At six o'clock they telephoned the state police station at the little town of Ponte Verde—the small, now crowded county seat. Somebody—Jody, probably—had made coffee. They had sat around in the hall by the telephone, pale and disheveled, drinking it, discussing whether or not to call the police for a long time before they finally decided to do so; there was, after all, so little to tell them. A scream that only Victoria had heard; a distant splash. And that was before Clistie had gone down the stairway and quietly disappeared.

"I simply don't understand it," said Bessie fretfully, looking at Victoria. "Why in the world did you let her leave like that? Alone! After what you heard. . . ."

Michael, standing beside Victoria, said quickly, "Clistie told her she'd call Judson. Victoria couldn't search the woods."

"If it wasn't Clistie that screamed, who was it?" said Thalia.

Nobody could answer that. Hollis, nervous and pale, said, "I hate to call the police."

"Better call them," said Agnew. "If Victoria wasn't dreaming . . ."

"She may have got ill, you know," said Bessie suddenly, staring at each of them with her great, haunted eyes, holding her coffee cup in both thick jeweled hands. "She may have had a—a stroke. A heart attack."

Nobody had thought of that. Clistie was like a tough little hickory nut and was never sick.

Hollis shrugged and at last went to the telephone. "I suppose we'll have to call the police. It's the only way to make a really systematic search. Besides . . ." He shrugged again and called a Ponte Verde number.

Everybody listened and watched. So everybody heard him describe, briefly, the situation. Everybody saw him stiffen, listening to the voice at the other end of the wire. And everybody saw the coffee cup he still held fall out of his hand and crash and splinter on the floor. Black coffee splashed all over Bessie's pink, trailing negligee, but she paid no attention to it. She put her arms around Hollis, who seemed to sag against the wall by the telephone. And, as he listened and said nothing, just stood there, sagging, clutching the telephone, she took it suddenly and strongly away from him. Hollis didn't resist. He turned around and looked at them with blank blue eyes, and said, "They've found a woman. In the river. An hour or so ago. She's—she's wearing a brown lace dress with a blue ribbon."

Bessie said into the telephone, hoarsely, "How old is she? What does she look like? Yes, yes, we'll come."

Agnew crumpled down on the stairway and began to cry. Thalia said, so softly her voice was like a chill little wind, "Is she dead?"

Hollis, staring at Bessie, didn't seem to hear. Michael put his arm around Victoria.

Bessie turned from the telephone. "Oh, yes," she said, huskily. "She's dead. She was murdered. But it can't be Clistie. They say it's a young woman, in her twenties. An unidentified woman. Only—only they say she's wearing Clistie's dress."

Agnew put his head up, choked back a sob and said, "But where is Clistie?"

Nobody could reply to that. Bessie looked all around the hall slowly, at each face, as if seeking the answer. When she reached Victoria her dark eyes changed. She said, in an appalled way, "Good Heavens! And your wedding day tomorrow!"

7

They all had to go to Ponte Verde to the police station. Hollis, looking ill and pale, explained it briefly.

The unidentified woman had floated downstream toward Ponte Verde where an early fisherman had seen the body. He had rowed near enough to see that it wasn't just a brown log, curiously limp, floating along there, turning and twisting sluggishly with the current. He had towed the body to shore and called the police. This had happened while the men were searching the pine woods only a mile or two upstream for Clistie.

There hadn't been time for an autopsy, but the police were convinced that it was murder. "They—they said she was strangled," said Hollis. "They don't know who she is, and as soon as they heard about Clistie—that is, that a woman was missing here, they said we'd have to see the body they'd found."

"It *can't* be Clistie's dress," said Bessie as if debating it with herself. "It's brown lace with a blue ribbon, but how on earth . . . *No! It simply can't be Clistie's dress!*"

"Clistie made it herself," said Thalia softly. "There isn't likely to be another dress just like it."

Nobody said anything for a moment. Perhaps all of them were remembering Clistie's thin, angular figure in her new brown lace the night before.

47

"She was wearing a dressing-gown when she went downstairs," said Victoria. "An old green dressing-gown. And turquoise satin evening slippers."

"We'd better look," said Michael, "and see if the brown lace dress is still there."

But it wasn't. Victoria and Bessie went with him. Clistie's few clothes were in orderly little ranks in the wardrobe; each one familiar, nothing added and only the new brown dress was missing.

Bessie said at last, heavily, "Well, we'd better dress and go to Ponte Verde, and insist on the police coming back with us to look for Clistie."

"Are they sure it isn't Clistie they found in the river?" asked Michael quietly. And Bessie said, shaking her head, "It isn't Clistie. Unless they are color blind. This woman's blonde."

Michael, sensibly, suggested breakfast. Jody and Ernestine could prepare it while they dressed; after all, they couldn't go to Ponte Verde dressed as they were.

"You mean undressed," said Agnew, with a rather sickly grin. "We look like people in a shipwreck, except Thalia." The pretense at a grin failed. He said soberly, "Of course you realize that at any moment Clistie will come walking in with a perfectly sensible reason for being away."

But they had dressed and had a quick breakfast, and were ready to start for the little county seat and still Clistie had not turned up and there was no word of her. The sun was far up, of course, by that time. It was a warm, bright day, with the sky blue, and the river bright and sparkling with gold, and the black and white silence of the previous night gone as if it had never been.

They went together, with Hollis driving the long town car. At the last moment Bessie had an argument with Agnew, who didn't want to go. "We have to go," she snapped. "The police want the woman identified. They say we all have to look at her. And if it's Clistie's dress . . ."

"You oughtn't to have admitted Clistie had a dress like that," said Agnew sulkily.

"Why on earth not! We reported that Clistie was missing. . . ." Bessie lost patience and stamped her high-heeled slipper. "Oh, get in, for Heaven's sake, Agnew. I don't want to go any more than you do."

Michael said soberly, "We'll get this over, and bring the police back with us to make a real search for her."

The Ponte Verde police station was in one corner of the courthouse. Victoria remembered it all too well. As they drove into the little town and turned the familiar corner, and the small, solid, red-brick courthouse, overgrown with bougainvillaea, rose before them, she had a very unpleasant sensation of repeated experience. They'd made her come to the courthouse many times during the investigation following Henry's death. The coroner's inquest had been held there, too. Michael had the same thing in his mind, for, as the car stopped, he said in her ear, "Brace up, Vicky. It won't be like that."

And, as a matter of fact, it wasn't. In a queer way, it was worse.

For they had to look at the woman who'd been taken out of the river.

But it wasn't Clistie.

It was a young woman, with wet, short hair that, dry, would be very light. She was not pretty then; but she had been pretty only a few hours before; there were blue marks at her throat. Victoria shut her eyes. There were two or three state troopers in the bare little room; one of them took her arm in a hard grip. "Don't faint," he said. "Just a moment— will you look again? Have you ever seen this woman before?"

"No," said Victoria. "No." And immediately was assailed by some fleeting recollection. It was nobody she knew. Yet she had an odd notion that somewhere, not long ago, she had seen her face. She opened her eyes again. And this time she saw the dress the woman was wearing.

It too was wet and draggled. But it was Clistie's dress, or one exactly like it. Limp brown lace and chiffon, torn and wet; turquoise ribbon, now stained and damp. Oddly, the girl was wearing one brown street oxford.

"Is it Miss Forbes' dress?"

"Yes. Or one exactly like it."

"Do any of you know who she is?"

No one did; at least, no one replied. Agnew looked sick. Hollis, after one quick look, stared out the window and wiped his face with his handkerchief.

Thalia, however, looked puzzled. "It seems to me I've seen her somewhere," she said, "but I can't think where."

"What is her name?"

"But I don't know," said Thalia, opening her pansy eyes wide. She saw Hollis and got out her own handkerchief and touched her lips.

"It *is* Clistie's dress," said Bessie heavily. "How *do* you suppose . . . ?"

No one answered.

"Will you come this way, please," said the state trooper, and pulled the sheet again over the young, tragic thing on the table and led them to another room. An office, this time, with sunlight streaming in the windows, and chairs brought for them.

Agnew, sitting on the edge of a table at Victoria's elbow, murmured unhappily, " 'Cover her face: mine eyes dazzle. She died young.' "

"Sh-sh," hissed Bessie sharply.

"I was only quoting . . ."

"Here is Mr. Beasley," said the state trooper. "The State's Attorney. He would like to ask you a few questions."

"Beasley!" said Michael. "I thought it was the other fellow. John Campbell."

Beasley, entering, heard it. "John," he said smiling, "is in the army now. But I'll endeavor to fill his place. Now then, if you don't mind answering a few questions. . . ."

The new State's Attorney was older than John Campbell. He was a thin, dark, suspicious-looking man of fifty or so, whose eyes were remarkably black and sharp in his yellow malarial face. His name was Eliot Beasley; his lined, long face wore the slightly sinister and mournful look of a bloodhound. He questioned them quickly. When had Clistie disappeared? When had they last seen her wearing that dress? Were they sure it was Miss Forbes' dress? Did any of them know the girl who'd been found in the river?

Thalia said again that she believed she had seen her, perhaps on the street. She wasn't sure.

"I think I've seen her, somewhere, too," said Victoria. "But I don't know where."

They questioned her about that. And then, at length, about the scream she had heard and her talk with Clistie. About the length of time she had waited for Clistie to return, and about the search for her.

It did not actually take very long. Certainly it added little to anybody's stock of information. It was Clistie's dress. The dead girl *could* have been put into the river in the vicinity of the pine woods; she *could* have screamed.

And no one knew anything of Clistie.

Beasley let them go very soon; a police car, he said, would follow. Obviously the fact that the dead girl was wearing Clistie's dress augmented his interest in Clistie's whereabouts. But that was all.

"Don't look like that, Vicky," said Michael, sitting beside her, on their way home. "It must have been over very quickly —poor little kid."

"In our own woods," said Victoria unsteadily. "So near . . ."

"There was nothing you could do. Even if—well, if she *was* put into the river along the pine woods, and if she screamed, and that was what you heard—it must have been already too late. There was nothing anybody could have done. Here. . . ." He pushed a handkerchief into her hand. Agnew said crossly and nervously, "She's not crying." And Thalia, holding onto her hat, for Hollis was driving very fast, said, "Suppose Clistie went down to the pine woods herself and met whoever it was that murdered that girl and he murdered her. . . ."

"*Stop that, Thalia!*" said Bessie, sharply. Her eyes looked haunted in their dark, weary pockets. Her hair was an untidy dark wad, her hat was crooked, she still hadn't removed her jewelry, and had put on apparently the first clothing that her hands touched, so she was wearing a flowered voile afternoon dress, rather soiled, a raincoat, in spite of the sun and the growing heat, and a black straw hat, which, with the jewelry, looked indescribably dowdy and a little rakish.

The police car arrived almost as soon as they did. But Clistie had not returned and there had been no word of her. Jody met them at the door and told them. Judson and his two assistants were still looking for her.

The four state policemen began to organize a systematic search; one which ignored the search that had already been made, and began with the house. Nobody was very clear, however, as to whether the police were looking for Clistie or for evidence concerning the murdered girl—wearing Clistie's dress.

It was the beginning of a strange and unreal day—a day that seemed to have broken loose from the moorings of the customary and comprehensible pattern of other days, and shot off into some nether world of such grotesqueness, of such chaotic and distorted strangeness that they themselves seemed to partake of that strangeness so nothing they said or did or thought was quite natural and normal.

Victoria thought that when she had drifted out onto the terrace and glanced down at the familiar—yet that morning unreal and unfamiliar—view of the river between the arches of liveoaks and Spanish moss. Beyond the gardens, men were then searching the pine woods—working slowly along the banks. Down below her was the pier where Henry had been found that late December morning. Henry who had died in the river, too, as that girl had died—who had been wearing Clistie's dress.

And only the day before John Campbell had said, again, that Henry was murdered.

For a moment, a different kind of uneasiness caught at Victoria—something quite different from her anxiety about Clistie, and the shock of the ugly and tragic sight she had been made to look at in the bare, damp-stained little room of the Ponte Verde courthouse. John Campbell had not only told her, again, that Henry Frame had been murdered; he had also quite frankly warned her. Not of any specific thing; not in any way that had seemed, then, credible. But he had warned her; he had talked of money in a way that seemed to associate his warning with her own inheritance. And then he had said he was sorry he'd talked to her; he'd told her to forget it.

But Henry's death, Clistie's disappearance, the ugly brutal murder of a girl none of them knew, could have no possible connection with each other! The trip to the Ponte Verde courthouse, the policemen in the house and searching the grounds, had reminded her, and probably all of them, of the days following Henry's death. That was why, she decided, she kept thinking of him.

But the lurking shadow of that new, different uneasiness hovered over her, nevertheless, like a pursuing, ugly bird, its black wings spread.

Bessie and Hollis were talking down at the other end of the terrace, where Victoria and Michael had talked the night before. Suddenly it seemed to her that the plans for her wedding and the talk she'd had with Michael the previous night belonged in an altogether different world, and had nothing whatever to do with her now.

But that of course was wrong. She must have a talk with Michael. And explain to Bessie. She crossed the terrace toward Bessie and Hollis, and Hollis was trying to make Bessie understand that he couldn't stay at the house and help with the search because he had to get back to camp.

Bessie was protesting; an official leave, limited to hours, meant nothing to her when she wanted Hollis. "I'll just telephone to Bruce," she was saying. "I'll explain to him. I'll tell him why you can't come back to camp. We're not at war yet. Surely you can break a few rules! I want to tell him about Clistie, anyway."

It was Agnew eventually who restrained her, while Hollis, consulting his watch, dashed for his own small car and camp.

But Bessie telephoned to Colonel Galant anyway. She did not tell the post-commander that one of his soldiers, and a mere private at that, would (if she'd had her way) have overstayed his leave, she did tell him the whole story of the dead girl and Clistie's disappearance.

Victoria, following her into the hall, heard it. ". . . just like that, Bruce. In her green dressing-gown. Walked down the stairs and disappeared. And then that poor dead girl in Clistie's new dress, and we all had to go to Ponte Verde and tell them it wasn't Clistie. No, of course we don't know who it

52

was. Nonsense, I knew everybody Clistie knew; Clistie didn't know that girl. And Victoria thinks she heard the girl—well, scream . . ." Bessie's voice wavered and she went on, "I do wish you'd come. Bruce, what *shall* we do? And there's the wedding tomorrow . . ." She stopped and listened and finally hung up.

"Bruce said he was busy and would rather not talk just now! But he thinks we ought to postpone the wedding," she said to Victoria. "Yet if Clistie comes back—and she might at any moment, you know. It does seem a pity. After all, it isn't as if we knew that poor girl."

Last night, thought Victoria wearily, she had decided there was to be no wedding. Again it seemed far in the past. Bessie said impatiently, "Really, Victoria, you don't look as if you'd heard me. I suppose you're tired after such a night. So am I, but still . . . Oh, there's Michael. . . ."

He came in from the driveway, looking hot and tired, and seeing the quick question in their eyes, shook his head. "No news," he said. "It's horribly hot in the woods—not a breath of air." He sat down on the lower step of the stairs and mopped his forehead. Victoria said, "Michael, we were talking about the wedding."

He looked at her quickly. "I didn't want to bother you, Vicky." He stretched out his hand and drew her down to the stair-step beside him. "What about it? If you don't want to talk about it now, we won't."

Bessie said agitatedly, "But Michael, it's tomorrow! If we're going to postpone it, we've got to let people know right away."

Bessie, of course, didn't know what Michael really meant. Victoria said slowly, "We were talking of—of postponing it. Bruce thought it would be best."

"Oh," said Michael. His gray eyes searched her own intently for a moment. Then he said abruptly, "Well, I don't agree. I think the best thing to do is to put off the people who were invited. I mean, call off the wedding party. But we— could be married tomorrow, just the same, Victoria. Quietly —only the family and the minister. We could cancel our plans for a trip and stay here until—until things are straightened up. That is, if we need to."

"But Michael, last night . . ." began Victoria. Bessie interrupted. "I hadn't thought of that," she said. "I suppose you're right. We can't have people here; that's flat. Not unless Clistie —if we only knew," she ended disjointedly. Michael got up.

"I've got to go back," he said. "I only came to get a drink and take back some water for the rest of them."

Victoria said unsteadily, "But I feel just the same, Michael.

53

Last night . . ."

"Today is—well, different."

But the situation between them was the same, thought Victoria unhappily.

"No," she began. "No, Michael. It's only Clistie . . ." Her voice broke in spite of herself, and she cried, "If anything has happened . . ."

"If anything has happened," said Michael. "I'd like you to be my wife." He turned to Bessie. "I think that may be the best plan. We'll see. I'm going back now." He said to Victoria, "But it's up to you. Anything you decide . . ." and went down the hall toward the butler's pantry.

Bessie looked at Victoria worriedly. "What do you think?" she said.

"I don't know," said Victoria uncertainly, trying to think, and failing. There were only two things she was sure of: one was still that she didn't love Michael enough to marry him—and wished she could. The other was that they ought to have heard from Clistie by then—if Clistie was able to communicate with them. She said to Bessie wearily, "Of course we can't have people here. If Clistie . . . If we only knew . . ."

She stopped as Bessie had stopped. And Bessie said abruptly, "In any case, I'd better let people know. What a situation! Really, I don't know . . ." She hesitated, thinking. "I'll write one telegram and give it and the list of addresses to the Western Union girl," she said practically.

It gave her something to do. Michael went down to the pine woods again and Bessie sat at the desk, writing telegrams and scratching them out, tapping her large, firm teeth with the pencil. "You can't say, 'We don't want you to come to the wedding luncheon to which we invited you because a girl was murdered near the place last night and somebody in the family has disappeared,'" she said at last irritably to Victoria and Thalia. "You can't say, 'On account of all this the marriage will take place as arranged, but we don't want you or anybody else to come.'" She shoved her pencil through her thick, untidy hair. "Really, I don't think there is a precedent for this kind of thing . . ." She broke off abruptly to look toward the hall and listen as the telephone rang. They did that all that strange, long day, for it might be news of Clistie.

It wasn't, however; it was a reporter, said Jody, coming to the door. He wanted to ask if it was true that Miss Forbes' dress had been identified. There was a moment of silence. Then Bessie said, "Already," with a kind of groan. "Jody, tell him we can't talk to him."

It was again like the days following Henry's death. Bessie said suddenly, "I'm not going to send any telegrams. Clistie

54

must come back."

"But something's wrong—she wouldn't stay away like this. Please do send them, Aunt Bessie."

"Nonsense." Bessie crumpled the papers she'd been trying this and that phrase upon and thrust them into the waste-basket. "Clistie *will* come back. You'll see."

Thalia said, her white eyelids flickering, "You're going to be married then, Vicky, just as if—just the same?"

"No," said Victoria. Bessie said, "Yes. Unless we—have to postpone it." And Jody, just then, his black face old and wrinkled and tired, came back to announce lunch. A lunch that Clistie had ordered, writing it out in her neat, slanted handwriting. Thalia and Victoria and Bessie ate alone; neither Michael nor Agnew returned.

After lunch, however, unexpectedly, Major John Campbell arrived. Victoria, finding it impossible to sit still and wait, had walked out into the gardens. It was very hot; the sun beat down warmly upon the roses and the banks of azaleas glowed brilliantly along the paths. Through a vista made by path and hedges she saw a car with a man in uniform driving, enter the drive and approach the house. Thinking it was Colonel Galant, she walked quickly along the path to intercept him, but, as she reached the graveled court in front of the house, Major Campbell swung out of the car, saw her and came toward her, his black head, with its rather arrogant lift, shining in the sunlight.

"Colonel Galant asked me to stop," he said. "Is there any news?"

"None. Except—that girl this morning . . ."

He nodded. "The Colonel told me. But you have no direct news of Miss Forbes?"

"No. Clistie would have told me if she meant to leave. It isn't like her. . . ."

He took her hand quickly in his own. "Please don't worry. Miss Forbes always seemed to me very independent. She would be quite likely to—oh, play a lone hand, if she took it into her head to. But she was sensible, too. Remember that."

She said abruptly, "I keep thinking of Henry. And what you told me yesterday."

"I never thought of anything like this," he said. "I only meant—what I said."

"She—that dead girl, I mean, could have had nothing to do with Henry's death. None of us even knew her."

He didn't reply to that. He said instead, rather casually, "Have you searched Miss Forbes' room for any note or clue to her disappearance?"

It was an obvious step to take. Victoria wondered why

none of them had done so. "I will," she said.

He glanced at his wrist watch. "I've got to hurry; there's a brace of Washington dignitaries I've got to meet at Ponte Verde and escort to camp and put back on the six o'clock train. Will you please tell Mrs. Isham that Colonel Galant will come as soon as we get rid of our visitors." He started back toward the waiting car and she walked beside him.

The sun beat down hard upon them. The windows of the long house, silent behind their awnings and screens and the bougainvillaea that draped them, were still observant, somehow, like so many eyes. The uniformed boy at the wheel of the car stared straight ahead so rigidly that it only emphasized his rather outstanding ears.

Major Campbell opened the car door and paused, his hazel eyes narrowed against the bright sunlight. She had put on that morning, quickly, a cool, blue chambray dress; she had pulled her hair up away from her temples and from the back of her neck and twisted it in a loose knot.

Something in Major Campbell's eyes gave her a sudden inner vision of herself, the dress she had snatched hurriedly, the scuffed white sports shoes, the quick, childish knot of hair. She put her hand to her hair, and he said quickly, "Don't . . ."

For a startled, queer instant they looked at each other. Then he said, "I mean—you look so—so young and . . ." He bit his lip. "What I meant to say is—if there's anything I can do, please let me."

"Thank you."

He got quickly into the car. The slam of the door awoke echoes in the silent, sun-drenched courtyard and apparently brought Thalia to the open front door. When the car had disappeared around a curve of the driveway and Victoria turned toward the house, Thalia was standing in the doorway. She said, "Wasn't that John Campbell?"

"Yes."

"Oh," said Thalia. And again, unexpectedly, Victoria had a fleeting impression of something amused below the velvet of her lovely dark eyes. It was an odd impression, and it was gone almost as soon as it had come. Thalia's eyes were all at once wide and candid. She didn't even ask why Major Campbell had come; she said merely, "I wish Michael and Agnew would come back and tell us if—what they are doing. Heavens, it's hot! Beasley, the new State's Attorney, you know, just telephoned to say she isn't in any of the hospitals in the vicinity. They tried every one—even as far away as Pine Beach."

Clistie's room yielded nothing in the way of clues. Victoria searched it at once. There was no note, telling them where she had gone or why; there was nothing, in fact. Except, gradually, a rather curious impression that the room had already been searched.

The dresses were pushed a little awry on their hangers, but early that morning, when they had looked in the wardrobe in the hope of finding the brown dress, everything had been in perfect order, and had been left like that. The blotter on the writing desk was crooked and the paper and envelopes shoved untidily into the pigeonholes. When Victoria looked in the chest of drawers she was sure; Clistie was, as a rule, as neat as a little brown cat. Now the stacks of underclothing and stockings and sachets were heaped together in frantic disorder. Victoria closed the drawers thoughtfully and went downstairs.

But when she asked neither Bessie nor Thalia knew anything of it. "And I don't think it was the police," said Bessie, looking puzzled. "They looked in the room, when they were searching the house for Clistie—as if we hadn't the wits to find her if she was here!—but they didn't make that kind of search, I'm sure."

The men were, then, still searching the pine woods.

Particularly they searched the river banks. This took time; all of it took time. Owing to the vagaries of the St. Sebastian, the river banks along the stretch of pine woods were irregular, sometimes quite abrupt and high, shelving straight down to the quiet, deep current of the river. The river had cut in here and there against the high banks and had veered unaccountably away at other points. The pine woods were long, too, stretching out over a mile along the river. Altogether it was a difficult place to search, even systematically as they did, dividing it into sections and quartering the sections.

They searched more carefully, of course, within hearing distance of the house. The bank there was not high but it was abrupt; therefore, they reasoned, if Victoria had heard a splash following the scream, it could have been the splash made by the girl's body, dropped down into the river which, just there, was deep. There were other, flat, low strips, rushgrown where nothing could have splashed, where the murderer would have had to wade out into the river in order to let the current catch the body.

The murderer. Under that white moon, in that silence, a murderer had crept along in the black shadows, somewhere near the house, while Victoria sat on the balcony. Yet she'd heard nothing and seen nothing, thought Victoria, in horror, until the scream which she knew wasn't part of a dream. Everyone else knew it too, now, whether they admitted it or not.

Eventually, Michael and Agnew came back with what news there was, which was little enough. The police were not giving up but were working farther downstream, toward Ponte Verde.

They had found no real clues.

The soil was muddy along the banks; there were pine needles; many footprints were found in the woods, but most of them were blurred and unclear, probably unidentifiable; all of those that had retained any clear outline were preserved and marked for, later, a mold. There was no telling when most of them were made; there had been little rain that spring.

Among them, however, were some small marks of high, French heels.

There was no straight trail of them, nothing that could be followed. Eventually, however, a fairly clear mark was found near the bank.

For a hundred feet around it, the bank was marked off for close examination. If the girl had been murdered at that point, her body would have splashed heavily as it was dropped into the river. Victoria on the balcony could have heard both the splash and the scream, for the spot where the heel print was found was not far from the garden hedge.

But nothing moved or walked in the gray, shadowy arches of the pine woods, twilight even in daytime, except for patches of light sifting thinly here and there through the Spanish moss. Nothing, that is, except the searchers, for Clistie was not there.

By late afternoon they were talking of bloodhounds.

And by late afternoon, too, the dead girl was identified.

Eliot Beasley himself drove out from Ponte Verde to tell them that, and to question them.

He arrived about six. A few moments after Clistie was found.

8

Agnew found her.

The police were far up the river toward Ponte Verde by that time. Judson and the other men had given up. Agnew and Michael had returned to the house, and the shadows were slanting long across the garden, when Agnew thought of the pump house.

He got up quietly, without speaking to anyone, and went down through the gardens again.

The pump house was behind the yew hedge, in a kind of small cave, hollowed out below the garden and plastered with concrete, like a little air-raid shelter. The house had its own water supply, naturally, as it was some distance from any town. It was an artesian well, dug when the house was built, and the water was pumped by a motor and stored.

Judson oiled the pump regularly; everyone else forgot it. They had searched everywhere else.

So Agnew, when he remembered it, went down quietly through the garden, turned on the other side of the yew hedge, followed it along the bank of the garden for the land was irregular there, opened the green-painted door, slanting like an old-fashioned cellar door, descended the short flight of damp, cold concrete steps, with the rhythmic murmur of the pump in his ears, and found Clistie.

He saw the green of her dressing-gown first; and then the huddle of her thin, horribly inert body against the wall, opposite the pump. There was an electric light bulb swinging over his head, but he didn't turn it on. He had seen enough and he felt sick and dizzy.

He knew, he told them later, that she was dead.

He turned stumbling, not sobbing this time, and ran to the house, cutting across the formal rosebeds, bursting upon them as they sat on the porch.

It seemed to Victoria, then, that they'd been waiting all that day for the sound of his running feet, heavy across the grass. For the look in his white face.

Bessie's hands went to her breast and her lips moved. Agnew cried in a thin, high squeal, "She's in the pump house. I found her. She's in the pump house . . ."

Jody had a pitcher of iced tea in his hand, and he was going to drop it. Victoria watched it shake and tremble in his shriveled black hand. Michael was at Agnew's side, his hand on Agnew's shoulder. "Is she alive?" The look on Agnew's face seemed to answer him. He whirled around. "Jody, telephone to the police; get Judson up here, too. I'll go down. Agnew, is she . . . ?"

Agnew, shivering, said between his teeth, "She's dead. I know she's dead. She's against the wall. . . ."

"I'll go," said Michael, and ran, as Agnew had done, across the formal beds, toward the yew hedge and the pump house. Agnew, rubbing his arm over his eyes, followed him and Victoria must have moved to go, too, for Bessie caught her arm. "Don't go down there," she cried, her lips gray. "Don't go—it can't help. If she's dead . . ."

Jody had got the big glass pitcher safely placed on a table. He turned around and ran back into the house. Thalia said, "Where's the pump house? Didn't the police look in the pump house? Didn't Judson look?" Her small face turned white and sharp all at once, and she said in a kind of scream, "Was she murdered? Like that girl—murdered . . ."

59

All at once the cook, old fat Ernestine in starchy white, was there, and Lilibelle, one of the little colored maids, in equally starchy gray—rolling her eyes widely, shocked and frightened. Ernestine put her fat, comforting arm around Victoria. Bessie said unevenly, "Thalia, stop that noise! Lilibelle, you tell Jody to telephone for Judson. Tell him to telephone the camp too and ask for Colonel Bruce and tell him I've got to have . . . No, I'll telephone. I've got to tell Hollis. I've got to—a doctor, too," she cried loudly, her breath coming in stertorous gasps. "Maybe she's not dead. Lilibelle, wait; tell Jody to call the doctor, first. Dr. Theobald. Jody will know."

Lilibelle ran into the house again. Victoria said stiffly, "If she's dead, Bessie, the doctor can't do anything." She shook off Ernestine's arm and started across the garden. The pump house, of course. She hadn't thought of it; nobody, then, had thought of it. Not even Judson. He took care of the pump; but nobody ever thought of the pump house or its inconspicuous, green-painted door. *Why had Clistie gone there?*

Michael was running across the garden again, toward her, his face drained of color. He caught her by the shoulders. "You can't go down there."

"Michael, is she dead?"

He held her tightly. "Yes." Victoria felt herself sway against his hands; he put both arms around her. "She's been dead, I think, for at least all day. Victoria, you'll have to know. Perhaps you've been expecting it—since that girl this morning . . ."

"Was Clistie murdered?"

"I'm afraid so."

Agnew suddenly was beside her also, his face rigid and white. Somebody was crying. It was Bessie, in loud vehement sobs. Then they were on the porch again—the wide porch with its gay wicker chairs and its beautiful view of the river. The sun was low, the sky tranquil and clear and reflecting itself in the river. Michael must have led her to a chair. Ernestine was crying, too, her white apron over her head. Jody was in the doorway, trying to make Bessie understand something he was saying about Colonel Galant, and just then Colonel Galant himself came out from the house.

"I just drove up, Bessie. Is this true, what Jody tells me?"

A tall, lanky man with a long yellow face had apparently arrived at the same time and was questioning Jody as if he had a right to. Then she recognized him; it was the man who had questioned them that morning; the new State's Attorney, Eliot Beasley. She wondered dimly how he had got there so soon. But Clistie was dead. *Clistie* was dead. Like that girl in Clistie's dress.

60

Colonel Galant came to bend over her. His face was kind and worried. "Vicky, Vicky, my dear . . ." He was patting her hands, comforting her. He straightened to his full, spare height and told Jody to bring brandy. Michael and the State's Attorney were talking. Suddenly the men were moving again toward the garden, toward the forgotten little pump house whose very existence no one had remembered. No one except Clistie.

Why had Clistie gone there? And what had happened?

Bessie was crying and stopping to wipe her eyes, her ringed fingers flashing. Thalia's face was white and still. Agnew was hunched on a bench, alone on the grassy slope below them as if he couldn't bear to be with anybody.

They'd waited all that day. Well, now they knew.

It didn't seem very long, really, until the men came back again from the garden, their faces very sober. Bessie saw them coming and rose. They trudged along, heavily, as if they carried a weight on their shoulders. The State's Attorney's yellow face was like a mask; he said nothing to Bessie, who stood directly in his path, but went around her and asked Jody to take him to the telephone. Colonel Galant wiped his face with his handkerchief and sat down on the divan.

"I'm afraid it's true," he said to Bessie. "It— I'll have some of that brandy, Michael."

It stood on the table with the big pitcher of iced tea. Michael poured some for the Colonel which he gave him, and some for himself. His hand was unsteady, and he set the decanter down loudly. The Colonel said, with an apologetic glance at Bessie, "It's been so horribly hot today. I—I wasn't prepared for . . ."

"Bruce, was she murdered?" said Bessie harshly, her great eyes showing white rims. "Was she murdered? Like that poor girl this morning?"

"Yes, Bessie. Strangled," said the Colonel, and drank his brandy quickly. Victoria put her hands over her eyes to shut out something that really she had not seen. Michael put down the glass he held and came to her.

"Bruce, who killed her?" cried Bessie loudly. "Nobody would kill Clistie. What happened?"

"I don't know, Bessie. She—that's all I know. She's there in the pump house. This man—the State's Attorney, whatever his name is—thought she'd been there probably since last night. Undoubtedly she was murdered."

"Victoria," said Michael in Victoria's ear. "Come with me. Quick—before he gets back." He took her arm and led her down upon the path, away from the porch. Bessie's voice rose loudly behind them. "I must have Hollis. I must let Hollis

61

know at once. Oh, Bruce, Bruce, *couldn't* she have committed suicide? Henry committed suicide. Maybe Clistie committed suicide . . ."

"No," Bruce Galant's voice sounded loud, too. "No, Bessie. She didn't kill herself."

Michael took Victoria's hands urgently. "Victoria, listen," he said quickly, his voice low. "It's been a shock, I know. I wish I could have kept you from knowing like—like this. But I—Victoria, that man Beasley, the State's Attorney, is going to question you. You and me and all of us, for that matter." A door closed. Michael glanced back at the porch. "It's Beasley already. What I wanted to say is this: when he questions you, don't admit anything. Do you understand?"

"You mean it will be like—like Henry's death."

"It's murder, Victoria."

"You're afraid they'll suspect me, again. As it was when Henry died. But I—I didn't—I couldn't have . . . Clistie . . ."

"I know, Victoria. But remember, ask for a lawyer. Don't let Beasley trap you into saying anything you don't mean. We'd better go back . . ."

They turned back toward the porch. Beasley was watching them. His yellow face long and lined, his black eyes bright under heavy yellow eyelids. He wore a wrinkled white linen suit and a pale yellow tie which seemed to match the ugly pallor of his long, heavy face with its pendulous lips. He watched them; he watched Thalia and Bessie and the Colonel and even Jody, all at once. He explained as they stepped upon the wide porch, that the police and the coroner were on their way.

"I'm not a coroner," he said, jerking his purplish lips over yellow, long teeth in a kind of grin, "as my predecessor was. I expect you all remember him very well. If I'm not mistaken, it's only been nine or ten weeks since"—he looked all around with his black eyes sparkling beneath those wrinkled yellow eyelids—"since Henry Frame was murdered."

Bessie said heavily, her face shocked and flabby, "Since Henry committed suicide."

"It *was* suicide, Mr. Beasley," said Colonel Galant. "That was the coroner's jury's verdict. Surely you knew that."

"Yes," said Beasley, "I knew."

Colonel Galant flashed a startled, comprehensive glance at Beasley.

"Then exactly what do you mean?" said Michael.

"Murder," said Beasley. "Of course."

"But that case—Henry's death—that case is closed," said Colonel Galant.

"It's reopened now," said Beasley. "Now, then . . ."

"But that's impossible!" cried Bessie, staring. "None of us even knew that girl! It has nothing whatever to do with Henry. Mr. Beasley, who murdered Clistie? What happened? Can we—can we bring her into the house? It doesn't seem decent to leave her—like that. . . ."

"Sorry," said Beasley. "I can't do anything till our coroner arrives. Except—well, I came out from Ponte Verde just now to ask you a question or two. If you don't mind. . . ."

Thalia put a dainty, lacy handkerchief to her eyes. The Colonel uttered a protesting but helpless murmur. Bessie seemed to gather her strength together, as one braces muscles. She lifted dark, white-rimmed eyes toward Beasley. "Why, certainly, if you must," she said. "You must understand, however, that—that this has been a frightful shock. If you could give us a little time . . ."

"I'm so very sorry, Mrs. Isham. Do you know anyone named Joan Green?"

It put a kind of period to the whole ugly scene.

Bessie leaned forward, her face slack. She tried to get up, and fell clumsily and slackly, half over the chair, half on the floor. One foot, absurdly small in a high-heeled pump such as Bessie always wore, scuffed up the grass rug.

They carried her into the drawing room and put her on a couch; she wasn't unconscious for more than a moment or two; she insisted on walking upstairs to her own room.

The doctor, their own family doctor, whom Jody had summoned, arrived a few moments later and said she was to stay in her room; she'd had a severe shock. No one was to question her yet.

Hollis arrived shortly after, and the police again, and the coroner.

The family doctor, old Dr. Theobald, went down to the pump house with the coroner and the police and came back after a long time, his face very grave. He told Victoria to stay with Bessie.

"It's a bad business," he said, shaking his head. He was a little, stocky man with a pointed gray beard and rather popped eyes. He looked doubtfully at Victoria. "I'll tell you this," he said suddenly. "Clistie couldn't have had more than a —a few seconds. If the pressure exerted is hard enough, and just at the right place, against these arteries"—he put his stubby hands against his own neck, one on each side—"it doesn't take more than a few seconds. It cuts off the blood supply to the brain, you know. You lose consciousness at once." He stopped abruptly. "Don't look like that, my dear. It's—it's a bad business." He shook his head again and trotted

63

away. Bessie stirred and sat up.

"He's gone, has he?" she said. "Vicky, has Hollis come? Has Hollis come, Vicky?"

He had arrived, but had gone down to the pump house. And when he returned to the house and came to his mother's room, Bessie sent Victoria away. "I want to talk to Hollis," she said. "Hollis, come here."

Passing Victoria on the way into the room, Hollis gave her hand a quick, comforting squeeze. He looked white and frightened, younger, more like Agnew. He stopped at the foot of his mother's bed and gripped the railing tightly, rather defiantly, Victoria thought, as she closed the door.

The house, on the second floor at least, was quiet. Downstairs there was a kind of subdued hubbub—footsteps, the hum of men's voices, the ringing of the telephone. It was like the time following Henry's death. Henry's murder, Beasley had said. As John Campbell had said.

Henry, and Clistie, and a thin, blonde girl none of them knew.

Victoria went to her room. From the windows she could see men—police in uniform, Beasley, a little man she recognized as the county sheriff—cross the garden toward the pump house and return.

She left the window and went out on the balcony; but in the growing twilight the river looked secretive and strange, as if it, and the house and garden and even themselves, she thought suddenly, had changed—had undergone a swift and sinister metamorphosis.

Murder.

A long time later, for it was dark and the moon was out bright and white again, Jody brought her some soup and sandwiches on a tray and coaxed her to eat them.

"What are they doing?"

"I don't know, Miss Vicky. They talking mostly. Mr. Hollis and Mr. Michael and the Colonel. Mr. Agnew, he sick and went to bed. Miss Thalia, she ate a good dinner. Lots of people downstairs—policemen, and lots of people. It's like the time when Mr. Frame died." He avoided her eyes, set the tray down and started away. She stopped him.

"Jody, who do they think killed her? Is there any—any evidence?"

His eyes roved around the room, everywhere but toward her. "I don't know, Miss. You eat your soup," he said, and went away quickly, as if afraid she would call him back.

She couldn't eat; she returned to the balcony; it was night again; there were lights glancing about the garden down there toward the pump house, beyond the thick yew hedge.

She was thinking of Clistie when they sent for her. Jody came, again, to tell her. Obviously he hated asking her to go downstairs and talk to the police; he felt sorry for her, she could see that, and he saw that she'd been crying.

She washed her face with cold water and brushed back her hair. Her eyes felt as if they were on strings. She followed Jody down the stairs where Clistie had descended the night before, while Victoria stood and watched her and had no premonition that that was the last time.

The library was lighted and there was a high-backed chair at the long table in the middle of the room, with the light from above shining brightly down upon it. Men were waiting there.

But not Michael, not Colonel Galant, not even Hollis, whose face would have been friendly. Instead there were two state policemen in uniform, standing back in the shadows, the State's Attorney, Eliot Beasley, sitting at the end of the table but outside the rim of light so the direct glare was not upon him, and two other men in civilian clothing—the county sheriff and a stenographer, with a ruled pad of paper on his knee.

Then she saw John Campbell, in uniform, standing at one of the windows, his back to the room. As she entered, he turned, saw her, and made a quick move toward her. Eliot Beasley said peremptorily: "Come in, Miss Steane. Over here, please."

Major Campbell stopped, folded his arms and stood before the window.

She moved forward slowly and then saw something on the table. It was the only object on the table which had been swept bare of its usual clutter of books and ashtrays and flowers.

And it was a thin, red leather belt with a small gilt buckle. It was a belt that belonged to her; it went on a white, silk dress with red buttons. It was a queer place for her belt to be.

The State's Attorney said in a rasping voice: "I see you recognize that belt, Miss Steane. It belongs to you, doesn't it? Do sit down. No—here, in this chair."

She sat down, staring at the belt which looked lithe and thin, coiled there under the light like a small scarlet snake.

"That," said Eliot Beasley, "was around Clistie Forbes' neck when we found her."

9

The night was hot. The state police had shed their tunics and were wearing brown shirts. Beasley had taken off his white-linen coat and pulled his collar open and his long, yellow face glistened. The windows were open but not a breath of air stirred the heavy draperies. The light pouring down on her face was hot too.

But that scarlet, thin belt couldn't have been around Clistie's neck!

She was sitting upright in the high-backed chair, hands tight on the carved arms. The polished, bare surface of the table reflected the glaring light from above—only the coiled, sinuous red belt broke the reflection. She moistened her lips.

Beasley said, "It *is* your belt?"

"I—I don't know . . ." Whoever murdered the girl in the pine woods couldn't have entered the house, Victoria thought dazedly. If somebody the girl knew, somebody who'd wanted to murder her, who had met her in the pine woods and killed her there and dropped her little, tragic body in the river—and then, later been intercepted by Clistie so that, terrified and shaking with the dreadful thing he had just done, he had felt that he had to kill Clistie, too—if all that had happened (and it was the only logical explanation for Clistie's murder) then how had he got Victoria's little scarlet belt?

Beasley said, "Look here, Miss Steane, you may as well understand this: I'm going to break this case and I'm going to do it quickly. The sooner you and everybody else understands that the better for everybody. Now then. That belt was twisted around Clistie Forbes' neck when we found her. Undoubtedly it was the weapon of murder. I examined the marks on that dead girl's throat; we'll have experts look at it later. But I'm sure now, anybody would be sure who looked at it, that the belt could have been used to strangle that girl. And then removed and used to murder Clistie Forbes, too. What have you to say about it?"

"But I—I don't know anything about it! I don't understand how anybody could have come into the house and taken the belt. It . . . There *must* be some mistake. . . ."

"But it is your belt?"

Michael had told her not to admit anything. Yet anybody could have told Beasley that she had a red belt like that one.

She said, "I—I have one like it."

"So I'm told. And your maid says it's not in your dressing room. I sent her to look while you were with your aunt. There's no use, you see, in trying to evade. This is your belt. Now then when did you last see it?"

She tried to think back. The slim strip of red leather was horribly fascinating; it looked as if it might move. She made herself look at Beasley, and his sparkling black eyes had a triumphant glitter. "I don't know," she said. "I don't remember."

Beasley glanced at the stenographer who was making jerky marks on the tablet he held.

"You don't remember. Miss Steane, how long have you known Joan Green?"

"Joan . . ." That was the name he'd asked Bessie about, and Bessie had fainted—not, Victoria had thought, because of the name, but rather from what the doctor had called delayed shock. "I don't know anybody by that name."

"Oh, you don't know anybody by that name. You've been at Camp Blakoe frequently, haven't you?"

"Yes." But Camp Blakoe (and Joan Green) had nothing to do with Clistie.

"So I understood. You know quite a number of the officers and their wives, don't you?"

"Yes, I suppose I do. Mr. Beasley, this has nothing to do with Clistie's death . . ."

"You know Colonel Galant very well, don't you?"

"Yes."

"I expect you've been in his office occasionally during the building and organization of the camp. Haven't you?"

"Why, I—yes, I suppose so."

"You suppose so." Beasley glanced sharply at the stenographer as if to be sure he had written her answer. Major Campbell hadn't moved. Beasley said, "His office is in the administration building, isn't it? But you don't know Joan Green?"

"No. Is that the dead girl? Has she been identified?"

"'Is that the dead girl!' Yes, Miss Steane." Beasley's voice was sharp with sarcasm. "Yes, Miss Steane, that is the dead girl. Joan Green. She has been identified. She worked at the administration building. Her desk was in the outer office, connecting the Quartermaster's office and Colonel Galant's. You had to pass her desk every time you went to Colonel Galant's office. She took the telephone calls for both offices, so you had to talk to her every time you telephoned to Colonel Galant. She was at the Colonel's tea party yesterday and you were there, too. But when you saw her this morning, dead, you didn't know her. Oh, no. You only thought her face was familiar. Sit down, please."

Victoria had started to rise; she sank down into the chair again.

"But there were so many people," she said, slowly. "The camp is so big. I don't remember stopping at Colonel Galant's office more than once or twice. If she was there I don't remember her. I do though, now, remember seeing her at the tea party."

That was why the dead girl's face had been faintly familiar. She remembered her, suddenly—standing beside Bessie, taking a cup of coffee and moving away. It had been just as Major Campbell approached and spoke to her.

"Oh, you remember her, now, do you?" said Beasley. "Now that there are so many people who can prove that you have seen her many times!"

Major Campbell's figure moved a little forward. Victoria said, "It's true, exactly as I told you. I didn't know where I had seen her until you spoke of Colonel Galant's tea. Then I knew."

John Campbell had stopped; his voice came from the shadows. "Have you any proof to the contrary, Eliot?"

Beasley shrugged, shot a quick glance toward John Campbell and said, "No. Not yet, and you know it."

There was a short silence.

Beasley's long yellow fingers were tapping the polished surface of the table. Major Campbell's tall, uniformed figure, just at the edge of her vision, moved back again quietly into the window embrasure. Beasley leaned forward and continued with an air of frankness and a stretching of his thick, purplish lips that went for an ingratiating smile. "Well, Miss Steane, let's forget Joan Green. Let's go back to last night. You say you heard a scream; you say you thought someone was being hurt; you say it seemed to come from the pine woods. You say that you ran out into the hall and called Miss Forbes and Agnew Isham. At least that was your statement this morning when I talked to you. Do you want to change it?"

"No. That is what happened."

"Do you want to add to it?"

"That is all there is to tell."

"Really," said Beasley. "Oh, I think not quite all. For instance, why did you call a boy of eighteen when there were men in the house? Why did you tell Miss Forbes that you had heard something in the pine woods, and then let her go alone and unaccompanied to investigate? Why didn't you go with her or send someone with her?"

"I meant to call Hollis," said Victoria. "But I made a mistake and opened the door to Agnew's room instead of Hollis'; the rooms are beside each other. And I called Clistie because . . ." She knew her voice wavered and she made herself speak steadily. "Because we always called Clistie. She always saw to things. That's why I let her go downstairs and, when she told me to, I went back to my room. She said she was going to telephone Judson—that's the gardener. She—all of us did what Clistie told us to do. We always have. If I'd known—if I'd dreamed . . ." Her voice wavered again, and this time she had to stop. There was a brief silence, with the light pouring down into her eyes and reflecting itself upward from the bare table, so wherever she looked there was a glare.

Beasley said, "Whom did you call first, Agnew, or Miss Forbes?"

"Agnew—well, as a matter of fact, I went to Clistie's room first. But she wasn't there and hadn't been to bed. Her dressing-gown was across the bed. I called her—I think I called her—anyway, I started toward Hollis' room and opened the door to Agnew's room instead, and woke him. Then as we went into the hall, to call Hollis, there was Clistie. She'd put on her dressing-gown and she still had on her turquoise satin slippers."

"Was she wearing the brown lace dress then?" broke in the State's Attorney.

"I don't know. I—why, no, I'm sure she wasn't wearing it under the dressing-gown for I remember noticing her slippers. The dressing-gown wasn't as long as the dress would have been; it came about to her ankles. No, I'm sure she wasn't wearing it then."

Again Major Campbell's voice came from the window embrasure. "What was she wearing when she was found? I don't remember that anyone told me."

"Dressing-gown, underclothing. No dress. Stockings. Blue satin slippers."

"What of the girl's dress then? What happened to it?"

Beasley looked irritated. "If I knew that, John, I'd know why she was wearing the Forbes woman's dress—which is more than I know now. Go on, Miss Steane. What happened then?"

"It's as I told you this morning. She asked what was wrong, and I told her. She said she'd call Judson and see to it and sent me to bed, and Agnew. She said she'd come back and tell me—but she didn't come. And then . . ."

"Then you and Agnew called Hollis Isham and Bayne and roused the house to look for her. But what about this scream? What time did you hear it?"

"I'm not sure. It was around midnight, I think."

"Can't you be more specific?"

"It was a little after eleven when I went out on the balcony. I was there a long time. When Agnew and I realized that we must look for Clistie it was nearly two, and Agnew thought she had been gone about an hour. I must have heard the scream about twelve-thirty. Perhaps a little later."

He glanced at the stenographer. "What time did Hollis Isham and Miss Frame say they returned from the movies?"

The stenographer flipped back pages. The little, quiet

69

county sheriff got out his handkerchief and mopped his round face. She remembered that he had been like that after Henry's death—an unobtrusive figure, appearing and disappearing with no explanation, yet adding a kind of passive weight of officialdom to the inquiry.

The stenographer stopped flipping pages. "Here it is, Mr. Beasley. Shall I read it? 'Question: What time did you return? Answer: I'm not sure; a little after twelve, I suppose.' That's Mr. Isham. And Miss Frame says . . ." He paused to turn another page. "Miss Frame says, 'It was ten minutes, almost exactly, after twelve.' She says . . ."

"All right. Now, Miss Steane, did you know they had returned?"

"I heard a car I supposed was Hollis' car."

"You didn't see either Hollis or Miss Frame?"

"No."

"But it was after that you heard the famous scream?"

"Yes."

"How long after?"

"Perhaps—a quarter of an hour. I can't say exactly."

He drummed on the table again for a moment, thoughtfully.

"And you sent Clistie Forbes to see what was wrong and an hour later you 'realized you must look for her.' It took you rather a long time," said Beasley, again sarcastic. He was right, though. If only they had not been so dependent upon Clistie, so assured of her efficiency and so blindly, childishly obedient! Major Campbell stirred uneasily in the shadow by the window. Beasley said, "Did anybody else hear that scream?"

"No. At least—no."

"What were you going to say?"

"It just seemed to me so loud and—and shrill. I thought everyone must have heard it."

"But in point of fact no one else did. The night was very quiet too. You're sure, Miss Steane, that someone screamed?"

"Yes. I wasn't dreaming . . ." Something moved in his eyes; she stopped, and after an instant said slowly, "You didn't mean that I was dreaming."

"No, Miss Steane, I'm afraid that isn't what I meant," said Beasley, stretching his lips over his teeth. He leaned forward so his long hand reflected itself in the surface of the table and the reflection looked exactly like a yellow, grasping claw. He said, "I told you I was going to break this case and do it quickly. Now, I've already questioned other people in the house: Miss Frame, Mr. Bayne, Hollis and Agnew Isham, the servants, everyone but Mrs. Isham and you. The whole picture isn't clear; there's no use pretending it is." He paused, and Victoria thought, queerly, with a kind of surprise: but he's honest. He was suspicious, clumsily sarcastic—with sparkling, hateful black eyes. But honest.

He said, "I suggest, Miss Steane, that there *could* have been no scream, for you alone heard it. I suggest that your story *could* have been only a ruse to get Miss Forbes out of the house. I suggest that this dead girl *could* have been dressed in Miss Forbes' dress merely in a desperate intent to confuse us. It would have been something a woman would think of. I don't know why Joan Green came here, or why she was murdered. So far—I'm being perfectly frank with you—I know only that Joan Green was a quiet, hard-working girl. She came from a little town near here, where she had lived with an aunt. She'd learned shorthand and typing in High School. She left home for the first time when she got a job at Camp Blakoe last winter while it was being built. She had a room in a hotel in Ponte Verde. That's all, so far, that I know about her. But that's not the point." He was leaning far over the table now, shaking his long hand at her. It was so still in the room that no one seemed to breathe. He said, "It was your belt, Miss Steane. You—and this boy—were the last to see Clistie Forbes. You sent her out into the night. You . . ."

Major Campbell came toward the table. "I think you're going pretty far, Eliot."

Beasley's long thin body twisted around. "It's my case, John, not yours. Although . . ." He smiled. "Well, no," he said. "I'm not so sure but what it *is* your case. Or *was* your case. You always said Henry Frame was murdered."

There was another silence in the hot room. Then Major Campbell said, "Exactly what is the connection?"

"I don't know yet. But mark my words, there is one. The Frame case is opened again, automatically. No doubt in anybody's mind now that he was murdered. So there's a triumph for you, my boy. You always insisted he was the kind of man somebody would murder."

There was another short silence before Major Campbell said, "I believed he was murdered, yes. But what about evidence?"

"Evidence of murder in the Frame case?"

"Evidence of that, and evidence linking it to the murders last night."

Beasley thrust out his lower lip and put his head on one side, judicially. "Concrete evidence, none. I doubt if we shall have any further evidence on the Frame case. *But* the big link is simply murder." His long hand dropped to his knee, his thick eyelids lowered over his black eyes. "Murder breeds murder, my boy. There was never anything truer said." He

71

chuckled a little and said almost gloatingly, "I'll tie up your case for you, John. Besides there's the important question of motive. Suppose this Forbes woman knew who murdered Frame. Suppose . . ." He checked himself abruptly, his eyes glittering yet secretive. "It's my luck to step in after you've gone out and wind up your famous unsolved murder. The Beasley luck," he said, and chuckled.

Major Campbell's face didn't change; nevertheless, a kind of shutter seemed to have closed over it, and whatever he was thinking. He reached inside his coat and got out a package of cigarettes. His brown belt glowed dully in the light as he struck a match. "Nevertheless, Eliot, I think you'd better let Miss Steane go now. She's had rather a bad time; you can't get much out of a—a hysterical witness," said Major Campbell, looking at Beasley as if Victoria didn't exist.

"I can get a confession . . ."

"I doubt it."

"But my God, John, *you* thought she murdered Frame!"

Michael had said, ask for a lawyer. Victoria got up. Campbell said, "I didn't prove it; remember that, too." Then he saw that she was rising and came toward her. Victoria put her hands on the table. "I'm going to have a lawyer," she said. "I refuse to answer any more questions now."

The small scarlet belt was so near her hand it almost touched it.

It was Major Campbell who broke the silence. "She's quite within her right, of course, Eliot," he said. "Besides—well, you can let her go for tonight, can't you?"

"I'll not have you interfering, you know, John," said Beasley softly. "I let you in on this tonight because you asked to come. All right, Miss Steane, you can go."

Major Campbell opened the door for her, his brown face and bright hazel eyes inscrutable. He said nothing; there was no way to know whether he was a friend or an enemy. Certainly he had seemed, once or twice, to defend her; yet obviously it was his case against her, after Henry Frame died, that led Beasley to suspect her now. For, obviously again, if the motive for Clistie's murder was some knowledge she possessed about Henry's death, then Clistie's murderer was also Henry's murderer.

But she hadn't murdered Henry—or Clistie. If Clistie had known that Henry was murdered, and had evidence leading to the murderer, she would have told the police, long ago. And Beasley's theory left out Joan Green altogether.

Yet there was her red belt. How *could* Clistie's murderer have got possession of it? Had he crept into the house—big, rambling, frequently left unlocked—found his way secretly to her dressing room, and got away again without being seen? But then who? And why go to such pains when a rope from the garage would have done as well?

The library door closed.

Michael was waiting, sitting on the stairway, an ashtray beside him full of cigarette ends. Thalia was there, too, sitting on the step above him. She was wearing the blue silk housecoat again and looking very pretty. "Oh, Vicky," she said quickly, getting up. "We've been waiting. Was it very bad? Of course, we knew about the belt—they asked everybody whose it was. Vicky, I sent the telegrams about the wedding. I got the list from Bessie. I . . ." She hesitated, her eyes very soft and dark and yet rather watchful under her long, soft eyelashes. "I didn't know what to say and you were in your room and so upset about Clistie, that I didn't—want to bother you. But I knew you couldn't have the wedding. So I said in the telegrams it was postponed; I couldn't think of anything else to say. I do hope that was right. Poor darling, you look simply dead." She paused for an instant. And a spark of something knowing and queerly speculative moved in her dark eyes, and she said gently, "Was John Campbell very difficult?"

"No," said Victoria shortly. Looking directly into Thalia's eyes, she found nothing secret, nothing amused, only sympathy.

"My God, I thought they'd never let you go," said Michael, putting his arm around her. "Vicky, darling, we'll get a lawyer right away."

He went upstairs with her. Thalia followed and went into Bessie's room. Ernestine was waiting for Victoria; fat old Ernestine with her troubled, faithful eyes. Hot milk was on the bed table. "She's got to go to bed now, Mr. Michael," she said. "Come, Miss Vicky. Ain't no use making yourself sick."

But she let Victoria tell Michael what Beasley had said. Michael listened in silence, holding her tight in his arms. "It'll be all right; you'll see," he said quietly. "We'll get at the truth. We did it before. Vicky, is there anything you've forgotten? Anything about Clistie?"

"Now, Mr. Michael," said Ernestine. "Miss Vicky's done up. Such a wedding day tomorrow! With Miss Clistie . . ." Scowling and troubled, she stopped.

Michael said, "It was all right for Thalia to send telegrams saying that the wedding was postponed; but we'll be married anyway. Right, Vicky?" He paused and said, "Vicky, I don't believe you've understood a word I've said. Put her to bed, Ernestine. Good night, dear."

Ernestine closed the door after him. "Now, now," said Ernestine. "Drink your milk. Hold up your arms, Miss Vicky—turn around . . ." Her loving old hands were more adept than the most skillful of French maids.

Victoria didn't remember Ernestine leaving the room. She didn't even remember putting down the glass of hot milk.

Agnew awakened her.

It was very late, the squares of moonlight on the carpet had traveled, slanting, across it. Agnew was sitting on the bed, tugging at her arm. She awoke and for a fractional instant did not remember what had happened. It was merely Agnew wandering the house at night, owl-like, as he often did. She could see him clearly in the reflected light.

"Toothache?" she said sleepily. And then remembered and sat up, "What's wrong? Agnew . . ."

"Sh—sh—don't yell! Nothing's wrong. I just wanted to—to talk . . ." He hesitated. He'd put on a winter bathrobe, hot-looking and woolly; his spectacles glimmered as he turned his head. "Vicky, why do you suppose Clistie went to the pump house?"

It was all back in her awareness now; the weight and the horror.

"I don't know. I wondered, too. There's nothing there . . ."

"No. Vicky, I'm going down there."

"Agnew, you're not!" she said sharply.

"There must be something—some clue . . ."

"But Agnew, you can't . . ." She thought quickly, seeking a reason with which to dissuade him. "The police have already been there. They wouldn't overlook anything. . . ."

"Yes, but why did she go there? And in the morning the police will be everywhere under foot again and I don't believe any of them are around tonight. I've got a flashlight."

With despair she recognized his arguing tone. It meant that nothing short of dynamite would sway him. She got up and reached for a dressing-gown.

"What are you going to do?" he whispered quickly.

"Tell Hollis. Thank Heaven, he managed to get a leave."

"Vicky," he said, "if you tell him and get him to stop me, I'll never tell you another thing in my life. I mean it."

He did mean it. There was a pause. He tugged the flashlight out of his pocket and turned toward the door.

"Wait," she said and fumbled for slippers. "I'm going too."

"No. Vicky, I won't let you . . ."

"I go or tell Hollis. Take your choice."

There was another silence while she tied the long crimson sash on her dressing-gown. Then he said crossly, "All right. Come on . . ."

The house was quiet. There was a small light above the

74

stairway; the rooms downstairs were dark. They crossed the drawing room, groping their way, and let themselves out the side door, very quietly. They crossed the porch and Agnew caught her wrist and whispered, "Follow the shadow of the hedge, just in case there *is* a policeman around."

But they crossed the garden and still no one stopped them. The tall yew hedge made a wide black shadow at the end of it. There was a gap in the hedge there; Agnew let Victoria precede him. On the other side of the hedge the moonlight fell full and strong upon them. Nothing moved in the moonlit strip between the hedge and the deep shadow of the pine woods.

Why had Clistie gone down the stairs—and instead of calling Judson, crossed the garden, walked along the hedge, entered the little, forgotten pump house? And then been killed.

But it had been a mistake to come; they'd better go back to the house—back through the still, white moonlight, back along those shadow paths.

Agnew whispered in her ear, "What's the matter?"

"We're going back. This was a crazy idea."

"Maybe it was," admitted Agnew. "But now we're this far . . ."

"Let's go back."

"Afraid? Well, I don't much like it myself. It's so darned white and black and—and still . . . But it's not much further."

"But there can't be anything there. I mean anything that would explain . . ."

"All right, go on back, then!" snapped Agnew fretfully. "But I'm going on."

He went ahead. The moonlight was bright and everything was quiet. Not even a bird moved in the black depths of the pine woods. The night before, if the police were right, Joan Green had been in those woods. A murderer had walked quietly in those black depths. Nothing moved there now; the police had combed the place. Still she'd been wrong to come and to bring Agnew with her. She followed his tall, bathrobed figure which was clearly outlined in the moonlight. He was carrying the flashlight in one hand. They moved again into the deep black shadow made by some shrubs which were planted thickly around the slanting door of the pump house. She could barely see Agnew, but she could hear him tug the door upward She couldn't see the steps; he was fumbling with the catch of his flashlight. "Go ahead, Vicky," he said. "If this thing's out of batteries . . ."

She groped for the edge of the steps and started down them Agnew was muttering impatiently and clicking the catch of his flashlight. She couldn't see anything below her,

75

but now she could touch rough, cold, concrete wall on both sides of the steps. She went down a few more steps, nerving herself to take each one. The pump wasn't running; it was perfectly still and quiet except that Agnew, above, seemed to be having difficulty finding the steps, scuffling his feet and bumping against the door. She turned around and said, "Agnew—where are you?" And the lighted, luminous sky directly above and the nearer black shadow of shrubs were blotted out.

All at once. Quickly. As if a curtain had been thrown over them—but a curtain that came down with a thud.

She cried, "Agnew—why did you drop the door? Where's the light?"

Agnew was coming softly down the stairs in the thick, damp, darkness, but he didn't answer.

"Agnew . . ." she said again. And stopped.

The footsteps stopped too. Suddenly she knew it wasn't Agnew.

10

Whoever was in the pump house did not answer. And must have heard her voice.

She could remember very little about the pump house. It was small, built around a pump which was run by electricity, and a tank for the storage of water; there was only one way to get in or out of it, and that was by the steps. That was all she knew of it. And with the blotting out of that rectangle of luminous sky, she wasn't sure, even, where the steps were. She was in a bewildering, damp, black space that smelled of oil.

Agnew was somewhere above. Why didn't he open the door again and come down the steps?

It was perfectly black and perfectly still. But someone was there, in that black little cave, and it wasn't Agnew, and she was caught exactly like a rat in a trap.

And anyone in the family, any of the servants, would have recognized her voice. Would have spoken.

She must move; do something—anything—not stand there frozen, rigid, waiting for the trap to close. She moved backward cautiously; her hands stretched into the darkness. If she could find the wall, it would guide her to the steps—if she went the right way. If nothing came out of that enveloping black pit and fell upon her, slid around her neck, tightened itself.

Her fingers touched something rough and cold, it was the wall; exactly as she touched it there was from somewhere near a sudden rasping hoarse murmur, like a beast rousing, and with a loud throb the pump started. She didn't scream; she couldn't.

The pump settled with a regular, loud beat which filled the tiny cellar, throbbing in her ears, making the darkness vibrant. Under the cover of that sound, she slid along the wall, instinctively toward the right. In a moment the wall gave way behind her. She stumbled, but the sound of it was covered by the noise of the pump; she fell upon steps, scrabbled up them, groped upward, found the door and pushed. It wasn't heavy; light came through the crack and showed a streak of white. It would reveal her clearly if she lifted it further, but she had to get out of the cellar. She pushed at the door and it fell back with a jarring thud. Moonlight poured down upon her, flooding the steps. The shrubs made black shadows. The pump was so loud behind her, waking all the black and white night to throbbing life, that she couldn't tell whether or not she was being pursued. But she stumbled into the shadow of the nearest shrubs, fell over something, was down on her knees again and, suddenly, tugging at Agnew's woolly bathrobe. He was there, in a heap. He said, mumblingly, "Vicky, what did you hit me for?"

She clutched at his arms; she dragged him to his feet. He was reluctant to move, and she had to make him come with her—had to make him hurry—had to urge him along while he stumbled and held back.

They reached the gate in the yew hedge. She looked back and behind her stretched a white alley of clear moonlight, with the silver yew hedge on one side and the deep black belt of shadow made by the pine woods on the other side. She could see the clump of shrubs around the pump house. The sound of the pump filled the night with its steady throb. No one followed them—or at least nothing moved along the white strip. But there were deep, concealing black shadows everywhere.

"My head aches," said Agnew thickly and loudly. "Don't make me run." But she did, clutching his arm tightly, dragging him along through the garden, ghostly and strange at that time of night.

They must rouse the house; they must hurry; they must get people to take lights and search—search the pump house, the grounds—the garden and the woods.

"Oh, *hurry*, Agnew!"

They reached the side door on the porch and it was lighted. They had left it dark. Someone, then, must be up and about. She pulled Agnew into the house and Jody was in the hall. He heard them and came running to meet them. He had, obviously, dressed in a hurry. His collar was open and his wrinkled old face looked worried. He peered at them uncertainly.

"Miss Vicky—was that you I heard?"

"Jody, call Mr. Hollis! Call Mr. Bayne! Hurry!"

"*Let me go*," said Agnew. "I'm going back down there—somebody hit me." He spoke thickly; there was blood on his face from a cut on his forehead, and a bump swelling rapidly above his left ear. Jody cried, "*Mr. Agnew—what happened?* You come with me!"

"I'm murdered," said Agnew, mumbling. "I'm wounded! Somebody tried to murder me!"

"You come right with me," cried Jody tremulously, taking his arm. "You come right along with me. I fix it . . ."

But they must search; they must hurry!

The amount of blood, though, streaming down Agnew's pale face was frightening. She followed Jody and Agnew to the butler's pantry. Jody snapped on lights. Agnew put his head under the cold water. Jody got out towels and ran around him in circles, muttering and anxious.

All in all, she thought later, several moments must have elapsed before Agnew announced himself as wounded but unmurdered, and Jody pulled himself and his scattered wits together. Victoria started for the stairs herself, but Agnew called her back, to hold the towel to his head. "I'm bleeding to death," he groaned. "I tell you I'm wounded." He broke off to hiss to Jody who was opening the pantry door, "Don't wake Mother."

"No, no. . . ."

"Jody, hurry—tell them in the pump house . . ."

"Yes, Miss."

She could hear Jody's muffled knocks, the low murmur of voices, and in a moment steps running down the stairs again. Jody went with them. After a little while, Agnew, fidgeting and murmuring, snatched the towel away, discovered his head had stopped bleeding and had only an inch-long cut in it. He went, too.

She followed him as far as the porch and waited. She could hear their voices and see the glancing gleams of flashlights.

But in the end they found no one.

Jody was the only one of them who was sure, really sure, that someone had been about the grounds on that still, moonlit night. He said it was the sound of footsteps on the gravel of the driveway that aroused him.

"I wasn't asleep," he said, wrinkling up his forehead like a faithful, worried dog. "I heard somebody run—light and quick—across the drive; I looked out the window, but couldn't see nobody. So after I worried about it awhile, I thought I'd better get up and come downstairs. Make sure nobody was breaking into the house. Soon as I got here and turned on the lights, you came . . ." He looked at Victoria.

Hollis said, rumpling his blond curls, that from their accounts of the thing there'd been plenty of time for anybody in the pump house to get away. "He was probably running for the gate by the time you reached the house," he said. "That is, if anybody really was there."

"We might call the police," said Michael.

"What for?" said Hollis. "I tell you nobody's there." He looked curiously at Agnew. "What *were* you doing there? Both of you, at this time of night. Looking for clues?" He laughed shortly as Agnew blinked and nodded.

They had, however, found the flashlight. Agnew pointed to it with grisly pride. It had been on the grass just outside the door of the pump house and along the edge of it, at one end, there was a perceptible, small smear of blood.

"*My* blood," said Agnew. "Probably there's some hair there too."

They had found his glasses too, unbroken, beside the flashlight; but they had found nothing else.

There were only two possible theories. One was that Agnew himself had managed to drop the door on his own head, dropping the flashlight and his glasses, striking his head for a second time, in falling, upon the heavy flashlight and knocking himself briefly senseless. The corollary for this theory was that Victoria, frightened, had heard some sound made perhaps by the pump and had taken it to be footsteps.

Agnew, clinging to the view that he had been the victim of a murderous attack, hotly denied this; Victoria agreed with him. The other theory, however, was not very pleasant. It was that somebody had come up behind Agnew, knocked him senseless with one blow of his fist, perhaps, and then given him another blow with the flashlight which would account for the traces of blood. And that that same person had then descended into the pump house, pulling the door down after him. Why (or who), nobody could guess.

"Certainly," said Michael, "there's nothing in the pump house but concrete walls. There's no place to hide anything and, anyway, the police searched it this afternoon."

In the end, Hollis looked at the clock, said, "My God, it's four and I'll probably have to drill all day," and got up.

"What's the use of having a Colonel practically in the family if you can't get longer leaves?" said Agnew irritably.

"If we were at war I probably couldn't get here at all!" said Hollis. "Come on, let's go to bed. We can't do anything more tonight."

They trailed upstairs, turning out lights with a feeling of

79

anti-climax. Michael went with Victoria to the door of her room. "Next time," he said rather grimly, "call me before you start out in the night. . . ."

"Michael, there was somebody there. I'm sure of it."

He said soberly, "There must have been some reason for it. We looked all over the pump house. There was absolutely nothing there and no traces of anybody's having been there." He looked tired; everybody looked tired. "Well, try to forget it and sleep awhile. Tomorrow's another day."

The sun was streaming into the room when Victoria awoke. Again someone awakened her. It was Thalia, standing beside her, calling her name. "Vicky—oh, you're awake! I hated to wake you, darling, but the police are here, and it's almost noon and they want to question you and—oh, I've brought your breakfast tray."

It was an unaccustomed attention on Thalia's part. She leaned over as Victoria sat up and put the yellow wicker tray across her knees and brought her an extra pillow. Thalia looked very pretty; as sleek and composed as a soft little bird, except she was wearing pink lawn with a very short skirt and a demurely ruffled white organdy collar. She stuffed the pillow behind Victoria's back. She said unexpectedly and softly, "I wanted to talk to you for a minute, too, Vicky. Before you marry Michael. You see—Vicky, I think you ought to know that it's only chivalry on Michael's part. Marrying you, I mean."

The sun poured in through the windows. The French doors upon the balcony were open and the river glittered in the sun. It was going to be hot again that day. Victoria's wedding day —only it wasn't going to be her wedding day. She closed her eyes to keep out the glare of the sun.

And Thalia said, her voice very soft, "I didn't mean to hurt you; you've been very good to me. But I—I do think you ought to know why Michael insists upon the wedding taking place today. In spite of . . ." She paused and said significantly, "In spite of everything."

"*Everything* . . ." said Victoria, opening her eyes quickly. "Clistie's death?"

"Yes. And . . ." Thalia's breath stirred the ruffles of white organdy. "And the evidence against you, Vicky. Of course I know—we all know that you didn't murder Clistie. But still— —well, there *was* your red belt, you know," she said softly. "And you *did* tell Clistie something that made her leave the house. Not, as I said, Victoria, not that any of us believe it for an instant. It's only the police . . ." She stopped, bit her lip, and said gently, "Don't be angry, Victoria. I'm sorry I've spoken so frankly. It's because it was a very difficult thing for

80

me to say. So I—I blurted it out."

Thalia never blurted anything out.

"Do you mean that Michael doesn't love me?" said Victoria.

"I—oh, Victoria, you are so direct. You make me sound so —so brutal."

"You said it was chivalry on his part."

"Yes, but—please, Vicky, don't be angry." Thalia leaned forward, her lovely little face beseeching, her hand stretched out pleadingly across the silk cover.

"I'm not angry," said Victoria slowly. "You don't understand." She poured a cup of coffee. Her eyes were caught by Thalia's hand, stretched pleadingly toward her. The sunlight lay full and revealing upon it. It was small; Thalia was small-boned and beautiful. But her hands were not; they were broad and thick, and her thumbs were curiously long with thick joints. She never wore rings and always used colorless nail polish. All at once Victoria wondered if it was because she didn't want to call attention to her hands. And then she knew that Thalia knew that Victoria was staring at her hand. With a kind of fascination Victoria watched the slight, almost stealthy motion with which those ugly thumbs moved inward, out of sight, and Thalia's hand withdrew, so it·was all at once tucked down softly into the folds of pink lawn. Thalia's eyelids were lowered, making misty rims on her face which looked as smooth as a gardenia and had the same pale ivory loveliness.

Victoria was suddenly and sharply self-reproachful.

Thalia said gently, "You see, I know Michael; better, in a way, than you do."

Victoria said abruptly, "Thalia, why did you tell me this? Did Michael ask you to?"

Thalia's long eyelashes stirred but didn't quite lift. She said, "No. But I . . ." She paused for another long moment. Then she got up, gracefully. "I know Michael so well. I know how he feels about things. I really don't think you ought to take advantage of his loyalty and—well, chivalry. That's all. If you hadn't met him, you know, Victoria, and—and taken him away from me, we would have been married. Michael and I. Michael, you know, has a future. He'll go far and I . . ." She caught her pretty lower lip in her teeth as if she'd said too much and stopped. She lifted her white eyelids, gave Victoria a long, full look and turned around toward the door.

"Thalia . . ." said Victoria. A glass tipped as she sat upright. "*Thalia*, what do you mean? Was Michael . . . ?"

"Michael was in love with me," said Thalia over her shoulder. "Oh, we weren't engaged; it hadn't come to that. But he

81

was in love with me. Or at least, very near it. Until he came here and saw you." Her small shoulders shrugged. She didn't turn her head. "That's all, Victoria. Only believe me—I know Michael so well, you see; and it isn't that I want to hurt you. Or stop your marriage. I only . . ." She stopped, opened the door and quietly went out of the room. The door closed gently behind her, as if she took the utmost care not to intrude upon Victoria even with the sound of a door closing hard.

Victoria stared at the blank panels of the door.

After a while it occurred to her that any other woman in the world would have at least closed the door hard. Thalia's demure, quiet self-control seemed to reveal, for just an instant, rather startling depths.

And Thalia, then, was in love with Michael. They had seen each other occasionally before Henry Frame's death; Victoria had known that, but she hadn't thought that there was anything more than friendliness between them. But Thalia actually had been in love with Michael; and then Michael had met Victoria.

And what about Michael?

Suppose Michael was, really, in love with Thalia. Suppose he had felt exactly as Victoria felt, that they had been thrown into each other's arms by circumstances. But Michael, a man, had been loyal to Victoria; had told her, when she would have released him, that she must take time to think, to be sure. And then Clistie was murdered. And Victoria was under suspicion. So he couldn't, according to his lights, have accepted the release she offered him, even if he wanted to.

There was the red belt. There were the circumstances of Clistie's death. There was the case of Henry Frame's death—reopened, Beasley had said.

"My God, John, you suspected her yourself," Beasley had said to John Campbell when, for an instant, he had seemed to defend her.

And so Michael had said, "We'll be married anyway."

She looked out across the river. Through the arches of live-oaks and Spanish moss there were glittering bright patches—as glittering and as bright and as calm as if no one had ever died, fighting in the darkness against that deep current. As if it had never been freighted with a slim, tragic young body.

Her hand jerked, turning over orange juice as Agnew opened the door unexpectedly and stuck his head in.

11

It was a bandaged head. Agnew showed her the bandage modestly but a little crossly, and helped her mop up orange juice. Agnew was always cross if he didn't have a full eight hours of sleep. He looked pale, his freckles standing out. He wore dirty, white duck slacks and a shrunken sweatshirt. His mother was better, he said moodily; she was sitting up in bed and having a large breakfast. Hollis had gone back to camp early. Michael was talking to the police, Beasley and a couple of other men.

"They asked me all about last night," he said, twisting the cord of the Venetian blinds in his fingers. "I told 'em all I knew. They didn't act as if they believed me—I mean as if anybody really was there. They had the bandage off my head and looked at it and Beasley seemed to think it was all a put-up job. Between us, I mean, you and me." His fingers stopped twisting, and he looked across the river, his eyes squinted against the glare, and said in an expressionless tone, "They said maybe we made up the whole story, just to make them think somebody *was* there."

"In order to divert suspicion from me?"

He nodded. "Nuts, of course. Remember the time Jody's yellow cat caught a young rabbit and hurt it but didn't kill it and ↠ . . ." He looked rather ashamed even now. "Neither of us could kill it, and we had to take it to Judson—who was only too glad to finish it off. *You* couldn't kill a fly! It's all nuts," he said, looking white and squinting out over the river.

"Agnew," said Victoria caught by a small and unexpected memory, "what did you mean by saying Thalia had funny thumbs? Last night—no, the night before. Remember?"

"Oh," said Agnew. "That. Criminal thumbs."

"*Agnew!*"

"Why, yes. Henry had them, too. I read all about it in a book. Vicky, was she here just now?"

"Yes," said Victoria rather faintly.

"I thought so; saw her come along the hall. Looking rather pleased in a quiet, purry little way."

"Agnew, don't!"

"Okay. Victoria, listen: they keep talking about Henry's death. What do you think? Do you really think it was suicide?"

"Yes!"

He turned around, peered at her, and said with unexpected gentleness, "No. You don't really think so. If you did you wouldn't say it—that way. You're scared, Vicky. Well, I guess we're all scared. Beasley keeps talking about Henry. He says if Clistie knew who killed him . . . Vicky," he said abruptly, "if Henry *was* murdered, who do you suppose could have done it? I mean—well, there's so few of us. Yet—unless somebody followed him here from New York, or unless he had a secret feud with somebody living around here. Or maybe . . ." His face brightened a little. "Maybe some fellow at Camp Blakoe . . ." He paused, and then shook his head. "Doesn't sound very likely; I'll ask Thalia, just the same. But unless it *was* something like that and there was never any hint of it in the evidence, there's only—well, *us*. People who knew Henry, I mean. I didn't kill him and you didn't. Mother's capable of it, if she got upset but . . ."

"*Agnew!*"

"But still I don't think she did," said Agnew reasonably. "Because as far as I can remember she wasn't upset about anything just then. Michael is in the business; but the accountants gave Michael's office an absolutely clean bill of health, and he had nothing to do with Henry's office. So unless they just didn't like each other, I can't see that. Of course, Hollis . . ." He stopped for an instant. Victoria was sitting upright, staring at him uneasily. He went on, "Hollis is kind of a fool, someways. He's so crazy about the Steane Mills, always has been . . ."

"*Hollis!*"

"Why, of course. He would have loved being your father's son; wants nothing so much as to get through with the war and go back to the office. He would like to manage it, you know. He's—well, really crazy about it. Loves every damn tree and every contract; works like a slave and Henry wouldn't advance him an inch. Henry always said it would look too much like making a favorite of him—be bad for the morale. Henry was in the saddle for as long as he lived, and he was likely to live a good long while. Still, I don't really think Hollis would murder him. Do you?"

"No! No, I *don't* think so. Hollis didn't murder him."

"Oh," said Agnew. "Well, I don't think so either. I—well, only mentioned it. Not that I like Hollis very much. And it has always seemed to me, hatred or jealousy or both is the only real motive for murder. Unless it's—fear," said Agnew thoughtfully. "Have to cover everyone, you know. There's"—he swallowed and said hurriedly—"there's Clistie; but she was murdered, too. . . ." His Adam's apple went up and down. He said, "She didn't kill Henry. And there's Thalia."

"Thalia didn't kill Henry. Her own father! She—why, Agnew, that's cruel. She loved him. . . ."

"Oh," said Agnew. "Did she? Vicky, whatever happened to

Thalia's mother?"

"Thalia's . . . Why, I don't know," said Victoria, taken aback. "That is, yes, I do. She was divorced from Henry—oh, ages ago. Then she died. In Switzerland, I think. Why on earth?"

"I only wondered. You see, if Henry treated her very badly and Thalia wanted revenge . . ."

Victoria thrust her tray away abruptly. "See here, Agnew, you mustn't talk like this. Or even think—it's horrible. . . ."

"So," said Agnew unexpectedly, very white, "is murder. Clistie didn't hurt anybody." He swung away from the window. "You'd better go down and see the dear police," he said becoming childish all at once. "If they put you in jail I'll bring you a file in a chocolate bar. A nail file ought to work. I had a look at the jail last winter and the bars looked pretty rusty. Anyway," said Agnew with a morose scowl, "I'll see you later, baby."

He went away, working his forehead up and down moodily, apparently to ascertain the condition of his wound.

He was probably right about Hollis. She could see it now, looking back. Hollis' insistence upon going into the Steane Mills where Henry had put him in his own office, in an unimportant position—so unimportant, in fact, that in the family, there'd grown up a kind of feeling that Hollis was equal only to that position and nothing better. Yet he'd refused a job that paid better; suddenly she remembered that.

Other little instances which could be translated into a real devotion on Hollis' part came to her mind; he would never take an hour's more vacation than would have been due him if he had been the merest clerk and not a member of the family and one of Victor Steane's heirs. He had lived the year around in New York; he had worked hard. Yet, somehow, they had thought of Hollis as a favorite son, a playboy, making a kind of half-hearted gesture toward the family business.

Agnew could easily be right.

When she went downstairs Michael was in the morning room, in view of the stairs, smoking and waiting, his legs thrust out, his gray slacks and white sports shirt looking very cool. He sprang up when he saw Victoria.

"Hello." He took her hand, looking at her anxiously. "You're looking very pretty," he said unexpectedly. "I was worried about you after last night. Vicky, you couldn't possibly have—well, imagined any of that last night, could you? I went out this morning again to look at the pump house, and it seemed to me that Agnew could have knocked the door down somehow on his own head. And if you were confused in the dark, you know, and frightened . . ."

85

She knew that he wanted her to think that.

"Somebody was there. But that isn't . . . Michael, I want to talk to you about something else. About our wedding . . ."

"That's what I thought. It's all settled." He put his hand under her chin, tilting her face upward toward his own. He was smiling, his gray clear eyes direct and rather determined.

"Michael, please listen. It's exactly as I told you that night —Monday night. I was so tired last night I couldn't talk. But I . . ."

"But you can now," said Michael smiling. "All right. Let's go out on the terrace where it's less—well, public." He linked her arm through his own, and led her through the bright dining room with the open French windows letting in the sun and the sparkle of the river. The terrace, however, was shaded by the liveoaks; they walked along it, away from the windows. And Michael said, "This is our wedding day, Vicky. You're not really going to—leave me waiting at the altar. Are you?"

He was still smiling, but his eyes were sober as he waited for her answer, leaning against the balustrade, every line of his compact figure solid and dependable. With Michael, she thought gratefully, you knew where you were.

"Is it chivalry, Michael?" she asked directly.

"Chivalry!"

"I mean because I'm—well, it was my belt. And I did send Clistie out that night . . ."

"No. I'm not being chivalrous. And if it wasn't for Campbell, they'd never have dreamed of accusing you. Campbell made life hell for you after Henry's death. It's that that Beasley remembers now—Campbell and his suspicions. Vicky, you said Monday night that it was all too unreal—our marriage, I mean—that it was the happy ending, and all that. Well, at the time you were so sure that you convinced me, too. But now I think perhaps you were wrong. Hasn't it occurred to you that we are, both of us, plunged into exactly the same situation as that following Henry's death?"

"Yes. It makes it worse, somehow. Remembering." She looked out at the shining, wide river with its secret currents. "You know what's going to happen. Reporters, I mean. Photographs. Questions. Suspicion."

"That's it. Suspicion. Anxiety. A certain amount of apprehension. The fact of murder. Yet, in spite of your convincing argument it hasn't"—he hesitated and then said lightly, watching the river, too—"it hasn't driven us into each other's arms again. So you see you were wrong. Our love for each other wasn't based on that. It was—and is—based on something real."

But Michael was wrong. She had really turned to him as she had done before, counting on his loyalty; the difference was that this time, she knew it wasn't love.

She didn't know how she knew that. It was a stubborn, unwavering certainty in her heart. The only thing that mattered was that she knew it.

And she knew too that he was lying when he said he wasn't being chivalrous; lying like a gentleman, she thought, and smiled a little wryly, and put out both her hands toward him.

"I'm so very grateful, Michael."

He caught the implication in it instantly. He turned around, took her hands and brought them to his lips. "All right," he said. "I'm not going to try to make you marry me. Only— Vicky, if you need me, I'm here. That's all."

Footsteps on the terrace and a door closing interrupted him. It was Jody, hurrying toward them, his wrinkled black face a mask of worry. The police were asking for her, he said apologetically.

Michael went into the house with her. But the State's Attorney would not permit him to remain while she was questioned, although it proved to be, that time, a short interview. For when she told Beasley everything there was to tell of the incident of the previous night, he made no comments. And he asked only a few questions when she told him that she believed Clistie's room had been searched. She told him of that hesitantly, in view of the skeptical look in his face, but nevertheless she told it.

"When did you search her room?"

"In the afternoon. Late. Before she was found."

"And you suggest that this mysterious intruder of last night was searching for something in her room as well as in the pump house, too? Dear, dear. A fabled, fatal jewel, do you suppose? Or plans for a new bombsight—doubtless Miss Forbes coaxed the secret from Colonel Galant."

"I told you because I thought you ought to know. If that's all . . ."

"No, no, Miss Steane. That isn't all. Another moment, if you please." His voice purred. He put his yellow hand on her wrist.

He asked her to do a very curious thing and that was to take the telephone, the extension which stood on a table near him, and to ask Central for a Ponte Verde number, three, eight three O.

She did so. A man's voice at the other end said very promptly, almost as if he was waiting for it! "Ponte Verde Hotel . . ."

Beasley, watching her with beady black eyes, said, "Ask for

Miss Joan Green."

"Miss . . ." Her throat choked. Beasley snapped, "Go on. Say 'Is Miss Joan Green there?' "

"Is Miss Joan Green there?" said Victoria.

No one spoke at the other end. Beasley said, "Repeat it. Louder."

She did so.

Still no one answered, and Beasley rose and took the telephone from her. "That's all now. You can go," he said. He held the telephone, without speaking into it, waiting for her to leave the room.

It was the beginning of a hot, packed day which was very different from its predecessor.

The investigation, fully launched that day, was very different, too, from the investigation following Henry Frame's death—although to those directly involved it had its likenesses, and they were not pleasant.

It was true that the inquiry about Henry Frame's death was automatically reopened—in the minds of the State's Attorney, the sheriff, the state troopers, and in the minds of newspaper readers, if not formally. But there was, now, no question of murder, as there had been in Henry's death. Clistie had been murdered—with a belt knotted around her neck; Joan Green had been murdered, possibly by the same weapon—or at least one very like it, which was not found upon her body when it was taken from the river. This time there was no need to prove, first of all, that murder existed.

And if in the investigation into Henry's death the State's Attorney—then John Campbell—had been hampered and at last defeated by a lack of evidence, now the police were, if not defeated, at least hampered by too much evidence. Too many leads. Too many small threads to explore to the end which too often raveled off into nothing.

As, for instance, Beasley's attempt to discover who had searched Clistie's room, and when, and above all why, as he did attempt to do that day in spite of the skepticism with which he listened to Victoria's story of it. For when he inquired of the servants, when he questioned everyone in the house, directly and indirectly, from Bessie on down to Lilibelle, the little colored chambermaid, no one knew—or at least admitted knowing—anything of it. Early in the morning they had looked quickly for the brown chiffon and lace dress; the room they thought had been in order then, although no one remembered anything but the wardrobe. After that, however, no one had been in her room (except Lilibelle to make the unused bed); no one had seen anybody entering the room

88

or coming from it. Except, of course, the troopers and later Victoria. No one knew of anything that Clistie had had, that anybody would want. It was a complete blank which annoyed Beasley almost as much as the blank he drew at the end of long, detailed questioning designed to discover who—if any-one—had been in the pump house the previous night, and why.

But those were only two evidences of Beasley's energy, patience, and minute and tireless gathering together of a mass of information, much of which was unimportant and irrelevant. It soon became evident that the case was almost entirely in his hands; that it was by its very nature already prominent and much publicized, and that Beasley was determined, one way or another, to solve it with credit to himself. That he was also honest, and no one could doubt it for an instant, made him the more formidable.

"But I rather like him," said Michael, with a little laugh. "If only because he's so exactly the way I want him to be, so I can hate him. He's mean; he's covertly insulting when he questions you, as if he'd already made up his mind that you were lying. He employs a brand of sarcasm that is as subtle as an axe. He's everything that you want somebody you hate to be."

"He's not very pretty," said Bessie.

Agnew said thoughtfully, "He's nobody's fool."

Certainly he was indefatigable, restless, full of nervous energy that sent him prowling everywhere about the place, driving at full speed to Ponte Verde, or to Camp Blakoe and back again, questioning them in abrupt, unexpected forays, letting them go again. He pre-empted the library, to Jody's disapproval, but nevertheless was likely to turn up anywhere, his long, yellow face and glittering black eyes suspicious and concentrated, to question them with what seemed almost indiscriminate favor, for he interviewed them separately, together, in groups, without apparent plan, with much repetition, with spasmodic bursts of energy and with, even then, an air of accusation behind the simplest question. State troopers came and went at his behest, apparently; the county sheriff occasionally (although not that day) formed a passive but authoritative background—more than a little forbidding, as if he might be called upon to make an arrest at any moment and enforce it with the gun he wore, constantly, in a heavy leather holster at his waist.

They were fingerprinted that day—it was not a new experience; they had been fingerprinted at John Campbell's orders after Henry's death.

There was however no inquest. It was to come later.

"When Beasley can calm down and stay in one place for an hour or so," suggested Agnew morosely.

"Well," said Bessie, looking hag-ridden, with great brown pockets around her large dark eyes, "it's confusing. After all —that girl. And Clistie. And now they say, Henry too. There's no—link between them."

"Except Clistie's dress," said Agnew. He added with an attempt at flippancy which deceived nobody, "I do think confusing lies in the realm of understatement."

Soon, however, out of a mass of facts which might be evidence, and which might not be, which were often contradictory, unrelated (and certainly, as Bessie said, confusing), certain facts began to emerge, certain odd inconsistencies came out, and certain even odder consistencies.

Such as the matter of the maid.

"The little maid," said Agnew later, "who wasn't there."

The maid who, as a matter of fact, did not appear to exist. And yet was seen twice.

12

That developed late in the morning, when Beasley (in an attempt to piece together Clistie's actions, just before Victoria and Agnew had talked to her for the last time, there in the hall), pounced upon them to ask about time: exactly when and under what circumstances had each of them last seen Clistie?

They were sitting together at the time, feeling already a little battered from Beasley's swooping onslaughts.

Thalia said promptly that she and Hollis had gone to the moving pictures about nine-thirty; had seen Clistie in the hall as they were leaving and she, at any rate, had not seen her again. Michael said he had not seen her at all, for only Agnew was downstairs when he came into the house, about twelve or a little after. Bessie said that she had seen Clistie come downstairs, in her brown-lace dress, and go down the hall toward the kitchen about, she thought, ten-thirty; at any rate, just before she herself had gone upstairs. Agnew agreed with this; he had been reading when his mother went upstairs but had looked up to say good night and had seen Clistie going into the butler's pantry. Later, while he was reading, he'd had an impression that Clistie came back along the hall from the butler's pantry, but he couldn't be sure; he'd been reading, he repeated rather plaintively, and if it was Clistie, she hadn't spoken to him.

However, went on Agnew, after Victoria had gone to her

room and just before Michael came in, someone had gone upstairs and it was one of the maids.

"*Maid!*" said Beasley, his eyes snapping.

"Yes, of course," said Agnew calmly.

"Which one?"

Agnew hesitated. "Well, I told you I didn't pay any attention to her. Her back was turned toward me, and anyway it was shadowy just there on the stairs." He went on to explain: he had heard footsteps, glanced up in time to catch a shadowy glimpse of her at the turn of the stairway, had thought nothing of it and had gone back to his book. Then in a few minutes Michael had come in from the porch, and had said something to him and gone through the drawing room and up the stairs and he, Agnew, had looked at his watch and decided to go to bed, too, and had turned off the light and gone.

"That was just after twelve," he said. "I didn't have my glasses on, and I'd read till I had spots before my eyes."

Michael corroborated the time, for he had heard Agnew follow him upstairs.

And Michael also corroborated the mysterious maid. He had seen her crossing the strip of lawn between the house and the garden.

"I was sitting on the porch, smoking—or rather, just at that minute I think I was strolling up and down, there on the lawn beside the porch. I just saw the girl slip from the garden hedge, cross a patch of lawn where the moonlight was fairly bright and then disappear around the corner of the house. I supposed, if I supposed anything, that she'd been out with her boy friend and was taking the most unobtrusive way she could back into the house. Past the driveway and the front entrance, I imagine, and around to the kitchen entrance on the north end of the house. I thought nothing of it, naturally. But I did see her."

"Which maid was it?"

Michael shook his head. "I don't know."

"She couldn't have gone in the back entrance," snapped Beasley. "I just talked to the butler and cook. They said they finished washing up about a quarter after ten, and bolted the back door, *on the inside,* as usual, and went to bed. They say Miss Forbes didn't come into the kitchen before they went upstairs. They sleep in the house; this girl Lilibelle sleeps in the house. Your other maid . . ."

"Emma," said Bessie. "Sleeps out. Leaves, as a rule, as soon as she can get away after dinner."

"Yes, Emma. Well, she left as usual; the cook saw her go. Anyway, this girl Emma is as big as a house." He turned to Agnew. "Was it Emma you saw or Lilibelle?"

91

"Well," said Agnew doubtfully, "I didn't see her very clearly. I didn't have my glasses on. But I guess I thought it was Lilibelle."

Beasley batted his eyes exasperatedly. "You don't by any chance guess you thought it was Emma?"

"Oh, no," said Agnew definitely.

And the odd part of it was that when Lilibelle was summoned, and stood twisting one thin, long calf over the other and doubling up her white apron in nervous brown fingers and threatening to giggle—or cry—at every word, she said, and stuck to it, that she hadn't been out that night at all. Not even Beasley could shake her denial. And so far as anyone knew she hadn't a boy friend and there was something about her frightened, incoherent denials that sounded honest. It injected another troublesome and perhaps important fact into the already troublesome fabric of fact and surmise that Beasley was gathering into his long yellow hands.

For if Lilibelle was telling the truth, then who had entered the house and subsequently entirely disappeared? For no one had seen her again.

"The Yellow Peril," said Agnew, when Beasley had darted away again, "can't make up his mind whether it's an inside or an outside job. But I did see her. And I don't think Lilibelle's got the brains to make up a lie and stick to it."

"*Stop* calling him the Yellow Peril," snapped Bessie.

It was, however, clear enough that while Beasley doled out suspicion generously to those closest to Henry, nevertheless he did face just that problem; was one of them responsible for Clistie's death and Joan Green's—and Henry's—or was there a possibility of an outsider? An unknown? Someone who could enter the house at will and disappear into thin air.

As the mysterious maid had done.

His belief was, obviously, that someone close to them had murdered Henry and Clistie; it provided a motive for Clistie's murder. Besides, there was concrete evidence against Victoria. But savagely, grudgingly, yet honestly, he had to set himself to eliminate all other possibilities. For that reason, perhaps, he presently had a talk with Thalia. Had her father any enemies? Did she know of anything in his past that would lead anyone to follow him south and murder him? Thalia reported it briefly.

"What did you say?" said Michael curiously.

Thalia's eyebrows lifted a little. "I said, no, of course," she replied.

But obviously too, Joan Green's death fell outside Beasley's choice pattern of inquiry, unless he could prove that one of them had known her.

John Campbell did not appear and Agnew commented on it. "Major Campbell," he said crossly, "is conspicuous by his absence. I suppose he's got to keep the army in step." He brooded and said, "All I hope is Colonel Galant makes him work so hard he stays away from us."

"Well, it's not his business anyway," said Michael. "He's no longer State's Attorney. He's in the army. Where I'll be if we get into the war."

Thalia looked out at the shining river and said nothing.

Some time after lunch, Beasley went away again, zooming off with a great clatter in a small, shabby old coupe in which he folded up his long legs like a jackknife, and drove at such unexpected speed that it was all the state troopers could do to keep up with him.

Bessie sighed with relief when she heard him leave and demanded the newspaper—the little daily Ponte Verde paper, which had enormous black headlines.

Later, there were other papers: from Pine Beach, from Atlanta and New Orleans and Jacksonville. And that day, too, reporters, representatives of the big news agencies, began to arrive to cover the story. They came, stayed in Ponte Verde, went away, came back again, to hover, ubiquitously, near the place. The accounts of Henry's death had been sensational enough until the verdict of coroner's jury had stopped them as a blanket smothers a fire. Now, however, the story blazed up wildly, as if all those weeks it had smoldered. Double murder, said the columns of black print; tragedy breaks out again in Steane mansion, on the St. Sebastian. Beautiful Steane heiress questioned. Double slaying.

But just at first it was Ponte Verde's own story, complete in double columns, with a résumé of the circumstances of Henry's death, a not too brief history of the Steane family and, in the little society section (boxed in heavily, between the account of a bridge party and an invitation to all soldiers in town that night to come to the Ladies Club rooms for fruit punch and a free motion-picture show), a paragraph to the effect that the wedding of Victoria Steane and Michael Bayne, announced to take place that day, had been postponed.

Bessie nodded approvingly when she read it.

"Quite right," she said to Victoria. "You can't have a wedding at a time like this. It wouldn't do at all." She dropped the newspaper and stared at the river. "This reporter says outright that Henry must have been murdered and Clistie knew who murdered him."

"In that case," said Michael, "what about Joan Green?"

"Yes," said Bessie rather flatly, after a moment. "As you say, what about her?" She picked up the paper again, leaving

93

the question to repeat itself, mutely, in the hot afternoon air.

Why had the girl come to the pine woods? thought Victoria. If it was to meet someone (and she could have come for no other reason), then who? A great deal depended upon the answer to that question. For if it was to meet a stranger, someone who had no connection with them, someone concerned only with Joan Green, then suspicion of murder moved from them; and Clistie was murdered because, perhaps, she came upon Joan Green's murderer.

But if Clistie was murdered because of Henry, then, as Michael had said, why was Joan Green murdered? Why was she in the pine woods? Why was she wearing Clistie's dress?

It brought her around the full circle of conjecture. Oddly enough, no one then perceived an answer that was from the beginning inherent in those questions.

Bessie said suddenly, "Beasley asked me all about Clistie. The most absurd questions, really. All about her life and whether she was ever married and—oh, all sorts of nonsense. Really," Bessie sniffed, "I think for a moment Beasley had a wild idea that this—girl was something to Clistie. Her long-lost child perhaps. Then he swerved to your father, my dear, and his life and times. After awhile I began to perceive he had some idea she was your unrecognized half-sister."

"Good Heavens!" said Victoria blankly.

A smile flickered over Bessie's face. "Yes, it's funny. If he'd known Victor! He was like a rock of faithfulness, and frightfully fastidious." The smile vanished. She looked uneasily away from Victoria and said, "Of course, what Beasley was trying to do, was to establish some connection between the—the dead girl and us."

"Beasley," said Michael, stretching out his legs, lazily, "has read too many Victorian novels. But I suppose it's routine. He questioned me, too. All alone, early this morning. He wired to Seattle and to New York to confirm everything I told him. Apparently thinks I knew Joan Green. Well, I didn't—poor child. Never saw her in my life till yesterday morning. Beasley's typical of his policeman's job; he's got all the answers. If it wasn't a crime of passion it was blackmail; he did everything he could to get me to admit having known Joan Green somewhere. The suggestion was obvious: she was blackmailing me, on the verge of my marriage to you, Vicky. Neat," said Michael, "if not very pretty. I don't care though so long as it—well, distributes suspicion. The only trouble is it should be easy to prove just who the girl knew and who she didn't know."

"Well, I certainly saw the girl exactly once," said Thalia. "No more. *I* had no motive for killing her." She shuddered a little, daintily, and added, "So Mr. Beasley and John Campbell needn't try to make a suspect of me."

There was a scarcely veiled note of mockery in her voice. Michael said, "You don't like John Campbell, do you, Thalia? Never mind, he seems to be out of this."

Thalia looked at him with wide, candid eyes. "None of us have reason to like him, Michael. Especially Victoria." She turned to Victoria. "You remember Joan Green, don't you? At the tea party. Dressed in gray."

"Yes," said Victoria, thinking of the thin, efficient-looking girl in gray. She had stood at Bessie's side and Bessie had given her coffee. There had been no shadow of a change in Bessie's pleasant, polite expression; so Bessie had not known Joan Green.

"If we only knew *why* she came to the pine woods," said Michael, and added thoughtfully, "And whether or not Lilibelle is lying."

Bessie shoved her untidy hair into a still untidier wad. "It's not very nice," she said, her voice suddenly uneven, "to think of somebody coming into the house. Like that. In the night."

It was not at all nice. No one spoke for a moment. Jody came to say another car with reporters had arrived.

Michael went to talk to them. They were accompanied by photographers who took pictures of the pump house, the garden, the house. They didn't need to take pictures of Miss Steane or any of the family, they told Michael good-naturedly, for they already had pictures in their files. Pictures from the Frame case. They could use those.

He gave them a statement, brief and non-committal, which they accepted, as non-committally but not as briefly, for they asked questions. Quick, skillful questions designed to be revealing. Bessie and Thalia and Victoria remained cautiously out of sight until they went away.

It was some time after that that Colonel Galant telephoned. He talked to Victoria.

"Can you come to camp? Right away?" he asked her briefly.

"Yes. Unless the police . . ."

"They won't stop you. Come straight to my office. It's—about Clistie." He hung up.

Michael took her in his car and Thalia and Agnew went along. Agnew went because he could never resist any excuse to get inside the gates of Camp Blakoe. He folded himself up cheerfully on the small seat behind the wide driver's seat, where Michael sat with Victoria and Thalia.

Victoria glanced at Thalia whose profile under her shady pink hat looked very gentle and calm and—what had Agnew said?—purry. But that was wrong; everything, it seemed to Victoria suddenly, conspired against Thalia; there were the circumstances of her father's death; there was her feeling for Michael.

Yet Thalia had been really a very good sport about it all. No one had guessed, not even Victoria, until that morning, that she was in love with Michael.

Thalia and Michael and herself! It was like a child's scrawl on a blackboard; Thalia loves Michael—Michael loves Victoria—Victoria loves—well, Victoria loves nobody.

And all of it belonged to another world. It had nothing to do with the grim errand that brought them, then, to Camp Blakoe.

"Turn in here, Mike," said Agnew, hunching forward. "Turn in here and tell the sentry we want to see Colonel Galant."

Agnew knew every twist and turn of the multitude of roads through the camp; Michael turned in and stopped as the sentry came forward. He was expecting them and waved them through. A new regiment was arriving that day and a band had been sent to the gate to welcome them. They looked hot but zealous, with the sun glinting on their instruments. The leader stepped forward to ask over the sentry's shoulder: "Seen anything of a convoy along the road, sir?" Michael shook his head. Agnew thrust his head forward.

"Maybe they came the other way," he said helpfully. "Along the new road for construction, where they are building the new magazines; there's no gate there. It's that way . . ." He waved toward Ponte Verde.

"Thanks." The band leader grinned and wiped his face. "It's going to be a big place when it's finished! We just got here ourselves."

"We'll need all that unfinished space when war comes," said Michael. "Which way do we go now, Agnew? You seem to know the lay-out here."

"I've watched every foot of it," declared Agnew. "Now that they're getting organized and the army is arriving, I suppose they'll tighten up and not let us in without a pass. But we're not in the war yet. Turn left. Then go right around the recreation hall. That brings you to the hospital. . . ."

The low roofs glittered in the sun, and the blue lake glittered too. It seemed a long time since the day of the Colonel's tea party when Victoria and John Campbell had walked along that lake and talked.

And he had warned her then, but not about Clistie Not about a thin, tragic dead girl in Clistie's dress.

The administration building was, as the organization of the

96

camp was being completed, a hive of industry; cars were parked close before it; men in uniform were everywhere; the sound of typewriters and telephones came from the open windows. "Park in Colonel Galant's space," directed Agnew over Michael's shoulder. "It's the first one at the left of the door."

Small white boards with names in black letters on them hung from chains and designated the parking spaces: Major Huntley; Lieut. Col. Sanders. Colonel Galant's was the favored spot nearest the door.

Agnew crawled out quickly. "If they'll still let me, I'll show Michael around," he said, "while you see the Colonel." For an instant his eyes looked sharp and hard. "Unless you'd just as soon let me go with you," he said to Victoria.

"No, wait for me."

Agnew shrugged. "Confidential, huh? Well, that's silly, because if it's about Clistie, we're all in it together."

"I don't know what it's about," said Victoria. She went up the flight of wooden steps. Michael said, "Don't be too long,"

Inside it was hot but shady. She went down the narrow, deserted corridor; there was the smell of new wood and paint everywhere. A new girl sat at Joan Green's desk, who glanced at her curiously when she gave her name and said, eyeing her, "Colonel Galant said you were to come right in."

Victoria remembered that Joan Green had been very silent and very unobtrusive; so unobtrusive that no one really noticed her. She knocked at the door labeled Colonel Galant, and went in when he spoke.

She was suddenly struck with a very odd and very unpleasant thought. For Bruce Galant turned a perfectly strange face toward her; a face that, almost literally, Victoria had never seen before. She thought, curiously, that murder was like that; it revealed new faces among people one thought one knew. It was like a peephole into otherwise hidden emotions. It was like a revealing shaft of light into a dark room.

Colonel Galant looked older; his face was gray and lined; his blue eyes were as cold as ice. He wasn't just Bruce; he was Colonel Galant. He said, "Oh, come in, Victoria. I was expecting you." He put a paper weight on a stack of papers, rose and closed the door behind her, before he went back to his desk. "I've got an unpleasant job ahead of me," he said directly. "I'll do it as quickly as I can. What do you know about Hollis and Joan Green?"

"*Hollis* . . ."

"Yes. He knew her."

"But he didn't! He couldn't have! He . . ."

"I'm afraid he did, Victoria."

97

"But—but none of us knew her. None of us could identify her. . . ."

"None of you *would* identify her. That is, in Hollis' case, I mean."

"Colonel Bruce . . ."

"Don't try to defend Hollis, Victoria." He leaned back in his chair. "He knew her; there's no doubt of it. Beasley was just here and brought the hotel clerk. Beasley had managed to give the clerk a look at Hollis when Hollis didn't know it. He was drilling, and—but the point is the clerk identified him, picked him out at once. Said Hollis used to call for her and take her out. One of the girls in the office knew it too. It seems that Joan Green was a very quiet young woman; she knew almost nobody; he was the only man whom she went out with at all."

The telephone rang; he answered it. "Send him in. And don't put any calls through for a while." He replaced the receiver.

Victoria said stubbornly, "When we went to Ponte Verde to —to see her, Hollis didn't know her. He didn't even look as if . . ."

He shook his head. "That's the point. *Why* didn't he admit it? Openly. If Hollis had merely had a friendship for an attractive girl, why shouldn't he . . . ? Oh, come in." He jerked his head toward the door as someone knocked; Major John Campbell came into the room.

"Major Campbell," said Colonel Galant. "You know Miss Steane. Well, of course, you do. Sit down. Now then, Victoria," he frowned at the papers on his desk. "Hollis refused to identify her; refused to admit that he knew her at all. Well, then, why? You see—well, the point is that Joan Green had . . ." He bit his lip and tapped his fingers on the desk. "She could have had a detail of military information," he said shortly, the words like fine-edged icicles. "It was part of her job to take dictation from the listening-post. Her murder might mean—anything."

13

"L-listening-post?" said Victoria uncertainly, after a moment. Colonel Galant glanced at her sharply. For the first time a look of personal concern flashed across his gray, lined face.

"Is it too hot in here, Victoria? Major, will you turn on that fan, please?" John Campbell got up and turned on an electric fan near by. Colonel Galant went on, raising his voice against the whir of the fan.

"Yes. Listening-post. You see much of our business is done

by long-distance telephone. It's always important to get orders and detail exactly, consequently, whenever we talk to, say, Washington, we put a good stenographer on the listening-post, that is another telephone, and she takes a complete transcript of the whole conversation. Naturally, we pick a girl who's quick and accurate and . . ." he hesitated and said, "dependable. I mean, somebody we know something about." Major Campbell's black head moved slightly, and the Colonel shot a quick look at him and said rather hurriedly, "That is, don't misunderstand me. I'm not starting a foreign agent scare here. There's nothing here that would be worth very much to a foreign agent. Anybody who flies over the camp or visits it is welcome to take a look; all camps are very much alike. We have no"—he hesitated again, frowned at the sky beyond the open window and said—"no secrets."

Major Campbell looked out the window, too, and said nothing. Colonel Galant went on, after a moment, "There are ways, of course, in which anybody could do us harm; sabotage, I mean; fires in the storehouses; trouble with the water supply. Later, when we are fully organized, that will be impossible. Just now, in the confusion of building, with half the camp still open and most of it unfinished and armies of workmen coming and going, we have to watch out for such things. We are tightening up rules every day; we are not yet at war, but we intend to take and enforce every precaution that we would enforce during war. Just now, during these days of organization, as I say, we want to be particularly careful. It's a tremendous thing to organize. Now then, this girl . . ."

Major Campbell said abruptly, "I'd tell her about the . . . I'd tell her, Colonel."

Colonel Galant gave him one glacier-blue glance. "It's easy to see you're not yet accustomed to the army, Major," he said. "I'll say what I think best to say. I called you in because of your previous rather specialized experience."

"Yes, sir," said Major Campbell promptly.

"If there is any connection between this girl's death and Camp Blakoe's—welfare, then naturally the thing must be thoroughly investigated."

"Yes, sir. Although Beasley," he added quietly, "is a very capable fellow."

"That doesn't matter! We've got to go into it from our point of view! From the army's point of view. If that girl . . ." A bleak look came into his face.

John Campbell said, "Did you look up the records, Colonel?"

"Yes," he said. "Yes, John, I did."

"And she did know?"

99

"Yes. The records are there," he nodded at a file in the corner. "You can look them over when you've time." He looked at Victoria. "What he means is that while we have no great military secrets here, we do have a"—he bit his lip and said reluctantly—"some secret radio equipment."

Major Campbell said, "It's really secret, you know. The one thing that we—and any other camp that has it or anything like it—guard with our lives." He said it lightly; his eyes were intent and suddenly sober.

Colonel Galant leaned forward. "You see, Victoria, this comes very close to me. In any case I would have to take steps, naturally—quickly. But if Hollis . . ." He glanced at John Campbell. "There's enough there . . ." He jerked his gray head toward the filing cabinet again. "There's enough there to be, conceivably, of interest. There are no detailed manufacturing plans, naturally, but the bare fact that it exists, that it has been sent here, that we intend to make secret trials —that's enough to make us . . ." He bit his lip again.

"Nervous," finished Major Campbell, looking extremely composed, except for his intent, watchful eyes.

Colonel Galant flashed him another icy blue look and said to Victoria, "Frankly, I didn't want to tell you any of this. It was Major Campbell's suggestion. He thought that you, seeing so much of Hollis, might know something—something that you . . ."

"The only thing I know is that Hollis wouldn't sell any information to anybody!"

"My dear child," said Colonel Galant gravely, "I don't believe you realize that . . ." He stopped, drummed on the table with his fingers and gave Major Campbell a helpless look.

"Colonel Galant believes," said Major Campbell, "that if there is a link between Joan Green and Clistie, and there must be, then the chain goes on to Henry's murder. Thus, someone close to Henry, someone in a very small circle of people, must have . . ."

"Must have murdered them," cut in Colonel Galant, his face gray. "It's not safe there for you, Vicky—for anybody. Yet I can't come and stay in the house. I . . ." He took a long breath and said curtly, "About Hollis—as I say, it was Major Campbell's idea to talk to you."

"Why don't you question Hollis?" said Victoria.

Colonel Galant's blue eyes flashed. "It's not what I expected of you, Victoria—to take that tone, I mean. Do you realize that we may soon be at war! People have been asked to do more for their country's welfare than what I'm asking you!"

Major Campbell said easily, although rather quickly, "On the information Colonel Galant now has, a point-blank denial on Hollis' part is enough. He may admit he knew the girl, but that's all. Honestly, I don't think we've got any attempted espionage to worry about, and, in any case, the only thing Joan Green knew was that we've got some secret radio equipment. She knew nothing about it. And almost every camp—lots of them, anyway—have that. Aircraft detectors . . ."

"*Major!*" rapped Colonel Galant.

He swung around toward Colonel Galant. "Believe me, Colonel," he said impetuously, "These murders have nothing to do with espionage."

"What is the purpose then? What's back of it all? If you've got an opinion, what is it?" demanded Colonel Galant, angrily, rapping on the table.

John Campbell's face sobered. "Well, I don't know," he said slowly. "But I think it's some very deep and personal motive—something so strong, and something so urgent that—that there was no way out."

No way out—but murder.

No one moved for a moment. Then Colonel Galant said testily, "But this girl—this Green girl. My God, John, I've got to *know* if there's a leak in my own office!"

"Yes, sir," said Major Campbell a little grimly.

"There's some connection with the camp! That girl—Clistie's dress . . ."

"And Henry Frame?" asked Major Campbell.

"Yes. No. I don't know. It's your business to find out!"

"Certainly, sir," said Major Campbell, his mouth tight. He turned to Victoria. "You see, Miss Steane, there's no one but you in the house whom we can ask, like this, for information. Mrs. Isham . . ."

"Bessie would have a fit," said the Colonel gloomily, staring at the desk.

"Agnew is only a boy. Thalia Frame is—Henry Frame's daughter."

"What information do you want?" said Victoria stiffly.

"Anything! Everything!" snapped the Colonel.

Major Campbell said quietly, "Anything that strikes you, in view of this, as suspicious. Anything, particularly, that seems to be connected in any way with Camp Blakoe. Anything about Hollis, such as—oh, if he had more money than he ought to have had. If he's been seeing, or writing to, or talking to anybody who might possibly be a foreign agent."

"Perhaps Joan Green was quite innocent, you see," said Colonel Galant. "Perhaps she gave information without intending to; indiscreetly and against definite orders, but unintentionally. But suppose then she realized what she had done and intended to try to fix things—to tell me—to try to undo the harm she had done. And suppose Hollis was afraid she would do just that; suppose he—stopped her . . ."

"He couldn't have done that!"

No one spoke for a moment. Then Bruce Galant said heavily, "The girl *was* there in the pine woods. He *did* know her. And he did lie about it."

"But Hollis was not with Joan Green that night. He went to the movies with Thalia."

"If the scream you heard was uttered by Joan Green, then she died after Hollis had returned," said John Campbell. "And besides, the little moving-picture theatre was so crowded with soldiers that he and Thalia couldn't get seats together. He sat, according to him, some rows back of her. The show lasted a little over two hours; it is a fifteen or twenty minute drive from Ponte Verde to your house. They left about nine-thirty and returned about twelve-ten. But Thalia and Hollis didn't actually see each other from the time they entered the theatre until they left. And Beasley—the State's Attorney, you know—says the exact time of Joan Green's death is not possible to determine. But he also makes a point of the fact that you said you heard the scream after a car had driven up to the house, and you thought it was Hollis."

"How did Joan Green get there?" said Victoria, suddenly. "Somebody must have brought her from Ponte Verde; she couldn't have walked. Somebody—whoever murdered her—could have left his car at the other end of the pine woods. There's a road and a place where you can turn into the pine woods for a little way. He could have . . ."

Major Campbell was shaking his head. Colonel Galant was staring bleakly at her. John Campbell said rather gently, "She came by bus—the eleven o'clock bus from Ponte Verde to Pine Beach. At the corner below your house, she got out. The bus stops there at about eleven-twenty; it's about a quarter of a mile from the entrance to your place. And at about a quarter to eleven a woman's voice had talked to her over the telephone at the Ponte Verde Hotel where she lived. The driver of the bus identified her. She got off the bus at that corner and was never seen alive again."

"That's why . . ." began Victoria, and took a long breath. The room was very hot and the fan very loud. "That's why he made me telephone—to see if it was my voice the hotel clerk heard. But I didn't telephone to her. I didn't . . ." Again she stopped. Then she said: "What was she wearing when she got off the bus?"

Major Campbell shook his black head again. "The bus driver doesn't know; he says he didn't notice. He told Beasley that the only reason he remembered her is because she got off at such a lonely part of the road."

"But—then when she left the hotel? What was she wearing then?"

"The clerk didn't see her; no one (except the bus driver) has yet been found who remembers seeing her after about seven o'clock when she ate dinner in the hotel dining room; nobody remembers exactly how she was dressed, except that there was nothing unusual about her. And they don't change for dinner at the hotel, as a rule. Probably she was dressed in whatever she'd been wearing during the day. The telephone call for her came at about a quarter to eleven. Clistie Forbes was wearing the brown lace and chiffon dress at about ten-thirty that night. Between ten-thirty or eleven and the next morning . . ." He stopped with a kind of shrug. Sometime between a quarter to eleven Monday night and five o'clock the next morning that strange and tragic transference had been effected.

Major Campbell turned to Colonel Galant. "May I ask, Colonel, if there is anything else in the transcript which struck you as being of any possible importance?"

"No," said the Colonel. He looked at the back of his hand and said again, his face bleak and lined and old, "No . . ."

Major Campbell waited. Victoria waited too. And Colonel Galant said suddenly, "That is, it can't mean anything." He looked at Victoria. "Victoria, do the words," he lifted his voice over the roar of the fan, "Do the words 'Cara Nome' mean anything to you?"

John Campbell's brown face looked startled. Victoria said, "Why—a face powder. A song."

"That's not what I mean," said the Colonel. He glanced at Major Campbell. "It probably has nothing at all to do with—with anything," he said.

Major Campbell waited. Colonel Galant gnawed his lip, and then said shortly, "It's only a bit of idle conversation, really. Between Bessie and Clistie. But it sticks in my mind, and I keep trying to remember . . ."

"What was it?" asked John Campbell.

"Well, as I say, it probably means nothing. It was that night, you know, Monday night, after dinner. We were having coffee—Bessie and Clistie and I. Thalia and Hollis were at the piano; Agnew was in a corner with his nose in a book. So none of them heard it. Anyway, Clistie—she was looking a little odd, you know; thoughtful and quiet—at least I think so now—Clistie all at once asked Bessie."

He stopped as if he'd finished. After a moment Major Campbell said, "Asked Bessie what?"

"Why, what I asked Victoria! About the words Cara Nome. Did they mean anything to Bessie? Bessie said, like you, Victoria, a song and a brand of cosmetics and literally the English meaning, dear name, and that was all. Clistie, though, insisted a little. I thought it was a little queer; it seemed so unimportant. Finally Bessie said it seemed to her to have some sort of special familiarity, but she had no idea what and wasn't even sure of that, and tried to change the subject. But Clistie turned around to me and asked me if it meant anything to me."

"What did you say?"

"Good God, I said no, of course," exploded the Colonel.

Major Campbell waited again. The Colonel cast him an icy blue look, tapped his fingers on the desk and said, "And it didn't. At least—not then. But—well, it's annoying, you know, John, but since then I—I keep thinking of it. As if I did remember something, do you see? Except I don't. Clistie was very earnest about it. And—well, the fact is, John, I think, too, that I've seen those words, just lately, somewhere. I can't remember where; at the time certainly I paid no attention to them at all. But now . . ." He whirled around impatiently so the swivel chair squeaked. "Now I keep trying to remember some special connection. . . ." He frowned at John Campbell, who said, "Connection with what, Colonel Galant? The camp? Clistie?"

Colonel Galant eyed him frowningly for a moment and shook his head.

"Advertisement?" suggested Major Campbell. "Concert program? Opera?" His voice was casual; his hazel eyes very bright and intent.

"How should I know!" snapped Colonel Galant. He looked at his desk clock, worriedly and added, "A tremendous volume of detail goes across my desk." The telephone whirred and he lifted the receiver. "Who is it? Oh—oh, all right, all right, put him on. . . ." Holding the telephone, he looked at Victoria. "It's the commanding general for this area!" He glanced at the clock again and then at the stack of papers on the desk. "Well, what about it, Victoria? Is there anything that you know—anything unusual . . . ?"

There was nothing, of course. Nothing and no one, except —she leaned forward. "Someone did enter the house that night," she said. "Agnew saw her and Michael saw her, but no one else. I don't mean she came to see Hollis I don't believe Hollis could bring himself to sell any information even if he had it. But someone did enter the house and . . ."

But they knew about the maid. Colonel Galant said, "Beasley told us. I think it was the colored girl—what's her name—the upstairs maid."

Major Campbell said to Victoria, "Do you think Lilibelle was lying?"

"No."

"The alternative, of course," said Major Campbell, watching her, "is not a very pleasant one. That is that someone you don't know, someone nobody knows of—yet knows enough of you to come and go in your house; somebody who has nerve enough to get hold of a maid's uniform and walk in the front door (for the kitchen door was locked) and up the stairway right under Agnew's nose. Somebody who must know, even, that he's near-sighted."

Colonel Galant spoke quickly into the telephone, "Yes, yes, put him on. . . ." He waved at Victoria. "Think it over, Victoria," he said rapidly. "And keep quiet about this; I don't need to tell you that. Perhaps Major Campbell is right; certainly that girl didn't know much, and we can protect what she did know. If there's any hanky-panky going on, I'm going to stop it. That girl, Joan Green, had, so far as anybody knows, only one possible importance to anybody, and that was her connection with Camp Blakoe and this office. Major Campbell will investigate. It's entirely in his hands. Unless I have to call in the F. B. I. Beasley knows about it, of course, and will co-operate. That's all now, my dear. Thanks." He said abruptly into the telephone: "Yes. Oh, yes, General . . ."

He nodded at her as she rose. Major Campbell opened the door and walked with her through the outer office, and into the narrow, deserted little corridor. There was a smell of new wood, a water cooler against the wall at Victoria's elbow, and the sound of steady typing somewhere near.

There Major Campbell stopped and turned to face her.

The night before, when Beasley had questioned her, with that little gleaming red belt upon the table like a red stain of blood, there had been something about John Campbell's presence that was friendly. He had said only a little, there at the last when Beasley all but accused her of murder. He had merely stood for the most part, listening, smoking, immobile. Yet there had been something friendly in his very presence; she had felt defended.

She realized it now because that intangible thing seemed to have gone. He looked now as he'd looked after Henry's death; remote, hard, with impersonal bright hazel eyes in a brown face and his black head a little arrogant. He said, "I really am sorry, Miss Steane. This rather puts me on the other side of the fence again, doesn't it?"

He didn't sound sorry. He sounded as distant and impersonal and as hard as a Diesel engine.

John Campbell, before, had said she'd murdered Henry
Frame. And now, it was her own red belt around Clistie's
neck. Material evidence.

The bare walls behind him softened and blurred—so did his
face against them; with a clutch of inward dismay she knew
there were tears in her eyes.

He saw them. He said, "Victoria," and put his arm around
her shoulders. His arm tightened; he bent so his face was
against her own suddenly. He said again, whispering, and
unevenly, "Victoria . . ." And unexpectedly, blindly, as if he
didn't mean to, as if he didn't know, his mouth moved to her
lips.

14

The sound of typing, the bare walls went away, didn't matter;
became immeasurably distant—and then gradually began to
come back.

As suddenly as they had moved together they were apart
again. John Campbell said abruptly, "I'm always apologizing.
This time—but I didn't mean—I didn't intend . . ." He
stopped, looked at her, and said, "Oh, the hell. Where's your
car? This way?"

Somebody, not Victoria, but somebody inside her body
turned and walked coolly along beside him. As they reached
the door, probably the same person thought suddenly: all
those doors—how idiotic—did anyone see . . .

Victoria's cheeks tingled.

It was absurd; it was preposterous; she was behaving like a
schoolgirl. Nevertheless, she glanced backward along the narrow, bare little passage. None of the doors was open; well,
that was just lucky.

The hot western sun blazed upon them as they went out the
door and down the little flight of steps.

Thalia and Michael and Agnew were sitting in the car in
hot, weary silence, drinking Coca-Colas.

There was a spark of laughter in Major Campbell's eyes as
he put her into the car. But he looked, too, a little shaken.

Michael said, "Hello, Campbell." Thalia smiled; Agnew
scowled.

Then the car was moving away. John Campbell turned
quickly into the administration building again. Victoria
thought with dismay that she had kissed him as closely as he
had kissed her. And Agnew hunched forward, to inquire why
Colonel Galant had sent for her.

What reason could she give? "He wanted to know about the inquiry," said Victoria. "He's very busy; he couldn't come to the house."

There was a short silence. Then Agnew said, "That girl, Joan Green, worked here. I suppose they have spies on their mind and are being very hush-hush about it."

"*Spies!*" said Michael. The car swerved as he glanced swiftly across Thalia, at Victoria.

"Agnew," said Victoria, "sees spies in his dreams. It's his idea of adventure. He's very romantic. . . ."

"Why, Victoria Steane," began Agnew in an indignant sputter and then, abruptly, fell silent. And Thalia murmured rather cryptically, "It takes a thief to catch a thief. Or do I mean a spy?"

"As far as I can tell from what you say, you don't mean anything," said Agnew, emerging momentarily and rudely from his sudden and brooding silence.

Thalia, unruffled, smiled at the road ahead of them. And after that there was very little conversation. Agnew said presently, that they hadn't let them look inside the new magazines that were being built. "Sentries everywhere, now," he said. "You'd think the war was starting tomorrow!" Thalia said after awhile that it was very hot and she'd seen a lot of soldiers drilling and wondered if Hollis was among them. Michael drove very fast so as to cool them, and the road, elastic and soft-looking from the heat, spun under the gray hood of the car. Once Agnew saw some cows in the road and shouted to Michael to look out; at the corner they had to wait for another arriving convoy to hurry past.

They arrived at the house to discover a minor commotion.

There were—or seemed to be—no police around, which was, again, like the days following Henry's death. Even when suspicion of murder was strongest, they had not been, really, under police guard. (None of them could have escaped, perhaps; and anyway, an attempt to do so was almost a confession.) But at the same time they had been actually under a certain amount of surveillance, and they were again. A motorcycle policeman was very busy with the engine of his machine when they passed the corner below the house—the corner where the bus had stopped on Monday night.

The commotion was due to Bessie. She was sitting on the porch, in a draggled mauve tea gown, sobbing into a large green chiffon handkerchief, with Jody hovering helplessly around her with a tray on which stood a glass of brandy, and Judson, the gardener, standing in dour and disapproving silence behind her.

The only word they could get out of her for some time was

"ashes." Eventually Judson, giving Bessie a scornful look, said that it was the police. State troopers; not Beasley. They had been there and had searched the place.

"The whole house," said Bessie, becoming suddenly lucid and dabbing at her great dark eyes. "And the attics and the wardrobes and Clistie's writing desk."

Michael said, "Well, did they find anything?"

"*Ashes*," said Bessie sobbing wildly. Judson said, his eyes little and hard as agates, "They took ashes out of the furnace, Miss Victoria. Took them out with a shovel. I saw them. They took them away."

"*Ashes*," squealed Agnew sharply. "What *kind* of ashes?"

Judson, who hated talking, shook his head once and said that he had to go back to the potting shed. "Can I speak to you a moment, Miss Victoria?" he said. "Alone."

Thalia sat down and took off her hat. Agnew said thoughtfully, "But nothing was burned. Not that anybody knows of, anyway."

Michael took the glass from the tray Jody held and gave it to Bessie. Victoria followed Judson down the path. When they reached the garden, he turned to her. "I didn't want to say anything before Mrs. Isham. She's a vurra uncontrolled woman," he said severely. "But—well, I've never thought that Mr. Frame was the kind of man to commit suicide." He stopped there and looked at the ground.

"Judson, what are you trying to tell me? Do you know anything about his—his death?"

He looked up quickly. "No," he said directly. "If I had, I'd have told the police. But Miss Clistie wouldn't have. That is, if she knew anything that involved—well, any of the family."

He was, of course, quite right. Clistie would have protected any of them with her life, if need be. Judson said, "It's the spade, Miss Vicky."

"Spade! What do you mean?"

He drew himself up; his deep-set eyes were secretive and stubborn. "I didn't tell the police. Or the State's Attorney when he questioned me this morning. It was none of his business. But Miss Clistie came to me, ye see, after you and Mrs. Isham and Miss Thalia had gone to Camp Blakoe that afternoon, Monday, and asked me for a spade. She didn't bring it back. It's nowhere around. Why did she want it, Miss Vicky? And what did she do with it?"

"But that"—Victoria pushed her hair back from her hot face—"that didn't have anything to do with the murder, Judson."

"How do ye know that, Miss Vicky?"

"Well, I—I don't know, of course. Only—well, nothing's

been buried anywhere." Death and burying; the words seemed wrong and out of place in the hot, still sunshine with the bougainvillaea over the porch in full blazing glory. Wrong and rather ominous, as if their utterance invited misfortune. She said quickly, "Well, it's nothing, Judson. Thank you though for telling me."

"Mind ye," he said emphatically, "if I thought any of this was evidence, it would be my duty to tell the police. But I do not consider it so." He looked fiercely at her, as if daring her to give him credit for either loyalty or affection, turned around and went down the path, his thick body obstinate and dogged in every move.

She turned slowly back toward the house. Probably the spade meant nothing. It had always been Clistie's habit to poke about the house and grounds, quietly accomplishing her own domestic ends without explanation. On the other hand, it was an odd thing to disappear, like that.

What remained of the afternoon was quiet. Bessie stopped crying and ate a large slice of cake, which Jody brought her. The police did not return; Michael fended off several telephone calls and two more reporters. Agnew sat hunched on the edge of the porch, reading a large book. Bessie, eventually, asked him what it was and he said, reading and engrossed, that it was about murder. "There's a fine chapter on garroting," he said.

"*Agnew!*" Bessie sat upright in the wicker chaise longue. "Where did you get such a book! Give it to me at once."

" 'The next step,' " read Agnew dreamily, " 'will be to examine the instrument of strangulation and its employment.' " He read on further, squinted across the river, thrust out his under lip and said in a faraway voice, "Well, we all know the instrument. That was Vicky's red belt. There wasn't anything special about the way it was employed. I asked one of the police. It was just put"—his voice faltered a little—"put around her" — he swallowed and went on—"her throat and tied once and —and pulled."

Nobody spoke. Then Agnew went on rapidly. "There are only two possible theories about Vicky's red belt. No, three. One: it was discovered accidentally somehow by the murderer —not in the house; which would mean either that Vicky lost it . . ."

"No," said Victoria, "I didn't lose it."

". . . or that somebody else lost it. Two: Clistie herself had it. I can't imagine why. I asked Lilibelle when she'd last seen the belt, but she never knows anything. The police had asked her, too; she told me."

"What's the third theory?" said Michael.

109

"Intention, of course. Somebody got into the house, and took the belt with the intention of using it exactly as it—as it was used. That is," said Agnew, conquering the tendency of his voice to falter whenever he spoke of Clistie's death, and going on quickly, "That is, whoever did it intended either to involve you, Vicky, or to divert suspicion from himself, or both. Himself," said Agnew, "or herself. For the maid I saw could have done it. So that theory has something to back it up. Victoria went to her room before I saw the maid, but Vicky says she was on the balcony. The maid—or whoever it was—could have gone into Vicky's room, got hold of the belt and then . . ."

"Then disappeared into thin air," said Bessie irritably. "I wish you'd stop talking about that. It was either Lilibelle or nobody." Her voice was defiant. Her eyes, roving the shrubs and hedges of the garden, were uneasy.

Agnew went on. "Then, of course, the maid—excuse me, Mother—the unknown quantity, could have waited in Victoria's room until Michael and I came upstairs, and the coast was clear. And then she came down again. Yes, that could have happened."

"I think it was Lilibelle you saw on the stairway," said Bessie stubbornly. "If it's an opportunity for some—some tramp to get into the house unobserved and take Vicky's red belt that you're thinking of, I should say a whole regiment of tramps could have walked right under your nose without your knowing it."

"A tramp," said Agnew somberly, "wouldn't have murdered Henry. And then come back to murder Clistie and Joan Green. A tramp wouldn't have remembered that Victoria was the choice suspect of the police when Henry was killed; that must be, you know, the reason for the red belt. To make Victoria the suspect again. Vicky, who hates you like that? Enough to see you charged with murder. You haven't done anything to anybody, have you?"

There was a rather stunned silence. Then Michael got up, walked across and put his hand on Agnew's shoulder.

"You're worrying Vicky, Agnew," he said rather gently, as the boy looked up.

Agnew gave him and then Victoria a startled look. "Oh, I say . . . I didn't mean—aw, now, Mike, Vicky's all right. She's got guts."

"*Agnew!*" said Bessie. "*Put that book away and shut up.*"

"All right," said Agnew sulkily. "If you don't *want* to know who murdered her . . ." He complied in outraged dignity, and returned to sit with a wounded and brooding air on the edge of the low porch.

110

"Dreadful boy," murmured Bessie. But she eyed him uneasily, as she lay back in the great wicker chaise longue.

The sun had gone down by that time and soft gray clouds covered the sky like a blanket; a mist crept up slowly from the river, clothing it in distance and mystery.

After dinner, with the river misty and the moon that night half-hidden by clouds, so the whole night, the sky and river and mist were pearly and luminous, Michael and Victoria walked in the garden again to the point above the river where there were chairs and a sundial. It seemed a long time since they had stood there together in the moonlight; a long time since the Colonel's tea party—where John Campbell had talked to her of murder. She had never told Michael of that. She did so then, looking out across the river through wraiths of Spanish moss and mist which, in the diffused pearly light, were strangely beautiful and a little ominous.

Michael was angry and astonished. "But good God, Vicky," he cried, "why didn't you tell me! The man was warning you of danger."

"I didn't believe him."

"Look here," said Michael suddenly. "Do you know much of Campbell? I mean beyond the obvious facts."

Victoria thought back. He lived in Ponte Verde; he had been State's Attorney, therefore he must be a lawyer. He was in his thirties, probably. He liked dogs and horses and didn't like murder and that was all she knew. All, that is, except that she knew so many other things—odd things, like the way he walked, and the way his eyes laughed, and the way he said Victoria. The way he held a woman and kissed her. She caught that thought back, quickly.

"What is the matter, Victoria?" said Michael. He couldn't see her face clearly in that pale and shifting light; nevertheless, she said hurriedly, confused, "Nothing. That is, I don't know anything at all about him. Why?"

"It struck me that it was queer the way he let the thing drop. If he still believed Henry was murdered, why didn't he do something about it?"

"He said he had to abide by the decision of the coroner's jury."

Michael uttered an impatient exclamation. "If it wasn't for him and the unwarranted stand he took against you, Vicky, you wouldn't be on the—on the spot you're on right now."

Clouds shifted so that gradually the light was less and the shadows came nearer; the pine woods and the river took on a quality of sentience, of awareness, of threat. She moved uneasily. "Let's go back, Michael."

"All right. Cigarette?"

They strolled back toward the house. But Michael was deep in thought and, as they reached the lighted house, said, "He dropped the case when he still believed it was murder. And then took the trouble to warn you just exactly then. The night before Clistie—and that girl were killed. Why?"

"But he couldn't have had anything to do with it. He didn't know any of us; there would have been no motive."

Michael said slowly, "Last winter, I mean after Henry's death, I thought Campbell was—well, a decent sort. Mistaken, but doing what he thought was right. Now, I'm not so sure that he's entirely disinterested, and I think it's time to . . ."

She interrupted him. "But he didn't know Henry! Someone would have known of it! He would have said so!"

"Would he?" said Michael after a moment.

And a little memory returned suddenly from that talk with John Campbell. He'd said, suddenly harsh, "You've forgotten one thing. The fact that he was the kind of man somebody might want to murder." He'd meant Henry Frame.

As if he knew.

15

The night was quiet and, for that matter, parts of the next day. Or comparatively quiet. Beasley darted into the drive a time or two at top speed in his chugging little car, and shortly went away again without, so far as any of them knew, accomplishing much. He talked to Lilibelle again, reducing her to tears but not to confession. He talked to Ernestine and Jody about the time when they'd bolted the kitchen door. He prowled the house on one occasion, spending some time in Clistie's bedroom. He visited the other bedrooms, too (according to Agnew), and went away with something wrapped in newspaper, under his arm, which was, as Bessie said later, a little unnerving, particularly as no one knew what it was.

But before Beasley left, he did tell Michael, who asked him, that the ashes from the furnace had yielded nothing of interest. He did not say what he had expected them to yield.

State troopers came, too, and took more fingerprints from the pump house. They were there for a long time. Agnew, hovering on the outskirts and watching them from the yew hedge, reported that they went away disconsolately. Certainly the bare, cemented, little pump house was not a fertile field for clues.

Again they saw nothing of Major Campbell. If, however, it was his job to read through the entire bulk of every telephone

112

conversation Joan Green had taken in shorthand and then typed, during the months of her employment at Camp Blakoe, it explained his absence. Or so thought Victoria; she could not, of course, say anything of it to the others.

"I don't like this Eliot Beasley," Bessie said once. "But anybody is better than Campbell. Thank Heaven he's in the army now and can't have anything to do with this. Or us." She fanned herself with a long, chiffon handkerchief.

Victoria could not tell her she was wrong.

The day was hot again, cloudy and very sultry. However, there was not a drop of rain anywhere in the vicinity—which later had its own small significance.

It seemed long because there was too much time to think. Yet in another way it passed very quickly. Certainly that day, plans were made and last desperate contingencies considered. But in view of the previous days it was quiet—at least to the outward eye.

There were, of course, newspapers in full cry now, and reporters. There were telegrams and a few rather cautious telephone calls from friends in the neighborhood. After one such telephone call Bessie came back to the porch fanning herself with long sweeps of her handkerchief, like an actress stealing a scene, and looking rather grimly amused. "That," she said, "was Eleanor Updike. She thinks a spy did it, and wanted to know if we had any Nazi servants! As if I'd have a Nazi even if we are not at war—yet." Bessie snorted. "She didn't seem to want to talk for very long. She acted as if I was Mata Hari in disguise."

"You'd have to be her ghost then," said Agnew grumpily. "She's been dead for years. Vicky, you're looking kind of peaked—come on and play some tennis with me. It'll do you good."

He made her go while Thalia murmured that nobody could possibly play tennis on a day like that, and Michael showed another photographer and two reporters the pump house and the pine woods. But the game of tennis was not a success. Agnew, a remarkably good player with or without his spectacles, was that day erratic and absent-minded, and before they finished the first set, Victoria missed a serve, slipped, skinned her knee and, sitting unexpectedly in the middle of the hot tennis court, burst into more unexpected tears. Agnew, appalled, leaped over the net and ran to look at her knee. "But my gosh, Vicky, it's hardly scratched! My gosh, what are you crying for! *My gosh*," said Agnew sitting beside her and eyeing her with horror. "Does it hurt like *that?*"

"N-no . . ."

"Then what's the matter?"

"Give me your handkerchief."

"Here. . . ." He watched her anxiously.

"Sorry," she said. "Thanks."

"Vicky, what's gone wrong between you and Mike?"

"Me and . . ." She stared at him. "How did you know?"

"Guessed."

"How?"

"I dunno." He shrugged. "No love light in your eyes, I guess. Besides you're so darned quiet. Too quiet—as if you're afraid to let down. Of course, none of us feels exactly jolly. And I know you feel like hell about—about Clistie. So do I. I know it's tough, too, with the wedding postponed and all. But still . . ."

"I don't think there's going to be a wedding," she said.

He got up briskly and gave her a hand. "Come on over to the bench," he said practically, "and tell me all. When did you decide you weren't in love with Mike and why?"

There wasn't really much to tell. Agnew, however, understood what there was. "Of course, I see," he said, balancing his tennis racket on his knees. "I thought at the time that it was all too, too romantic. Whirlwind courtship, love at first sight—well, second, anyway—then the big rescue and wedding bells. But don't go too far the other way, Vick. Mike's pretty regular, you know." The tennis racket fell over. He bent to pick it up and said, not looking at her, "I don't suppose there's anybody else? Anybody you've got your mind on, I mean."

"No!"

There was a long pause. Agnew put down his racket and got a tennis ball out of his pocket, bouncing it thoughtfully in soft little thuds against the turf. The air was very still; not a leaf in all the green around them seemed to move. She said, presently, "Agnew, who could have killed her?"

He didn't reply for a moment. Then he said abruptly, "Whoever killed Henry, I think. But I don't know who or why."

"I don't suppose that there's any doubt now that Henry was murdered."

He shrugged. "I always rather thought it was murder. But only because he was the kind of man somebody might want to murder. There wasn't any real proof. And there isn't now, and I imagine there never will be. His murder is important only because it happened. I mean, it seems to have launched —all this."

John Campbell had said that, too; but Agnew knew Henry.

"Agnew," she said impulsively, "do the words Cara Nome mean anything to you?"

114

"Cara Nome!" He turned his freckled face with a jerk to peer closely at her. "Why?"

"Because"—she could tell that much, she decided, without betraying Colonel Galant's confidence—"because Clistie asked Bessie that, the night she was murdered. Just that—she didn't explain. Do you know anything about it?"

He considered it slowly.

"Outside of *Rigoletto*, no," he said finally, his face screwed up with concentration.

Presently they strolled back to the house. When they came to the driveway Victoria stopped and put her hand on Agnew's thin wrist. "Thanks," she said.

To her astonishment, Agnew patted her shoulder almost tenderly. "You're a nice girl, Vicky," he said. He added quickly, alarmed, "But don't go and cry again. . . ."

"I'm not crying, I'm only . . ."

"Scared," he finished. "I know. So am I. By the way, I don't suppose you want to tell me why Colonel Galant sent for you in such a hurry yesterday?"

"No, I—can't."

"Oh," said Agnew. "I didn't think so. Well, Vicky, whether you're going to marry Mike or not, ask him about a lawyer. Get one down from New York. I—I don't like that red belt. And the way Beasley acts," said Agnew avoiding her eyes. "Not," he added somberly, "that a lawyer can change any facts."

They went back to the house.

Michael had already sent for a lawyer. "I talked to him over the telephone," he said. "I hope it's all right, Vicky dear. I didn't want to—to bother you, so I just went ahead and got him. It's Fabre Gleason; he's one of the best. He'll fly down from New York if you—if we," he amended it hastily, "need him. Right away. But if nothing breaks for awhile, he wants to finish a case he's on now. He'd read the newspapers. He said to tell you—that is, for all of us, to sit tight."

"Gleason," said Bessie thoughtfully. "That's the criminal lawyer." And added, thoughtfully too, "I wish Hollis would telephone."

Hollis, however, did not telephone; he arrived just before dinner.

It was, all in all, a quiet day. Yet, as evening came on, the sense of waiting—waiting for something that must happen, waiting for Beasley to sift and assort the evidence he had gathered so strenuously the previous day, grew almost unbearably tense.

They were all uneasy and, as Agnew said, too quiet. Yet there was not much they could say. Every hypothesis had been explored too many times; every theory had been uttered too often; every thought had followed the same well-worn circle—and eventually met the same baffling wall past which it could not go.

But so far as evidence went, or material clues, there was nothing that day that was new to Victoria; nothing she saw or heard or remembered that made the smallest chink in that wall.

Certainly there was nothing to suggest Hollis' implication in a plot to sell information to a foreign agent. Except, of course, the maid who walked upstairs and disappeared, but that could mean anything. And nothing.

And Hollis, himself, looking very tired, with fine lines showing around his hard, light-blue eyes, came in time for dinner. Colonel Galant had arranged a leave, he told Bessie shortly. Victoria could not tell from his bearing whether or not Colonel Galant had yet questioned him about Joan Green.

Almost immediately after dinner Beasley arrived too—with a large manila envelope, Major Campbell, two state policemen in uniform and a middle-aged woman in black. The manila envelope contained a detailed account of Henry Frame's death, the circumstances surrounding it, and the course of the investigation. One of the policemen was a stenographer and whipped out a tablet and a supply of pencils. Major Campbell, his brown face guarded, sat in one of the red leather armchairs drawn up to the library table. Victoria was sent for, and Hollis, and Michael. And the middle-aged woman in black looked at Victoria and at Michael and shook her head, and then at Hollis and nodded.

"That's the man," she said in a weary voice. "I'd know him anywhere. But I never saw the girl—Miss Steane—before, except, of course, her pictures in the papers a few weeks ago. If Joan knew her she never told me. And I never saw the other man. . . ." She looked at Michael.

She was Joan Green's aunt.

Hollis flushed a bright pink. Beasley said, leaning forward into the light so his long yellow face was in sharp relief and his black eyes gleamed, "Where did you see Hollis Isham?"

The woman had a plain, rather nice face, and an air of honesty. "In Ponte Verde," she said. "I had come to do a little shopping and to see Joan. It was the first time she'd been away from home, you know. She was"—her voice wavered a little—"she was a very quiet girl. She didn't make many friends and she was very keen about her job. Well, he was at the tobacco counter in the hotel. He didn't see us, but Joan pointed him out to me and then later told me he had taken her out a few times, to the movies and driving and to dinner.

116

He'd got acquainted with her at camp, at one of the dances there. She said he was rich, but that didn't make any difference to Joan," she said sturdily. "Except that—well," she hesitated, "I felt somehow that she liked him more than he liked her. Joan was—very quiet," she said again. "She didn't say much; that was all, really. But I remember telling her that there were lots of nice young men in the world and that she was very young."

Hollis put up his fair head. He said, "Mrs. Green, I can't tell you how sorry I am about—about everything." He turned to Beasley. "All right," he said, "I knew her. She was a nice girl. I liked her and I went out with her a few times. Now what are you going to make of it?"

Beasley said to Joan Green's aunt, "So you were worried. You thought there was something not quite . . ."

"Not at all," said Mrs. Green. "Joan was a nice girl. It's exactly as I told you. . . ."

Hollis interrupted angrily, "I'll tell you anything you want to know, Beasley. I didn't kill Joan."

"Why didn't you identify her? Why did you pretend you didn't know her?"

"Because . . ." Hollis began angrily and then stopped short, scarlet, angry—and afraid. Victoria saw that. And Beasley turned to Mrs. Green. "Think, now," he said. "Surely Joan talked to you about the Frame murder. Everybody was talking of it. What did she say?"

Mrs. Green drew herself up. "You've asked me that many times. My niece," she said with quiet dignity, "never mentioned the murder of Henry Frame. If she read the newspaper stories about it, she never spoke of it to me. I'm absolutely sure that with the exception of Mr. Isham, she knew none of the people concerned with it. And it's my opinion that she didn't know him until after the Frame murder."

"But you knew Isham's name," persisted Beasley. "You must have connected it with the Frame murder. You admit you read all about it."

"So did everyone else in the county, I imagine," said Mrs. Green heavily. "Yes, I knew Hollis Isham's name; at least his last name; Joan said it was Isham; and I've identified him. But I"—she looked at Hollis and said firmly—"I do not believe that this boy killed her. I am going now, if you please. It is a long drive home. . . ."

John Campbell said quickly, "We'll send you in a car . . ." He went to the door with her. At the door they met Bessie. She stared but drew back and let them pass and then, beads swinging and bracelets jangling, swept up to Hollis. "Hollis, my dear, I heard. I was listening," she said, and turned to

Beasley. "I'll tell you all about it," she said, twisting her big, swarthy hands. "It's all my fault. Hollis didn't kill her, but he didn't tell who she was either because I . . ."

"Take this," snapped Beasley at the policeman with the tablet.

Hollis interrupted, "I'll tell it, Beasley. I met Joan at one of the dances. I'd seen her in Colonel Galant's office. She was a —a nice kid. I liked her. But my mother . . ."

"I didn't approve of it," said Bessie. "I told Hollis to stop going about with her. I told him I—I wouldn't have it. And he stopped. When I found it was—was Joan Green who was murdered, naturally, I wouldn't let him tell anyone he knew her. It was absurd, to drag him into suspicion like that!"

Major Campbell returned and quietly closed the door. His eyes met Victoria's as he did so, briefly and without, apparently, any remembrance of the last time they had met—and a bare little hall with the sound of typing in the distance.

Hollis said: "I didn't kill her."

"But you failed to identify her the morning she was found," said Beasley. "You refused to admit that you knew her. That was before your mother knew her name; before she advised you to keep quiet."

16

"Yes," said Hollis. "It was crazy. Not to admit it, I mean. But I—I knew what they'd say. That she was murdered here. On the place. Thrown into the river. If I'd told the truth, then you'd have said—just what you're saying now. And she . . ." Hollis was quite white; his long obstinate upper lip set itself; his blue Steane eyes were very light and cold. He said, "It's as her aunt said. She was a nice kid. And I—liked her. It was a shock . . ." He stopped abruptly. Bessie gave him a long look and sat down. Beasley said, "But you must have known we'd discover it sooner or later."

Bessie said, "You must try to understand. He . . ."

"Mother . . ."

"Please let me talk, Hollis." She spread her jeweled hands out on the table and leaned forward fixing her large, dark eyes upon Beasley. "He guessed who it was when they described her over the telephone; that is, he didn't guess, but it —it sounded like her. He told me that later. And he was horrified and shocked. We all saw that at the time." Her eyes flashed around and she caught Victoria's eyes and Michael's and said demandingly, "Didn't we, Victoria? Didn't we, Michael?"

"Yes," said Michael. "He was shocked, and surprised."

Victoria remembered Hollis at the telephone. The way he sagged against the wall when the police described the woman they had found in the river.

"Yes," she said, echoing Michael.

"Yes," said Bessie. "But he didn't tell me. He didn't want to alarm me, and we—we'd had words about the girl, you see. He didn't . . ." She swallowed convulsively, "he didn't want to give her up. Yet he wasn't really in love with her, you see."

"Oh, Mother, *don't*," said Hollis. He turned brusquely away, walked over to the window and said over his shoulder. "Tell the truth. It was murder and I—I didn't want to be mixed up in it. I—it was an impulse. And I looked at Joan, there in that beastly little room and I—I couldn't say, yes, I knew her. I didn't even tell Mother until after Joan was—was identified. I couldn't . . ." He stopped. The room was very still for a moment. Then he said bitterly, "I was a fool. I know it. And a coward. All right. But I didn't kill her."

Bessie didn't move; only her great ringed eyes followed Hollis and her hands twisted. Victoria started toward Hollis, realized that sympathy would be another drop of humiliation, and stopped. Major Campbell said to Bessie, "Did you recognize the girl?"

Her great eyes flashed. "No; certainly not."

"Did you ever talk to her? Over the telephone, I mean."

"*No,*" she said violently.

"A woman did telephone to her," said Beasley. "Mrs. Isham, why did you want your son to stop seeing her?"

"Because, she—because I did."

"There must have been some important reason. Did she know anything about Henry Frame's murder?"

Hollis turned around. "Of course not. She knew nothing of it. How could she?"

Bessie said heavily, "I didn't want Hollis to marry her. That's all. I wanted Hollis to marry Victoria. There's the business, you see. Hollis could manage it." She glanced at Victoria. "You must have known that, my dear," she said breezily. "I never really wanted you to marry Michael." She glanced at Michael, too, gave him a queerly polite and self-deprecating smile, and added, "Not that I object to you, Michael. I just didn't want her to marry anyone but Hollis."

Michael, looking a little amused, said as politely as Bessie, "I quite understand."

"But Aunt Bessie . . ." began Victoria and stopped, with a feeling of helplessness.

Hollis said over his shoulder, "Victoria doesn't care a hang for me, Mike. There never was anything between us. It's just an idea of Mother's."

Beasley said, his voice still purring, "But Mrs. Isham, Miss Steane *is* to marry Bayne. She would have been married to him now except for"—his voice took on an added quality of softness—"except for the fact that Joan Green and Miss Forbes were murdered."

Bessie blinked and said violently, "I didn't kill either of them to stop Victoria's marriage. If that's what you mean!"

Major Campbell came forward. "Mrs. Isham, had Joan Green ever come to the house before?" he asked.

Hollis replied, "No. Never."

"Yet she did manage to find her way from the corner where she got off the bus, through the grounds, to the pine woods."

Hollis shrugged.

"How did she get there, do you think?"

"How should I know? I didn't meet her."

"But she must have met someone. Do you know who?"

"Certainly not," said Hollis. "Unless . . ."

"Unless what?"

"Well," said Hollis, "there's this maid that was wandering around."

"Oh, yes," said Beasley. "The unknown woman. You're going to make the most of her, aren't you?"

"It could have been a man," said Hollis. "That's all. . . ."

"I'm told," said John Campbell, "that Miss Green was very good at her job. Did you think so, Isham?"

Hollis looked at him suspiciously. "Why, I don't know. How should I know? Ask the officers she worked for."

"She did have a very retentive memory, hadn't she?"

"I don't know," said Hollis sulkily.

"Did she ever talk of Colonel Galant? Or—or anything at all to do with affairs in the office?"

Hollis whirled around. His face was red again and his light eyes were snapping. "Listen," he said. "Colonel Galant called me into his office late this afternoon. We've had all this out. Didn't he tell you? Or . . . I see! He did tell you, and ordered you to question me, too. Well, listen—I didn't sell any military information."

"*Hollis*," cried his mother. "*You!*"

"Oh, be still, Mother. I didn't sell any information. I didn't know anything to sell, and I wouldn't have known where to sell it if I had known anything. And I wouldn't have done it, anyway. So that's that."

There was a long silence. Then Beasley said softly, "Well, let's just go over all this again."

An hour later he let them go. Without, so far as Victoria could see, adding a scrap to his stock of information, except the fact that Bessie had told Clistie about Joan Green.

"So Clistie Forbes knew the girl!" he cried in triumph.

"Certainly not," said Bessie. "She'd never seen her. She only knew of her——her name and where she worked and how Hollis had got acquainted with her."

"You told Clistie to telephone to the girl. You told her to get the girl here. Then you got rid of both of them."

Beasley's method of questioning was almost entirely accusation. Bessie turned purple. *"I did not!"* she shouted.

In the end, both Hollis and Bessie stuck to the explanation they had given him.

And when they'd gone he turned all his guns upon Victoria. Michael would have stayed, but Beasley made him leave. "We'll come to you again, later," he said with a little smile on his wide, purplish lips. "Just now I want to talk to Miss Steane."

So Michael had to go.

And then, with the heavy oak door closed, the light from above pouring down, the thick notes about Henry Frame's death and its subsequent investigation before him, Beasley began.

Her thin scarlet belt around Clistie's neck. Her story that had sent Clistie out into the dark, mysterious night. Her quarrel with Henry. Her position as principal suspect when Henry Frame was murdered. Everybody now called it murder.

Obviously, Beasley's inquiry about Hollis and Joan Green, his accusations that Hollis had murdered the girl, that Bessie had murdered her and Clistie, constituted only his own manner of inquiry. Victoria herself was still his principal suspect; he made it abundantly clear.

Major Campbell listened——tracing figures on the table with his fingers, his face inscrutable. Once he got up and went to the door and had Jody bring some ice water and poured a glass of it for Victoria. Once he got out cigarettes, gave her one and lighted it and put the package near her. Beasley went on.

He referred to the notes of the investigation following Henry Frame's death. John Campbell's notes, on file in the office that now was Beasley's; notes that with every word emphasized the case John Campbell had built up against her. He read aloud in a rasping, inexorable voice her own admissions, her quarrel with Henry, what she had said to him, what he had said to her. She had told Henry she was determined to investigate the business; hadn't she?

It was all down in black and white before him; questions John Campbell had asked, questions she had answered.

"Yes," said Victoria.

"You told him you were determined to be given control of

your money, didn't you? And when he told you that you could do nothing so long as he lived, you said you realized it." He looked at the notes before him and quoted. "Answer: 'I said, Yes, I realized that. But there must be some way to get rid of him.' Question: 'What did he say?' Answer: 'He said—I think he said, "There isn't any way, I tell you. As long as I live." ' Do you remember, Miss Steane?"

John Campbell, his face hard and set, lighted a cigarette. Victoria said in a low voice, "Yes. Yes, I said that. Lilibelle heard it as she was going through the hall. Mr. Campbell induced her to tell it."

"Why didn't you fire her? Certainly her story didn't improve your situation."

"I didn't kill Henry. She only told what she heard. She was —made to tell it," Victoria said wearily. "She didn't mean to make things worse for me."

John Campbell said suddenly, "There's not much use in going back over that evidence, Beasley. We got everything we could get at the time. I don't think, honestly, at this date, you're likely to get anything further."

"Oh, *don't* you, John," said Beasley. "That remains to be seen. If Clistie Forbes was murdered because she knew something about Frame's murder, there are motives in plenty. Or rather suspects in plenty, all with the same motive. Frame kept Miss Steane—and Hollis Isham, and his mother, to say nothing of the kid, Agnew—from using money that belonged properly to them. Not only that, but there was nothing they could do about it as long as he lived and, since he was embezzling every cent he could, there was a sound reason for him to refuse, utterly, to permit any kind of meddling on their part in the business. He let Hollis work in the office, but it was an unimportant clerk's job; nothing that gave Hollis any insight into the way the business was run. Oh, there was motive for murder, there! Even Michael Bayne shared that motive; he wanted to marry Miss Steane and—supposing for the sake of argument that it was her money he was interested in and not Miss Steane—he couldn't get hold of that money until Frame was dead. So he had a good motive too."

John Campbell's lips tightened. "Not at that time, I believe," he said. Victoria said, "Michael scarcely knew me, then!"

"All right, all right," said Beasley, wagging his black head. "But everybody had a motive just the same. Bayne profited by Frame's death—or will profit as soon as you are married to him, Miss Steane. Unless," he grinned wolfishly, "you have a prior engagement."

John Campbell got up suddenly, shoving his chair violently

behind him. "You've questioned her long enough, Beasley. It's late. . . ."

Beasley smiled. "That's funny coming from you." He glanced at the thick sheaf of notes and thumped them with his yellow clawlike fingers. "She was your suspect, you know, John." He whirled around to Victoria again. "You telephoned to that girl and told her to come here. Why?"

John Campbell interrupted again; still standing, his hands tight and hard around the back of the chair before him, his black head high. "The hotel clerk wasn't sure it was Miss Steane's voice," he said.

"This is my case," snapped Beasley. "I'll thank you to remember that, John. And I was under the impression that you were under orders from Colonel Galant to investigate the case from the Joan Green angle. Not to undertake to defend Miss Steane."

John Campbell didn't look at Victoria. "I'm not defending anybody. I only say that Joan Green's murder gives the whole thing a new slant."

"Well, then," said Beasley, "find out who murdered Joan Green. And why." He glared at John Campbell and turned to Victoria. "Miss Steane, I want to ask you a question point-blank, and I want you to answer yes or no. Did you, on Monday night, enter the pine woods?"

Something a little perplexed came into John Campbell's face.

"No," said Victoria.

"You're sure of that?"

"I am sure."

"You would swear to it. . . ."

"What are you getting at, Eliot?" asked John Campbell.

Beasley smiled mysteriously. "Nothing; nothing. Merely a statement." Michael knocked on the door and came in; he looked white and angry.

"Haven't you done enough for tonight?" he demanded. "You've questioned her for hours. Come with me, Vicky," he said, and led her toward the door. Beasley made a motion to stop them. John Campbell, his face rather pale, too, under its tan, said quickly, "Oh, let her go, Beasley. You can't do any more tonight."

At the door Victoria glanced back. John Campbell was putting together the notes of the investigation into Henry's death. Beasley was still sprawled in the chair, staring into space with narrow, shiny black eyes.

They went away soon after. Victoria, in her room with the doors open upon the balcony, heard the cars leave. The night was hot and dark; there were clouds, so only occasional moonlight filtered through the clouds, and gave a ghostly, shifting radiance to the garden and the trees and the river.

"Well, at any rate," Michael had said with comforting calm, when she told him of the interview, "they've got nothing new."

Except, of course, Hollis. But they hadn't arrested him and John Campbell's questions sounded as if they had little if any real evidence against him.

Yet it seemed to her then that there had been something evasive in Hollis' eyes, something guarded—something not told.

It was then just after eleven—not as late as it had seemed. And it was shortly after that that she made a singularly unpleasant discovery. For she took down the shrouded wedding dress, still hanging beside the window, intending to fold it away in a drawer. Thinking of Clistie's little hands adding the last stitches to the dress, she took off the cover. And the white satin was hacked and slashed and shredded—almost as if it had been a live thing, stabbed to death.

It was, of course, only a dress.

It seemed to her presently, though, that that very fact gave the thing a peculiarly wanton and brutal quality.

She wrapped it up again, and put it away.

The little gold clock pointed at twelve when she put out the light. She decided finally to tell Beasley or John Campbell, although she could not see any possible connection between that and Clistie's murder.

It was still cloudy and still hot. She pinned her thoughts to something safe, something everyday and reassuringly commonplace. And rather oddly she was thinking of the fan in Colonel Galant's office, the steady buzz and whir of it, when she finally went to sleep.

It was odd because at that very moment the fan was still going and the windows were still up with insects whirring against the screen and vying energetically with the whir of the fan. Colonel Bruce Galant was at his desk. His coat was off, hanging over a chair, his collar opened, papers stacked on his desk and cigarette ends overflowing the ashtrays. That was at twelve.

At about twelve-thirty someone shot through the window at him. The clouds were heavier by that time and the moon hidden. The lighted window made a bright square. Colonel Galant's khaki-colored shirt was a perfect target.

Victoria, naturally, neither knew nor dreamed of that. She was asleep and did not awaken until some time later.

When she did awaken it was because she was dreaming of the night Joan Green was murdered and the scream she had

124

heard. And the splash—very clear and distinct; so clear. indeed, that she sat up abruptly, awake and listening.

It was very dark and very still. So she heard someone running heavily along the grassy slope below the balcony from the river, she thought.

She got up, sharply awake, and went quietly out onto the balcony.

It was dark, yet the clouds were moving over the moon and a faint luminous light was beginning to break through them. The sound of running footsteps had stopped.

Vines brushed her shoulder. The faint luminousness over lawns and river was increasing. Black blotches that were trees began to stand out against it.

And all at once someone was walking along the terrace— lightly, like the soft steady patter of rain upon the stones. She leaned over the balcony railing; in the daytime the open terrace, east of the house and adjoining the porch at the south, was visible from her balcony. Now it was only a faintly lighter strip in surrounding darkness.

But the light was increasing, and she thought now that she could see a moving figure, close to the house wall. She could hear the footsteps distinctly in that stillness—light, soft, quick. If only the moon would come out. . . .

A clear patch of moonlight lay suddenly and whitely on the lawn, and the figure on the terrace was almost out of earshot now and, by contrast, less clear. In another second or two it would reach the corner of the house.

It did.

And just at that instant the broadening patch of moonlight reached it.

A woman in a maid's uniform slipped around the corner of the house and was gone.

The soft patter of footsteps stopped.

The moonlight lay white and clear upon an empty terrace.

17

It wasn't Ernestine. If it was Lilibelle, the uniform was different, somehow, than she customarily wore—longer, and bulkier.

Whatever, whoever it was, she must alarm the house, wake everybody—set them to searching. Agnew had seen the mysterious maid and Michael, and now she had seen her, too.

It was important; it was the outsider. The unknown. It proved her existence. Yet the night was so quiet and still that she thought suddenly, have I been dreaming? Did I really see her?

But there was the memory of the soft patter of footsteps to convince her. The light, clear splash in the river that had been in her dream and yet had awakened her. The footsteps running across the grassy lawn.

The clouds were shifting rapidly again; already a band of shadow had crept across the terrace.

She must hurry; as she turned, she glanced downward over the other side of the balcony railing to where a clear patch of moonlight still lay upon the lawn, making a deep, sharp black shadow of a tall hibiscus there at the entrance of the garden path. And in that patch of moonlight stood John Campbell.

His back was turned toward her. He was perfectly still and seemed to be watching something in the garden. His tall figure was unmistakable. The moonlight gleamed on his wide leather belt. Then the advancing edge of shadow reached him and swiftly blotted out hibiscus and silvery lawn and the silent, motionless figure.

She leaned over the railing, intending to call to him. Then again she heard the sound of running footsteps on the grassy strip below—a rapidly diminishing sound that seemed to go toward the driveway. Then she could hear it no longer.

It was all strange and unreal, like a shadow play, blotted out by darkness.

If he went that way, though, he would meet the woman in white, coming from the opposite end of the house. Perhaps— in any case she must rouse the house and find the woman, and grasp at the clue which up to then had been so extraordinarily unsubstantial and evasive.

She ran into her room just as someone knocked softly at the door. Her heart turned over with relief as the door opened and Michael's voice said, "Vicky—are you awake?"

"*Michael . . .*"

"Are you all right? Where's the light?"

"Michael, there was a woman on the terrace. Michael . . ."

She ran against a table with a lamp on it and fumbled for the light. He was in the doorway, his brown hair rumpled, a dressing-gown hanging over his shoulders. He took a long breath. "You're all right then. Did you hear it too?"

"Michael, it was the maid again!"

"*Maid!* Vicky, are you sure? Where did she go?"

"Around toward the end of the house—the kitchen end. . . ."

"I'll look! I didn't see her. I just heard something—a door, I thought, and steps on the terrace. I—I had to make sure

126

you were all right. I suddenly thought of those French doors onto the balcony. You've got to keep them locked after this, Vicky. I—well—the maid! We'll get her this time! Stay here, Vicky . . ." He whirled around and ran down the hall.

She couldn't stay there while they searched. He was pounding at Hollis' door by the time Victoria had snatched up a dressing-gown and flung it over her white pajamas and slid her toes into flat little red slippers and followed him.

Hollis roused at once. He was indeed instantly awake and slipping a gun from a bureau drawer into his hand. Agnew awoke too and Bessie and Thalia.' Afterward, Victoria tried to think whether or not one of them had seemed to awake too easily, too soon, too fully; whether or not one of them had shown too little—or too much—surprise at the reappearance of the mysterious maid.

At the time there was nothing that indicated anything of the sort.

Everyone was obviously in a state of undress—hastily snatched dressing-gowns, pajamas, and—in Bessie's case—a silk and lace cover off a chaise longue—snatched up hurriedly and draped over her nightdress in a startling profusion of disorder, with a large blue taffeta bow hanging below her bare feet. Everybody was about as she would expect them to be— Hollis, pale and excited; Agnew, blinking and full of theories; Bessie, questioning and exclaiming; Thalia, perfectly collected and cool, but joining in the search.

It was a real search. They undertook it almost in a body. They searched the house, although, that night, they found every door locked. And when Victoria told them she had seen John Campbell standing there in the moonlight, Hollis and Michael went to find him, too. They shouted his name and went down the driveway to find his car. But if he was there, he did not reply, and certainly his car was not there.

And neither was the maid.

Eventually, they awoke Ernestine and Jody and Lilibelle. Their rooms were in the little L beyond the kitchen and above the drive where it circled in front of the door. None of them had seen or heard anything.

They were bewildered and sleepy and, as far as anyone could tell, they were telling the truth. Lilibelle, hearing of the maid, turned a kind of grape color, and instantly began to cry.

"It wasn't me, Mr. Hollis," she sobbed. "It wasn't me! Please don't tell Mr. Beasley it was me. He's so p'sistent!"

"It wasn't you, Lilibelle," said Victoria. "I saw her, and it wasn't you."

"Well, then who was it?" said Bessie, rolling her great dark eyes almost as vehemently as Lilibelle.

"I don't know. I just saw her like that, for an instant. But I did see her."

"So she does exist," said Agnew. "You see, I was right. It must be the same woman."

In the end they were no wiser than that. Search disclosed neither the mysterious maid nor any evidence of her visit. And John Campbell might have been a mirage.

Hollis was inclined to doubt that she saw him at all. "Where did he go, then, if you saw him? Where's his car? Why was he here at that time of night?" And, as she couldn't, naturally, reply, he added, his light-blue eyes very cold, with hard, shiny black pupils, "I think you just saw a shadow."

"I heard the footsteps," said Michael. "So someone did cross the terrace."

"Who?" said Hollis.

And again there was no answer.

Eventually, since, as Bessie said, no one was hurt and nothing had happened, they did nothing. There was certainly no point in calling the police. Hollis and Michael took up their post in the morning room in case the visitor returned. This was a strategic post since, when the room was darkened, they had a view of the terrace, the front door, and the stairway. "We'll stay awake and watch," said Hollis, and put the revolver on the arm of his chair. The rest of them, there being nothing else to do, drifted back to bed.

Michael, questioned, had not heard the splash in the river that Victoria was so sure had awakened her and, lying in bed watching the shifting clouds, she decided that that, really, might have been only a part of her dream. Nothing in the house apparently was disturbed. Certainly, as Bessie had said, nobody was hurt, by which she meant that no one had been murdered.

It was a rather horrible thought. She remembered what Michael had said about the French doors leading upon the balcony and got up again and closed and locked them. And then, for the first time in her life, locked the door leading from her room into the hall. Although when she opened it for a moment she could hear a murmur from below that meant that Hollis and Michael were still discussing the mysterious, and apparently purposeless, visitation.

It was then that Victoria, in spite of herself, began to question whether or not one of them—Thalia or Bessie, Ernestine or Lilibelle—had shown the faintest indication of knowledge. Or for that matter any of the men; a man could have dressed himself for purposes of disguise in a maid's uniform. And she had had only that glimpse of the vanishing figure—too rapid a glimpse to permit her to identify it even if it had been someone she knew. But there had been time, she decided, for any of them to enter the house (by a door, perhaps the kitchen entrance, which could have been unlocked from the inside before leaving the house) and come upstairs. She had listened and stared toward the spot where the maid had vanished, possibly for two or three minutes. She had stopped, naturally, when she saw Major Campbell. Oh, yes, there'd been time; time even for Michael, if he'd hurried. Time even for anyone to get rid of a disguise which might have been assumed in case, on that night of shifting sudden light, someone was watching, as she had watched.

It did not, however, prove that any of them had done so.

Besides, Agnew had seen her going up the stairs the night of the murder. *In the house, walking coolly up the stairs as if she knew her way, and certainly had some purpose!*

That, too, in its way was a queerly terrifying thought. Walking up the stairs, coming from nowhere, vanishing into nothing.

In the end, however, if it did nothing else, the incident of the night underlined the attack upon Agnew at the door of the pump house. It left no doubt in anybody's mind about that.

But then, who was it who had access to the grounds, and, on at least two occasions, to the house? Someone who came and went freely. Someone who searched Clistie's room in the full light of day—and who struck swiftly, murderously, almost within a stone's throw of the house.

There was, obviously, no real police guard about the place. That was because Beasley believed the murderer would not dare strike again. The next night, she resolved, she would ask for a police guard.

She went to sleep however with an uneasy conviction that bolts and bars and police were not likely to be of much use. As Clistie had said, the place was so big, with the pine woods —and the river.

Morning brought the news of the attack upon Colonel Galant.

Morning, indeed, brought many things, for it was a day of swiftly moving events. It was hot again that morning, with a mist over the river rising up toward a gray, pearly sky and the roses drooping in the garden.

It was that day also that, finally, an inquest was held—two inquests really, one upon the death of Joan Green and one upon the death of Clistie Forbes. But that was later in the day. The first thing that happened was the arrival of Major Campbell and the State's Attorney.

Bessie burst into Victoria's room with the news. She was already dressed—after a fashion, that is. The most charitable conclusion was that she'd flung on the first clothing that came to hand. She wore a beige chiffon afternoon dress, dirty white sports shoes and a knitted purple beret. Coral necklaces and great gold bracelets jangled with the speed of her entrance. "Vicky, Vicky, wake up! Somebody shot at Bruce! Last night. At camp. No—no, don't look like that, he's not much hurt."

She put her thumb on the bell. "I'll ring for your breakfast. You'll have to get up right away. They're here. Major Campbell and Beasley. And we've all got to go to Ponte Verde for the inquest—a double inquest. And Vicky, it *was* John Campbell last night—the man you saw! He said so just now. He *was* here. He drove here after the attack on Bruce, but must have left just as you saw him. He says he didn't see the maid, and he wants to question you about it. He's already talked to Michael and to me—but of course I didn't know anything—and to Lilibelle and Ernestine. Nobody knows anything. . . ."

"Bessie," said Victoria, trying to pin her down to facts and speaking very distinctly, *"What about Bruce? Is he hurt?"*

"Bruce!" said Bessie, as if she'd forgotten. "Oh, yes, of course, Bruce. Not at all. Well, that is, I believe he was shot through the shoulder—or intercostal muscles or something. Through the window of his office. It was about twelve thirty and his orderly heard the shot. It was an army 45. They got out the bullet and put the Colonel in the hospital right there and nobody is to know of it; that is, naturally, the doctors and nurses know, and they told us, but we're to keep it quiet. It's Bruce's orders. Anyway, the orderly—he was in the outer office—ran to pick him up and Bruce sent him for the doctor and Major Campbell. Major Campbell came here as soon as he was sure Bruce was all right and they'd got the doctor." Bessie stopped and took a rather unsteady breath.

"It's not very nice, Vicky, but the fact is he seems to think one of us—*us*, my dear—drove out to the camp, managed somehow to get into the camp through some of the unfinished construction, and shot Bruce. Because of Clistie and—and Joan Green. He feels there's some connection apparently. I'm sure I don't know what. You'd better hurry."

She waited, though, while Victoria dressed. A quick shower; the first dress her hand touched. It was merely lucky that her wardrobe was not of the liveliness that distinguished Bessie's. She came out of the dressing room fastening a cool gray linen dress with a starched lace collar. "Will Bruce get well?"

"Oh, yes," said Bessie. "He's not hurt much. If only—well," her dark eyes clouded. She gave Victoria a defiant look. "If only they don't blame Hollis! Hollis does have a 45. He had it with him last night. He gave it to Beasley this morning." Someone knocked, and she said, "Here's Lilibelle with your breakfast."

But it wasn't Lilibelle; it was Michael. And he, too, had news.

Michael looked tired; his smile was, as always, reassuring and cool, but his gray eyes were worried. He came to Victoria and took her hand. "You've heard about Colonel Galant?"

"Michael, who could have done it?"

He smiled a little and looked down at the sapphire, still on her hand. She'd forgotten it, she realized suddenly; she must return it to him. But not with Bessie standing there, watching, ready to ask questions. He said, "Soldiers in a camp do not take pot shots at their commanding officer. It's one of those things that simply isn't done."

"But Bruce—surely they can't think it has any real connection with—with Clistie."

"It's the girl's murder that connects the thing with Camp Blakoe. At least, that's what they think. And from what Hollis says, it seems to have been Colonel Galant who started an investigation into any possible plot for obtaining military information. Colonel Galant started the investigation and last night he was shot."

Bessie said angrily, "But they needn't come *here!*" She stopped and thought and said with an air of triumph, "Besides, there are sentries! At the gates and—and even in the unfinished areas. No one could have got past them."

Michael, turning Victoria's ring so the lights in it moved, shook his head. "I'm afraid someone could if he knew the camp very well . . ." he began, and Lilibelle arrived with the tray, her face sulky. Agnew followed her into the room, hands in his pockets, his face, too, rather sulky.

Lilibelle put the tray on the low table, did not reply to Victoria's good morning, and stopped in the doorway. "All I have to say is," she announced, "there's plenty of other jobs. A girl don't have to stay where there's murders all the time. A girl don't have to answer questions all the time, either. And that goes for you, too, Mr. Agnew!"

Bessie gasped, "Why, Lilibelle . . ."

But Lilibelle had flounced away. Agnew said gloomily, "All I asked her was whether she was sure she didn't walk in her sleep. It just occurred to me. Well, Mike—they haven't arrested you yet."

"No " said Michael

"Why Agnew, what do you mean?" cried Bessie.

Michael sat down beside Victoria "Here, Vicky, eat your

breakfast while it's hot."

"Michael . . ."

"They won't arrest me," he said calmly. "It's like this. There is an unguarded area of the road near the incompleted end of the camp; it's not the regular way, it's a new temporary road, built for construction, past the unfinished magazine area. If one knew it and knew the way they think it might conceivably have been possible to avoid sentries. And— well, it seems that after the Colonel was shot, our little friend, John Campbell, drove here . . ."

"Hell for leather," said Agnew sotto voce.

"Oh, be still, Agnew," snapped Bessie. "Go on, Michael."

"And when he got here," said Michael, still smiling a little, but his eyes sober, "the engine of my car was warm. They're getting fingerprints from it now—the wheel and the door and the handle and all. They'll find mine, naturally. Probably whoever drove it wore gloves and they'll find only mine. The keys were in the car. I left them there so the boy—one of Judson's henchmen . . ."

"Albert," said Agnew.

". . . could put it in the garage. The garage is some distance from the house and apparently wasn't locked . . ."

Agnew interrupted again. "It is supposed to be locked, but Albert doesn't always do it. Anybody could have come in from the road—he'd only have to pass Judson's cottage and Judson never pays any attention to anybody coming in the gate. Especially at night. He's got a deaf ear," said Agnew practically. "And sleeps with it up."

Bessie cried, "Michael! They believe someone here drove it?"

Michael shrugged. "Even if the car had been driven, it doesn't mean that it was taken to Camp Blakoe; or that whoever shot Colonel Galant took it there. Here . . ." He poured coffee for her. "Sugar? Cream? Now drink that, like a good girl."

Agnew said abruptly, "Vicky, what slippers did you wear on Monday night?"

"Slippers? Why, I . . ."

Michael said quickly, "Let her have her breakfast, Agnew."

"Now, what is it?" demanded Bessie. "Nobody asked me if I drove Michael's car to camp and shot Bruce. And nobody asked me anything at all about slippers. What do you mean, Agnew? What slippers? Whose slippers?"

"I think you'd better tell her, Mike," said Agnew uneasily. "Give her time to—well, give her time." Agnew was worried, too. The freckles stood out on his face as they always did when he was either sick or worried and his light Steane eyes were anxious and peering.

Michael said, "It's the slipper heel, Vicky; or rather the mark of the slipper heel that they found in the pine woods. You see—well, that package wrapped in newspaper that Beasley took away with him was . . ."

"Was one of your gold slippers! It had mud on the heel," burst in Agnew. "And after he took it away he had somebody do a soil test on it, or analysis or something, and Beasley says it's the same kind of mud as that on the river bank and he wants to know how it got there. The troopers, when they searched the house the afternoon we went to Camp Blakoe, missed it. Beasley found it yesterday. He questioned the servants; you haven't put on a dinner dress since Clistie was killed; you haven't worn evening slippers since Monday night. Vicky, where did you get mud on your slipper? That's what they're going to ask you."

That then was why Beasley had made such a point of her statement that she had not gone to the pine woods on Monday night. Would you swear to it? he'd said. And his long, yellow face had looked satisfied, vaguely triumphant as the stenographer made a record of her reply. That was so, later, at a trial, he would try to prove perjury.

"But I—I didn't go to the pine woods. There couldn't be mud on my slipper! I . . ."

Michael cut in swiftly, "Victoria wasn't wearing gold slippers on Monday night."

"That's what Beasley asked me," said Agnew. "I told him I didn't remember."

Bessie said, "Michael's right, of course! She wore her yellow dress and there were yellow slippers to match. Wait . . ." She hurried into the dressing room. Agnew muttered gloomily, "My guess all along has been a homicidal maniac. Pushed Henry into the river; killed the girl and Clistie; shot at Colonel Galant. No possible connection between them all. Somebody just likes to murder." Bessie returned, flushed from bending over the shoe cupboard, with a pair of small yellow sandals in her hand. "Here they are," she said. "See, there's no mud on them!"

Victoria had a little mental vision of herself descending the stairway with the wrong slippers—the gold slippers—showing briefly, one and then the other, below her yellow skirt. She must have started to speak, for Michael put his hand down hard over her own. He said positively, "Victoria wore yellow slippers that night. She looked so pretty—I remember noticing the slippers. You are quite right, Bessie."

And Lilibelle came sulkily to the door again to say that Major Campbell would like to see Miss Victoria in the library.

"Right away," said Lilibelle.

Michael went down the stairs with her. "Tell him you wore the yellow slippers," he said low.

"I didn't. I . . ."

"Tell him so, anyway," said Michael.

But when Victoria went into the library, John Campbell's first question had nothing to do with the gold slipper stained with mud. Instead he showed her, in a crumpled heap on the library table, a maid's white uniform. It had been found, he said, thrust behind some shrubbery close to the front door. And he wanted to know, he told her, watching her, whether it was the dress the woman she had seen the previous night had been wearing.

18

It was a short but in its way important talk that she had that morning with Campbell—in the library again with the windows open, but not a breath of air stirring the heavy curtains. He questioned her but talked too—directly, as if he counted on her understanding. He smoked, he paced the floor, he came to sit with one knee over the edge of the table. He took a pencil and drew circles and interlocking squares on the pad of paper.

He said rather wearily when she looked at the dress, that naturally she couldn't be sure, but did she think it looked like the dress the woman she had seen had worn.

"I don't know. It looks like one of Ernestine's uniforms. But then they can be bought at almost any department store."

He nodded and got out cigarettes and offered her one before he lighted one himself. "Yes, I know. Ernestine says it belongs to her, but she doesn't know how it got there in the shrubbery. The laundry mark is right and she says anybody that got into the house could have taken it from a stack of newly arrived laundry that was delivered by truck from Ponte Verde late yesterday afternoon. Lilibelle was supposed to put it away and didn't, so it was left, like that, on a shelf of the linen closet off the butler's pantry. The point is, of course, the woman you saw may have worn it intentionally for a disguise. If that's true, the maid Agnew and Bayne saw could have been the same woman, wearing a maid's uniform for the same reason. Disguise. But it . . ." He frowned for a moment at the rug. "It doesn't—match up, somehow. It doesn't seem right. It doesn't fit. An outsider could have got into the house. Jody says he never used to lock the front door because he never knew when people were coming home at night and they

—meaning Hollis, I suppose, or you—never remembered latch keys. So a long time ago he got out of the habit of locking the front door. Since the murders he has made a point of locking all the doors—but they can always be unlocked from the inside, and besides"—he said quickly—"there are all the windows. There's always a way in or out of a house if somebody really wants to find it."

He got up impatiently, walked to the window and back again and said abruptly, looking down into her eyes, "Victoria, what about this gold slipper? A slipper of yours—perhaps Agnew or Bayne told you—with mud on it. I—please believe me, I didn't know about it last night. I didn't know what Beasley was driving at with his questions, getting you definitely on record with a statement that he hoped later to prove false. He's gone now; had to go to Ponte Verde. He told me to question you about it. He . . ." He hesitated. Was he giving her time to think, she wondered; time to prepare an answer? He sat down on the edge of the table again beside her, and, rather absently, took her hand—her left hand as it happened and as Michael had done. He looked at it and turned the ring on it slowly.

"You see, I'm forced to be on Beasley's side. It's my job; Colonel Galant gave me orders to investigate; that means of course, to work along with Beasley—with his consent. His permitting me to know what goes on, his giving me what evidence he has, depends mainly upon a kind of—courtesy. But it's his case, and it's a chance to solve a case I couldn't solve. That is, of course, the murder of Henry Frame. Nobody, now, doubts that it was murder; but there's no more evidence than there ever was."

"You believe that—all this—is a result of Henry's death?" she asked him.

"I believe that when we have the answer to Clistie's death, we'll have the answer to Henry's, too," he said obliquely. "Certainly Clistie was murdered and Joan Green, and it's rather against the law of averages—three murders without some connection between them. Murder is, luckily, not a usual kind of thing," he said rather dryly, and turned her ring thoughtfully. "But the fact is, of course—Beasley and I don't really see alike."

"He thinks I did it," said Victoria soberly.

He glanced at her quickly. "It's the concrete—what he calls jury evidence. When Frame was killed, too, the evidence pointed toward you. I"—he looked back at the ring—"I didn't want to think it was you. Even then. And now I . . ." He stopped abruptly, relinquished her hand and got up.

"Beasley believes Hollis' story implicitly—or says he does.

135

He agrees that the murder of Joan Green does seem to connect the affair with Camp Blakoe, but he believes that her murder was in the nature of an accident. That is, that she saw or knew too much through her friendship with Hollis. He may be right." He walked to the window and back and said, "You said Clistie was wearing blue slippers when you saw her in the hall—after you heard the scream. Are you sure—about the slippers, I mean?"

"Yes. Turquoise. She'd got them to go with the brown dress."

"Turquoise," he said thoughtfully. "She was wearing them still when she was found, you know. I looked at them this morning, when Beasley told me he'd had the mud on your gold slipper analyzed, and that it was the same as the soil along the bank where the heel mark was found. I thought it might have been Clistie's slipper that made the mark. It would fit it all right, but then most evening slippers have heels that would fit it—or almost. Her slippers were soiled, damp-stained, as if she'd been walking in the dew. There could have been mud on them, and she could have wiped it off. Afterward, I suppose."

"I didn't go to the pine woods that night."

He said suddenly and very directly, "I believe you, Victoria. I'd better tell you that before Beasley left he asked Thalia what slippers you were wearing Monday night. Agnew, you see, had said he didn't know. Bayne caught on apparently from the manner of Beasley's question and said you weren't wearing gold slippers that night; that he'd particularly noticed because you"—a little tight mask seemed to slip down over his face—"because you were looking especially beautiful that night at dinner. As soon as Beasley let the cat out of the bag and said there was mud on your gold slipper, Bayne swore up and down that you didn't wear gold slippers that night. But then—well, you see, Beasley had Thalia Frame in; she said gold."

Tell them yellow, Michael had said. Well, it wouldn't do any good now. But John Campbell didn't give her a chance to lie. He said gravely, "You see, Victoria, if anybody remembered the evidence against you, and the lack of evidence against anybody else at the time of Henry Frame's murder, that person might think it a clever move to arrange evidence against you now. Such as your belt. Your slipper." He paced the floor again, his black head bent and his hands clasped behind him. "It would mean an enemy, you see. Somebody who really wants you to be charged with murder."

Agnew had said that too. And there was the wedding dress. He came back to sit on the table edge and watch her while

136

she told him of the dress. His hazel eyes were very bright and intent, but when she finished she couldn't tell what he thought. He said, after a moment, "It might have delayed the wedding, of course. On the other hand, you could have been married in another dress. Do you know when it was done?"

"No. But the state troopers searched the house the afternoon I went to Camp Blakoe to see Colonel Galant and you. And yesterday Beasley searched it too. Surely they would have seen if it had been cut to pieces then."

"Not necessarily. I'll find out. You say there was a cover over it; they might have merely glanced at the cover or at enough of the dress to see what it was, instead of removing the cover as you did." He lighted another cigarette and said, through smoke, "When did you look at it last—I mean before last night?"

She thought back. "Monday morning. I tried it on." Clistie had crept around her, she remembered, adjusting the hem, pleased with the dress and Victoria in it. And a sudden little memory floated apart from all the things that had happened directly afterward. She said slowly, "I think Clistie must have worked on the dress that afternoon, for that night there were scissors . . ."

"Scissors! Where?"

"On the floor. At least I—I think so. It was dark in my room; but as I went to the balcony my foot struck them. . . ."

"When? Before or after you heard the girl scream, I mean."

"Before. Oh, a long time before."

"Did you pick them up?"

"No."

"Did you see them again? What did you do?"

"Why, nothing. I'd forgotten, you see. I never thought of it again until now. I suppose someone else must have picked them up and put them away. I don't remember seeing them at all. But . . ."

"Well?"

"The scissors made me think of it. It's nothing really but—well, that night just before I heard the girl scream I thought that someone came in my room. I was so sure I went in and looked. No one was there. I went back to the balcony. It was such a trivial thing. . . ."

"How long before you heard the scream?"

"Not long. Only a moment or two, I'm sure. I had barely got out on the balcony."

"Did you see the scissors, then?"

"I don't know—that is, I don't remember."

"Probably somebody else did remember." He looked down

137

at her hand, on the table. The blue sapphire glittered, and he said suddenly, "I understand your wedding is postponed." And before she could reply, he walked to the window and said rather quickly, over his shoulder, "About last night. They say that you saw me?"

"Yes. I started to call to you—to tell you about the woman I saw—but then you were gone."

"I don't suppose it would have made any real difference. Whoever it was had had time to"—he paused, and then said —"to get away. Bayne's car was out last night. There's no doubt of that. I came here as soon as I could."

"Why?"

"Obviously—to catch Hollis. If it was Hollis. You see . . ." He turned around again. "You see, it's the only—at least it's the most probable motive for the attack upon Colonel Galant. Day before yesterday he started an inquiry into any possible activity in the way of attempted espionage. Joan Green was the link to Camp Blakoe. She was murdered here. Hollis knew her. As soon as I was sure Colonel Galant was not hurt much, I came here. I was too late to catch whoever drove the car. But the engine, as I expect they told you, was still warm. The car had been taken out. In case somebody— whoever drove it—was still around, I took a look around the place. The house was dark and apparently everybody was sleeping. It wouldn't do much good to rout everybody out and ask them point-blank if they'd been asleep. Naturally they'd say yes—especially whoever took the shot at Colonel Galant —if," he said quickly, forestalling the words on her lips, "*if* it was somebody here who did it. I imagine I would have done just that, but I thought I heard a noise somewhere . . ."

"I heard it. A splash and then somebody running. And then a little later the woman on the terrace. We looked, but . . ."

He nodded. "They told me. Everybody peacefully asleep. Especially Hollis. And that maid's uniform in the shrubbery this morning. It could have been put there any time, of course. And yet . . ." He stopped again for a long time, and then said suddenly, "You see, Hollis could have heard about —well, about Cara Nome (whatever it is, and if it's anything) that afternoon in Colonel Galant's office. The window was open, the fan was going, you were sitting near the window and, in order to make his voice heard over the fan, Colonel Galant practically shouted. Hollis wasn't drilling that afternoon. I found that out this morning. He was sent to the administration building on an errand. So he could have passed on the outside of the window. Thalia Frame could have heard it; she was strolling around outside the prohibited area, it seems, alone. She said, when I asked her, that she didn't know

138

one building from another at camp and doesn't know whether she was near Colonel Galant's office or not. I didn't tell any of them why I asked. Agnew says he and Bayne drove around over camp a little. He wanted to show Bayne as much as they were permitted to see of the camp; then they came back and parked in front of the administration office. And Agnew went, he says, to get Coca-Colas for them all. The nearest stand is down the road. Conceivably he could have passed the Colonel's office, though he says he didn't. Conceivably, while he was gone, Bayne could have strolled that way and heard what the Colonel said. Conceivably, too," he said wearily, "none of them did. Let's have your story again, Victoria. About last night, I mean. What exactly did you hear?"

She told him, quickly.

"The splash in the river could have been a dream, I suppose," he said. "Yet, running footsteps coming up from the river . . ." He paused and said thoughtfully, "It was an army 45, you know. The gun with which Colonel Galant was shot; they've got out the bullet. But if the revolver was tossed into the river, we'll never find it. They're doing what they can do at camp; but identifying one revolver in an army camp is almost comparable to the needle in the haystack. Well, not quite that really—but nevertheless I think that probably there's another clue that is no clue at all. I wish I knew. . . ." He sat on the edge of the table and swung his long legs as boyishly as Agnew, his face intent and concentrated. "I wish I knew whether or not it was Clistie that telephoned to Joan Green, and if it was, then *why*—what had happened that was so urgent. I wish I knew who is stacking up evidence against you, and exactly why. I wish I knew more about Clistie's dress and why it was on that girl. I wish I knew the meaning of Cara Nome—is it really poison to somebody, and why, and what connection is there between that and Camp Blakoe—if there is one. And I wish I knew the motive."

He laughed shortly, staring at the rug. "That's—how many —five main lines of inquiry. Somewhere in the answers to those questions is the answer we've got to have. Motive is the big one. Motive . . ." He sprang off the table and began to pace up and down again, his head bent. Finally, he said, "Let me see the wedding dress."

She brought it to him—wrapping it in its muslin cover and hurrying along the hall and stairs.

His face hardened as he looked at it.

"It's—it's so senseless," she whispered.

"Yes," he said briefly and wrapped it up again. "Put it away."

That was all he said of it. Bessie came to the door and said the car was waiting, and it was time to go to Ponte Verde. She bustled away again, and John Campbell said, "You'll have to go. About Cara Nome—it seems such a senseless thing really. Yet it worried Clistie—or something about it. And it's still on Colonel Galant's mind. I spent most of the day yesterday looking through the files of the transcripts Joan Green made and found exactly nothing but a guarded mention or two of the radio equipment, nothing that could be of any possible value as news to a foreign agent. So far as I'm concerned that's out as a motive. Completely. But—there was nothing about this Cara Nome affair either. I've got girls now, today, going through all available office records. But unless you . . ."

She shook her head. "I asked Agnew, too. He didn't know."

Someone honked impatiently outside. "Oh, by the way," he said. "I've asked Beasley to put a policeman or two in the house tonight. It's safer. I may be at the inquest."

He was gone when she came downstairs a moment later, after having put the torn wedding dress back in a drawer and locked it. She had her hat in her hand. Bessie and the others were already in the long town car which Hollis was driving.

The inquest, or rather the double inquest, was from the beginning an obvious formality. It took place in the coroner's courtroom in the little, vine-hung Ponte Verde courthouse with its damp-stained walls. Beasley was there but sat for the most part with his long legs crossed, a not over-clean white canvas oxford wagging nervously, and his chin in his hand. Major Campbell did not come, although Victoria looked for his tall uniformed figure and black head every time the door opened or closed.

It was not pleasant. And it reminded all of them too strongly of those other times when they had sat in that room, listening to a much more detailed inquiry into the death of Henry Frame.

Little in the way of evidence came out. The two women had died violent deaths, and that was all. But in neither case was there a verdict. Adjournments were again, as Agnew said on the way home, in order.

"They didn't ask us to identify the dress or Victoria's belt or anything," he said morosely. "All they did was give Beasley the formality of a go-ahead signal."

It was still suffocatingly hot and breathless when they reached the house, with the long, gray-green wisps of Spanish moss drooping languidly from the liveoaks and the river as quiet as a painted river.

Bruce Galant was better. Bessie telephoned to the hospital

and was told that, although she was not permitted to talk to him

Late in the afternoon, however, Victoria went to see him. That was because Agnew found what he found.

That was a slip of paper, torn from a memorandum pad. It had on it a telephone number, Ponte Verde 3830 and, below it, in Clistie's handwriting, the two words, Cara Nome.

19

There was no doubt of its being in Clistie's handwriting.

Agnew brought it to Victoria, dancing with excitement. She was then at the telephone. Everyone had known Clistie's wishes about her funeral. She had often told them she wanted to be buried quietly, "without fuss and feathers," in the little Vermont town where she'd been born. It seemed queer, thought Victoria, to make arrangements like that for Clistie— little, efficient Clistie. Later, when the investigation was over, she herself would go to the little Vermont village and see that things had been done as she wanted them done.

All Clistie's life had been bound up with the Steanes. She had a few old friends, fewer relatives. She finished the last telegram as Agnew came to her. "What are you crying again for?" he said, stopping short, and then, in his excitement, didn't wait for an answer.

"Look," he cried. "Look—it's in Clistie's writing. It's the telephone number of the Ponte Verde hotel where Joan Green lived. And it"—he lowered his voice with a quick look down the hall as if to be sure no one was listening—"and it's Cara Nome. So she did know something! And, Vicky, that isn't all. I found it just now on the memorandum pad where Clistie used to write the grocery orders. Well, since she—since Monday, Ernestine's been making the grocery orders and she didn't use that memorandum pad. Just used her memory, she says. But the point is, this was written after five o'clock Monday because . . ." Agnew's eyes were sharp and bright behind his thick glasses. "Because the grocery order arrived about five and Ernestine always tore off the order when the groceries came so as to check the items. And she did Monday, as usual. So the pad was clear until—well, until some time later when Clistie came to the kitchen and wrote that. So it proves—well, it doesn't really prove it, but it looks as if it might be so—that Clistie telephoned Joan Green, I mean. And maybe asked her to come. And maybe—well, pretty certainly, had the words Cara Nome on her mind. Now then, why?"

141

Victoria didn't know why. She looked at the scribbled few words. "We'd better tell Colonel Galant," she said slowly.

Agnew looked at her sharply. His rather prominent ears all but moved forward. "Why Colonel Galant?"

"Just—oh, because," said Victoria. "Where is Hollis? And Michael?"

"Swimming," said Agnew. "They just went down to the pier. Thalia's all done up in a very pretty suit, too, but so far she's sitting on the pier swinging her legs. They said to tell you to come down and take a swim too. I'm going. . . ."

"No," said Victoria. "You're coming with me."

It was an odd impulse of secrecy, she thought, as she backed out the old station wagon that she always drove. It looked very small and shabby in the long garage between the big, black town car, and Michael's gray coupe. Agnew wanted to drive and was as usual restrained with difficulty and contented himself with smoking a forbidden cigarette. "I can drive perfectly well," he said. "And you know it. I guess the police have finished examining Michael's car. They swarmed over it like bees early this morning—fingerprints and whatnot. Say, Vicky, what do you suppose she meant by Cara Nome? I mean, I don't see why she would telephone to Joan Green about a—well, a lipstick. Or a song. Clistie never used lipstick and didn't know one song from another."

That day one of the sentries at the gate into Camp Blakoe did some telephoning before he admitted them. At the hospital, while Agnew waited in the station wagon, Victoria was taken to see Colonel Galant only after the nurse had taken her name, disappeared for a long time and then returned. "He'll see you," she said shortly, "but for only a few minutes." She eyed Victoria with frank curiosity and escorted her along covered runways to the low new building in which there were private rooms. Colonel Galant was well-guarded. There were soldiers (on duty, businesslike and alert) in the corridor outside his room, and through the windows Victoria could see other soldiers, doing a steady sentry-go up and down.

He was sitting up in bed, however, looking more annoyed than ill and signing a large stack of letters, in spite of his bandaged shoulder.

"I'm all right," he said testily, when she asked him. "But things have come to a pretty pass when the commander of an army post gets shot. If I hadn't heard a kind of sound at the window and turned around, it might have killed me. It was a near thing, Vicky, and no mistake. I couldn't get to the window in time to see anybody, either. We've turned the camp inside out of course—discreetly and all that—but

142

haven't found any real evidence yet. I am convinced it's nobody in the camp; it's someone—and something completely outside. Well, well, Vicky—any news?"

She told him quickly. She showed him the slip of paper and explained.

"I see. Yes—yes, I see," he murmured thoughtfully. "Cara Nome again. Yes, that was worrying her, Victoria. But why? That's what I'd like to know. Why? And why does it ring some sort of bell in my own memory? It's nothing I can put my finger on, is the trouble. And it's not, I assure you, a face powder. Or that blasted song!" He brooded angrily for a moment. "This young Campbell seems to think I ought to be able to remember. But, my God, I've got other things to do. . . ." He gave a harassed glance at the stack of letters on the bed table. "Well, Vicky—thanks. I'll give this to Campbell. But you did right to come to me. Kiss me, my dear, and thanks for coming. And better not take any chances. It's a—a damned nasty business," he said gloomily. At the door he called her back. "Look here, my dear—you're keeping your ears and eyes open regarding Hollis, aren't you?"

"Yes, but he . . ."

"Now, now, you don't know whether he did or not. Somebody had Bayne's car out last night. Maybe Bayne, maybe somebody else. All of you drive—don't you?—except maybe Bessie. Not," he said hastily, "that I think *you* drove over here and got past the sentries along the new road and shot me. But Hollis—Hollis did know that girl. You can't get around that." She went away, again escorted by the starchy, curious little nurse. Driving slowly home through the hot, still air, she thought of Hollis. She had felt, always, that she knew him so well. Yet apparently she hadn't known him at all. There was his friendship for Joan Green of which she knew nothing; there was his driving ambition and love for the Steane Mills which Agnew had seen but, to which, again, she'd been blind. Probably there were many other things going on behind Hollis' light Steane eyes which were equally imperceptible to her own observation.

Certainly she'd had more than once an odd impression of evasiveness, of guarded silence, of something withheld. Yet it was only an impression. Hollis was never talkative.

"What'd the Colonel say?" inquired Agnew eagerly.

"He said . . ." She avoided two cows and a truckload of soldiers. The soldiers waved cheerily at her and she waved back. "He said he'd tell Major Campbell."

"Oh," said Agnew and shot a glance at her. "I suppose Major Campbell's on the job on account of this Green girl."

"I suppose so."

"Dear me," said Agnew, "how discreet we are! Listen, Vick, I may be near-sighted but I can still see anything if it's right under my nose." He lapsed into a sulky but a thoughtful silence. They arrived home to find Michael and Hollis in from their swim, on the porch with Bessie who was surrounded by newspapers. Thalia lay languidly back in a big chair, her smooth dark head beautiful against the yellow cushion, watching the river with dark, unfathomable eyes. Hollis looked up sharply to ask where they had been.

"For a ride," said Agnew shortly.

He disappeared soon after that. Victoria caught a glimpse of him strolling moodily, head bent, hands in his pockets, toward the garden where presently he vanished behind the screen of shrubbery and hedges.

She didn't see him again until dinner was half over. He came in hurriedly but as unobtrusively as possible as if in the hope of escaping Bessie's notice. He did not, naturally, succeed. Six lanky feet of—mainly—bones is difficult to dissemble. Bessie, however, was too dispirited herself to do more than hiss at him as he slid into his place. "Slinking," she said sibilantly, "and sliding in late. Did you wash your hands?"

Agnew, looking guilty, waved away soup. He also looked still very thoughtful and presently, when Bessie's attention had been diverted to a discussion of the heat, said in an undertone to Victoria, "Judson wants to see you. It's about a spade." He winked at her with much if obscure significance and took a large helping of potatoes.

"Spade?" said Bessie. "What spade?"

"It's a Scotch joke," said Agnew rapidly. "Calling a spade a spade. You've heard it, Mother. Everybody's heard . . ." Bessie opened her mouth angrily, and Agnew went on hurriedly, "Hollis, how long is your leave and how did you talk the Colonel into seeing that you got it? Did he call up your regimental boss and say you were to have it?"

It distracted Bessie, and Victoria did not listen to Hollis' reply.

If Judson wanted to talk to her about a spade, it was because he knew something of the spade Clistie had taken and not returned. She resolved to find the gardener immediately after dinner.

It happened, however, she did not see Judson then Instead she made another trip to the Ponte Verde courthouse.

Beasley sent for her.

Agnew came to tell her. That was perhaps half an hour or more after dinner. She had left the others having coffee on the porch and had walked along the winding driveway, shadowy already with the approach of another still, cloudy night, to Judson's cottage. He lived neatly and precisely alone, cooking his own meals, methodically taking care of the little house himself. He wasn't there when she reached the cottage and knocked and called to him, but he hadn't come in yet to cook his dinner, for the little kitchen, when she opened the door and looked in, was tidy and clean.

She sat down on the vine-sheltered step to wait for him. It was very quiet there, and the heavy shrubbery seemed to move stealthily closer to the cottage as the darkness grew. It was some distance from the house, too. Her heart jumped and stopped as Agnew came loping around the house from the driveway, before his white shirt and glasses gleamed out of the dusk and revealed who it was.

"I knew I'd find you here," he said. "Did you see Judson? Say, Vicky, they want you to come to Ponte Verde. Right away. The State's Attorney does. I don't think you ought to go."

He argued about it passionately all the way back along the driveway to the house. Michael, too, who met them as they reached the door, was against it.

"He's questioned you enough. You've told him everything you know. All he wants now is to trick you into some admission that gives him a handle for—well, arrest, maybe. Vicky, I'm going to telephone Gleason in New York and have him take the night plane. He can be here by morning, and you can let Beasley question you then to his heart's content. Don't go tonight, Vicky."

But Hollis, coming out from the house to find them standing there on the driveway arguing about it, said flatly that she'd better go. "I talked to him when he rang up," he said. "Maybe it's only the heat, but he sounded pretty frenzied. If you don't go, he'll send troopers to bring you; he said so. He's in that frame of mind. After all," said Hollis, "you don't have to answer his questions. And you didn't murder Clistie or—or Joan. So you don't have anything to be afraid of."

In the end Michael took her—in his gray coupe which, now that they had finished with it, the police had told him he could use again.

"Nice of them," he said, driving swiftly through the dark, soft night with the lights making long lanes ahead of them. "Vicky, if it hadn't been for all this we'd have been—let me see—driving through Virginia about now, stopping tonight at some little inn in the mountains perhaps . . ." He reached for her hand and brought it to his lips. And then she took off the big sapphire.

He refused at first to take it. And then, laughing, slipped it into his pocket. "All right," he said. "Wait till you see it on another girl's finger. Then you'll be sorry."

She thought swiftly, but did not say, that in that case she knew whose finger it would be.

The little town, when they turned into the main street, was hot and crowded. Soldiers loitered along the sidewalks, stood in a cue at the motion-picture theatre, crowded the lighted little drug stores. They reached the courthouse and most of it was dark, but lights gleamed from the windows of Beasley's office. A state trooper, hot and tired-looking, was waiting for them and took Victoria up the stairs. He wouldn't let Michael accompany her.

Victoria had scarcely entered the shabby, bare little office, with its odors of stale tobacco smoke, and sweeping compound, its littered golden-oak desk, its green-shaded lights—and Beasley sitting at the desk—before she realized that Michael had been right.

She ought not to have come; she ought to have let him send for the lawyer.

For that night Beasley was determined upon making an arrest.

She sat down where he told her to sit, in a small, golden-oak armchair, stiff and uncomfortable and directly under the light. The trooper went out and closed the door behind him. John Campbell was not there. No one was there but Beasley. And he, with a kind of simple, brutal directness set out to get her to confess.

His yellow long face jutted out into the light. His little black eyes were as glittering and yet opaque as a snake's. He thrust one clawlike, grasping hand toward her.

"This is my case," he said. "Campbell has his views. But I have mine. That girl Joan Green was an accident; she saw too much; she was there—to meet young Isham, I expect—at the wrong time. I don't know what happened to her own dress. It wasn't burned—at least not in the house furnace. Even her pocketbook—she must have carried one—has disappeared. It's in the river probably. But all that doesn't matter. The point is, I've got evidence. Real, material, jury evidence. And I'm going to stick to it." He paused and looked at her and said, "If you'll confess now, it'll save us both a lot of energy."

"Confess!"

"*Sit down,*" he said. And began.

Beasley's favorite method of questioning had always been accusation. When Victoria assayed a defense—such as the telephone number of the Ponte Verde hotel in Clistie's writing, and the words Cara Nome below it (for that implied, surely, something not yet known which might provide a motive for

146

the murders; it implied surely, if it didn't prove it, that Clistie had telephoned to Joan Green asking her to come), Beasley brushed it aside.

When, rather desperately, she pointed out how foolish it would have been on her part to strew clues about that led only to her, he brushed that aside too. "You'd had some police experience. You thought we'd reason that way—that you wouldn't be such a fool as to leave evidence that led directly to you."

"But the maid—the woman Agnew and Michael Bayne saw. The woman I saw . . ."

He laughed shortly. "The woman you heard about—one of your own maids probably. The woman that last night only you saw. Campbell was there on the place. You saw him, but you didn't speak to him. You didn't tell him a woman had just run along the terrace out of sight. You said nothing, because there was no woman." He leaned forward. "Listen, Miss Steane, I'm not pretending every little unimportant detail of this case is clear to me; there may be some that are never quite cleared up. That doesn't matter. I know enough. You killed Henry Frame, and Clistie discovered it. You killed her, and that girl was there waiting for Hollis and saw or heard something, and you had to get rid of her, too. What did she see? What did she hear? Tell me the truth. . . ."

"I am telling you the truth. . . ."

20

It was very hot. Insects buzzed against the black screens. The light from above, blazing down into her face was dazzling, confusing; the air was stifling.

Once Beasley poured himself a drink of water from the little cooler in the corner and brought a drink to her in a paper cup. "You could make it so much easier for both of us," he said rather plaintively, "if you'd just confess."

The distant street noises had stopped some time ago. It must be very late, she thought stupidly.

But it was much later and Beasley was sitting wearily on the desk, his own face moist and yellow and haggard, when someone came running up the stairs, his footsteps loud in the silence and flung open the door.

It was Major Campbell. He gave her a swift glance and came toward them. Beasley said, "Oh, it's you."

"I'll take her now."

"I've not finished."

Major Campbell crossed to the desk so his face was in the light. His eyes were blazing; his face a queer kind of gray below the tan.

"I said I'd take her now."

"Now, look here, John," said Beasley, "you've got no right —in my own office, too." He got down rather hastily and sidled around behind the desk. "Now there's no call to act like that. I haven't hurt the girl."

"Come on, Victoria. I'll take you home."

"You can't do that," said Beasley. "It's my case. I only let you in on it because Colonel Galant requested it. . . ."

"You've already made one arrest," said John Campbell. "That ought to be enough for one night."

Beasley's long teeth showed yellow. "Yes, I made an arrest. And I'm going to make another. That girl's in this thing up to her pretty neck, and I'm going to see that . . ."

Major Campbell leaned over the desk. She couldn't see his face, only his broad shoulders. He said, rather quietly, really, "I've told you, Eliot, I'm taking her away now. You can question her all you want to tomorrow—when she's got a lawyer; when she's had a chance to rest. But I'm taking her now. Do you want to try to stop me? You've got troopers downstairs; one of them guarding the jail. All you have to do is call them. But it's not going to sound very pretty when I tell what the trouble is about."

She couldn't see Beasley, for John Campbell was between them. Who had already been arrested? she thought numbly. Hollis? Beasley said suddenly, "Oh, all right, all right, John. Take her. No need to fight about it." He sounded fretful. He added, "If you don't get any more information than I got out of her, you won't get much."

Major Campbell whirled around, came to Victoria and half lifted her to her feet. He picked up a crumpled, limp little handkerchief that, some time, she had dropped, and looked at it queerly, with a kind of frozen expression on his brown face. He put it in his pocket and put his arm around her and led her toward the door. His arm was very firm and steady. Beasley said, quite goodnaturedly, "See you in the morning, John," as they left. Major Campbell said nothing. The little hall was deserted. No one was below either and, as they emerged into the hot night air, sweet-smelling and humid, he led her toward an army car parked at the entrance.

She said, troubled and vaguely perplexed, "Michael said he would wait." The sounds of the little town had died away. A few street lights here and there made haloes of brightness that showed only empty streets and strips of pale sidewalks with here and there great overhanging liveoaks that made caves of shadow. But Michael's long gray car was gone. John Campbell said, "I'll take you home," and took her to his own car,

148

put her in it and got quickly into the driver's seat beside her. He gave her a cigarette and lighted it before he started the car. They turned away from the courthouse and into the now almost empty main street.

She said, after awhile, as if he'd asked her, "I didn't . . ."

"I know that. I told you this morning." His voice sounded brusque and angry.

"Beasley thinks I did. He hasn't any doubt. He's—honest. He wouldn't have tried to make me confess, if he hadn't thought so."

John Campbell interrupted. His jaw looked stubborn and hard in the little glow from the dashlight. "Michael was arrested. They—put his car in a garage for him. Beasley, it seems, had told the trooper who met you at the door of the courthouse that, if Bayne brought you, he was to arrest Bayne. Quietly. Without your knowing."

"Michael!"

"It was his car out at Camp Blakoe. They found tire marks on the road they're using for construction, near the new magazines. The only road anybody could have taken to get anywhere near the camp in such a way as to—with luck—manage to avoid a sentry. Tire marks, I mean, that correspond with the tires on his car. And the only fingerprints they found were his and—on the handle of the right door a print of yours and two of Thalia's. There are some smudges—such as might have been made by anybody wearing gloves. But Beasley decided to arrest Bayne and did it."

"He—he didn't tell me. He said I did it. . . ."

"I suppose he was saving that bit of news for a coup de grace. When you were so exhausted that . . . Oh, well," said John abruptly, "Beasley's got his own little ways."

"Where is Michael? I must see him. I must get a lawyer. . . ."

"He's in jail, back there in the courthouse. The little jail in the basement. He's all right. I talked to him for a minute and gave him some cigarettes—he was about out. He said to tell you not to worry."

"But if that's the only evidence against him . . ."

John said slowly, "I don't know what Beasley's plan is. But I do know that he thinks—well, it's as I told you, Victoria. It's your money. Beasley says Bayne stood to gain as much as you by Frame's death."

"But he scarcely even knew me when Henry was killed. We weren't engaged till much later. John, please, please take me back to see him."

He didn't reply for a moment. She thought suddenly, why, I called him John.

149

Then he said, slowing the car, "I will if you want to, Victoria. But honestly you can't do anything tonight. Get him a lawyer. Give Beasley time to examine his own case. It may collapse of itself; cases do. Believe me—I'm not trying to keep you from seeing Bayne. But I want to get you home And Bayne's all right, really. He told me to tell you that. And I—I want to talk to you, too," he said. "I've found out something about Cara Nome."

"Cara Nome!"

"Yes. It's not very clear yet, though. In fact, it's—well, it's damned queer. But I know now where Colonel Galant saw the name. It's—of all things—a small construction company that sub-let a contract for the building of Camp Blakoe. Do you want to hear?"

"Yes."

"Well, it was a small contract. They were to supply some lumber to the larger company (the A.B.C. outfit that handled most of the job). It was ten thousand dollars worth of lumber. The girl found the name in the list of contractors—it was published, by the way, last week in the Ponte Verde paper in connection with a news story about the building of the camp. Well, anyway, the Cara Nome Company, it seems, got their contract—small as contracts go. The camp altogether cost something like thirty million. That was in November; but they didn't deliver any lumber. Instead, they sent a letter to the A.B.C. (and a copy to the Constructing Quartermaster—he has it on file and showed it to me) saying they couldn't fill the contract and forfeiting it. But the curious thing about it is that the Cara Nome Company has vanished. As thoroughly as the vanishing maid."

"Vanished! But there must be offices. What does Colonel Galant say?"

"Colonel Galant says," said John rather grimly, "for me to find out who and what they are. He doesn't say how. I got on the long distance telephone. It was about that time that Colonel Galant told me about Agnew's find. So—it looks as if Clistie really did telephone Joan Green. And as if whatever she knew was recent knowledge—and so urgent that she couldn't even wait till morning, but had to get hold of Joan Green instantly that night. But what was it?"

He avoided an oncoming car, negotiated a turn and said, "The Cara Nome letters were signed by one Philomel Jonson. The address was a post-office box in New York. I got Federal men working on it—rather Colonel Galant did. They've had very little time. So far all we know is that the post-office box was given up some time ago. That there's no construction company of that name with a business address in New York.

No address, no office, no Philomel Jonson, so far, who has any connection with it. Nothing. Except the Cara Nome Construction Company got a contract and then gave it up and disappeared. There's no obvious motive; there was nothing gained by it; there was apparently no attempt to defraud anybody, because the Cara Nome Company wasn't paid a cent. So—there you are! What's back of it? On the surface, it's an utterly senseless, motiveless, useless thing. It ended almost before it began." He lighted another cigarette.

He went on, "It adds to the puzzle when you stop to think that the Cara Nome Company can't be phony. Philomel Jonson can be a phony name—sounds like it. The post-office box, the lack of street address, all that sounds phony. But the Cara Nome Company has got to exist; it's got to have, at least, a charter of incorporation. Maybe nobody asked to see it—but nobody would dare take the chance of not having it. So we ought to have some news about it soon. If the company is legally incorporated, then the Secretary of State gave the charter and will have the record of it. We don't know what state; we're trying New York first. And, of course, when we find out, we may be no wiser."

He stopped again and said after a moment or two, "We got hold of the officials of the A.B.C. Company who sublet the contract to the Cara Nome Company. They said that their policy, as suggested by the government, was to sublet as many contracts for material as possible to the smaller companies. In the case of a good-sized bid for any kind of work, a check for a percent of the amount of the bid accompanies it—if the bid is rejected, the check naturally is returned to the company making the bid. In this case it was different. The Cara Nome outfit, whatever it is, offered to supply a certain amount of lumber for ten thousand dollars. It was like a grocer offering to supply eggs. The A.B.C. was subletting a lot of small contracts; they needed lumber and a prompt delivery; everything was done at top speed. About all the Cara Nome lot would need would be, as I say, a copy of their corporation charter. They might not even be asked to show that. It wasn't as if they were actually building anything and a question of their responsibility and past record was involved."

"I don't believe the Steane Mills had any of the Camp Blakoe contracts," she said. "If so, I didn't know of it."

"They didn't," he said promptly. "Naturally, we looked through the records for any connection with the Steane Mills. There wasn't any. Yet certainly Clistie knew something. If we could only reconstruct all of Clistie's actions that day and that night. Victoria, was she in any way—oh, different? Worried?"

A swift little memory of Clistie (looking earnestly into the thicket of pines behind her, moving up the slope nearer the house, talking—strangely—of watchdogs) returned to Victoria.

She told him of it. And then, driving through the hot black night, following the lanes of light ahead of them, she told him, as he questioned her in detail, everything she could remember of the night of Clistie's death. Everything, that is, except the substance of her talk with Michael.

She didn't love Michael; but he had defended her when she needed defense, and he had promised to do so again.

"Beasley thinks I murdered Henry," she said. "You thought so, then."

John said, his voice suddenly rough, "I didn't believe it. Not in my heart, in spite of the evidence. And I wish now I'd cut off my hands before I made those notes that Beasley is using now."

They passed the bus stop and turned off the highway before he said, "I asked Bayne about the Cara Nome Company. He knew nothing of it. I'll question Hollis. And Thalia."

"Thalia!"

"Why, naturally. She knew, I imagine, more of her father's affairs than she admitted. She's nobody's fool, you know. She might be back of this Cara Nome project. She's smart, and she's Henry's daughter, don't forget that."

"But Thalia! It's impossible; a woman . . ."

"Not at all. Some of the most successful business frauds have been conceived and carried out by women. And don't forget, or perhaps I didn't tell you—the date of the letter throwing up the contract was after Henry's death. Eleven days afterward. And that," he said, "is another possible lead that came to nothing. The envelope and thus the postmark was destroyed long ago. Everyone whom we know to be connected with the case was here at the time. Whether the letter was sent to some obliging friend in New York to be mailed—or mailed right here in Ponte Verde, there was no risk, for at that time there was no suggestion of this Cara Nome business. Victoria, what did Clistie know? What did she do that night? Who was the maid that Agnew and Bayne both saw coming into the house just before Bayne came in? You say you talked to him from the balcony just before he came into the house. That must have been about the time he saw the maid. What time was it then?"

At best it was only a guess. Twelve, she thought—perhaps a little after. It was before she heard the car in which Thalia and Hollis had returned from Ponte Verde.

"I keep thinking, why did Clistie go to the pump house?"

152

she said. "And why was Joan Green murdered?"

"Well, of course," he said, "as to that, there is a perfectly simple explanation for both. Joan Green was murdered because she was wearing Clistie's dress, and Clistie went to the pump house because she was trying to hide."

The gates loomed darkly ahead of them. He turned and passed Judson's little house, dark too. It made her think of Judson and the spade, and she told him as they went along the drive. "That was Monday afternoon?" he said.

"Yes."

They turned again along the dark tunnel of liveoaks. A light burned at the entrance of the house. He stopped the car in the circle before the lighted doorway, got out and went around the car to open the door for Victoria.

He put out his hands to help her. And then drew her down close into his arms and said, holding her, his mouth against her hair, "Vicky. Oh, my little Vicky. I love you so much."

21

He kissed her hair. And, turning in his arms with the soft, dark night enclosing them both, her face and her mouth met his. He said, against her lips, "I've known it for a long time. Even last winter when I . . . Oh, Vicky," he said, and kissed her. He held her as if he never meant to let her go.

How long had she loved him like that? Had she loved him, really, long ago, even when she hated him?

But it didn't matter, not in the faintest, smallest degree; she knew, now.

He said, "I'm going to get you out of this horror, Vicky. Do you understand? I could have killed Beasley tonight when I came and found you there so—so little and white and . . ."

Someone not far from them laughed. Very softly but clearly, so the sound carried in the quiet darkness. Victoria turned quickly. She would have moved apart from him, but John held her and said, over her head, "Oh, Miss Frame? I didn't know you were there."

Then Victoria saw Thalia. She was standing in the rim of shadow beyond the little area of light from the door. Her slender figure was outlined palely in white against the shrubbery behind her. She came toward them, her face emerging slowly from the shadows, disclosing itself in beauty.

"I thought you didn't see me. I didn't know that things were like this. So this is why you've arrested Michael?"

"I didn't arrest him," said John.

"He was arrested. It doesn't matter whether you or Beasley

did it. The fact remains he's evidently to be charged with murder." She came closer. So close that Victoria could see a sharper outline of her face, and all at once it wasn't beautiful at all. "But I think I'm going to have something to say about that. At last," said Thalia.

There was a small pause. Then John said, "So you knew."

"Yes, I knew," said Thalia, watching him.

"I see. Then why didn't you tell before now? I rather expected it."

Thalia said to Victoria, "He's talking about his quarrel with my father. You see, my dear, this man you seem so devoted to, in spite of your engagement to Michael, knew my father. And quarreled with him and threatened to murder him. And tomorrow I'll tell Beasley and Colonel Galant all about it. So you see, Michael will have me, my dear, to thank for his freedom. How do you like that?"

John said quickly, "Victoria, this really is unimportant and in the past."

"But it's true," cried Thalia, smiling. "You can't deny it. It probably does not reflect very creditably upon my father; but at the same time, my father remembered it so well that he didn't want to come here last winter. Because—are you listening, Victoria?—because John Campbell lived at Ponte Verde and my father was afraid of him. He told me so and he told me the reason why." She whirled around to John. "I didn't tell last winter. I could see you were afraid I would. You wondered—then you decided I didn't know of it and you were safe. But I did know. I only kept my own counsel for"— she hesitated briefly—"for reasons of my own. But now that reason doesn't exist. And Michael"—she said, very softly, as gently as a warm little breeze in the tree-tops—"Michael will have me to thank."

"So it was you who cut the wedding dress to pieces," said John, matter-of-factly.

Thalia caught her breath in a sharp sound that itself was like the tearing of silk. "Victoria, you saw . . ."

"You must have done it before you went to Ponte Verde with Hollis," said John. "But you forgot the scissors. So, later, you crept into her room again, after you returned from Ponte Verde. She was on the balcony. . . ."

Thalia cried again, "You saw me!" Her hands (strong, little hands with the thumbs Agnew had said were criminal thumbs) darted out toward Victoria, and John caught her wrists and held them quietly for a moment, looking down into her small, rigid face. Then he released her. "Nobody knows," he said. "Nobody but Victoria and I."

"I suppose that's a bribe," flashed Thalia.

154

"No," he said, and turned to Victoria. His face was in the shadow, the light behind him silhouetted his tall figure. "It's true, what Thalia says. I did quarrel with her father a long time ago. I did threaten him. But I didn't kill him. Believe me, Victoria—and try to trust me. Will you?"

Thalia gave a queer kind of whispering laugh

"I do trust you," said Victoria.

He put both hands around her face and kissed her mouth. And said low, "Good night, my darling."

She went with Thalia inside the house. The sound of his car gradually died away. Thalia looked indecisively at the door and then, with an odd half-glance at Victoria, she locked and double-locked it. "There's a trooper on the terrace," she said, "and one in the kitchen. But still . . ."

They walked upstairs in silence. At the top of the stairs, Thalia hesitated, and then said in a whisper, "You had everything, do you see, Victoria? I knew, at least I guessed—oh, for a long time, really, I knew that my father was stealing. There were things—but I didn't care. Not really. Then when he died and it all came out, I lost—well, everything. However, he got money, he had it. After his death, I had nothing except what you gave me. And I lost Michael too. To you. You had everything, and still you took what I had left. And that night, Monday night—it was like a wedding dinner. It was more than I could bear. I thought how you'd look in white satin at the wedding. So I . . ."

"Thalia . . ." Victoria put her hand upon Thalia's. Thalia flung it off. She said, "What's the evidence they have against Michael? I only know that they've arrested him. He telephoned; they let him do that. He talked to me; but he didn't tell me why; they wouldn't give him time. Of course I know about his car, the night Colonel Galant was shot. Is that all?"

She listened, her small face concentrated and thoughtful while Victoria told her of the tire marks. And then briefly of the motive Beasley attributed to him. Thalia said, still whispering, "I suppose Beasley thinks you were both in the scheme—you and Michael. Where are you going?"

Victoria, turning to go downstairs again, said over the banister, "To telephone to the lawyer in New York."

"I've already done that. He'll come tomorrow—as soon as he can get away." She smiled a little. "You see, I did that for Michael, too. It's true, you know, Victoria, what I told you about John Campbell. My father—well, it's true. I didn't tell anyone last winter. I was satisfied to—let the investigation run its course."

The shadow of a smile was on her lovely mouth again.

Victoria said, "Because I was the principal suspect. Is that why?"

"Listen, Victoria, I knew from the first that you were going to take Michael away from me. If John Campbell suspected you of murder, then why should I tell anything that would—well, divert suspicion to him? Why should I go out of my way to be a friend to you? I thought, Let him go ahead and arrest you; let him charge you with murder. It"—a little cold look crossed Thalia's lovely face—"it wouldn't have come to—well, to a conviction. You're far too pretty for one thing. And I didn't think John Campbell would go that far. Not," said Thalia suddenly, in a sharp vindictive whisper, "that I cared. So now you have the truth. . . ."

"Thalia," said Victoria wearily, "surely you know now that Michael and I are not going to be married." She turned and walked down the hall.

When she reached her own door, Thalia came running softly after her. "Victoria," she whispered, and caught at her arm, "that doesn't make any difference, you know. I'm going to tell them that John Campbell threatened to kill my father. And that he—Victoria, aren't you listening?"

She went into her room, leaving Thalia standing there. She closed the door. After she'd locked it as she'd done—half incredulously—the night before she heard Thalia's light footsteps tiptoeing down the hall. John had said—oh, a long time ago, beside the blue and gray lake at Camp Blakoe—that Henry Frame was the kind of man someone might want to murder. As if he knew. Well, he had known.

But John hadn't murdered him.

It began to rain about two—a steady, rhythmic rain that sounded like stealthy, even footsteps on the terrace below. Walking up and down, never quite loud, never quite definite, always furtive and pursuing, haunting the house and all within it. But it was only rain; twice, at least, she went to listen to that steady, furtive patter on the terrace, to make sure that it was only the rain.

It rained all night.

It was still raining in the morning—a gray, chilly morning with the rain like thin impenetrable shrouds over everything, so the gray river and the gray Spanish moss all blended with it.

Bessie stayed in her room. Hollis disappeared, and no one knew where he'd gone. Thalia met Victoria coolly and announced that she intended to take a car to Pine Beach to meet the lawyer who would telegraph the time of his arrival at the airport. She asked Victoria politely which car she could use and said she wouldn't need anyone to drive her as she drove very well herself.

She hadn't talked to Beasley yet, she said, or to Colonel Galant; she preferred seeing Michael's lawyer first.

But she had already told Agnew of it. He sought out Victoria to tell her that and that he was going to see Beasley.

He was excited, and white and in a hurry.

"It makes Campbell a suspect," he said. "If what she says is true. And I think it is."

"Yes, it's true. He admitted it last night."

Agnew whistled. "And all that time when he was building up a case against you, Vicky, he knew that he himself had threatened Henry! That's what she says, anyway. What was their quarrel about?"

"I don't know."

"I'll bet Henry cheated him about something, some time. Same as he did with us. But still—when was it, do you know?"

"No."

He screwed up his face thoughtfully. "It must have been some time ago. Campbell's lived here for years; father was a doctor in Ponte Verde. Only time Campbell was ever away from Ponte Verde was when he went to school and a trip or two to Europe."

"How did you know that?"

He shrugged. "Asked. Michael thought it was queer that he —Campbell, I mean—just let the inquiry drop, when he still believed it was murder. Mike and I talked about it a few times; seemed queer. Of course, Mike hates him because if he hadn't made such a case against you before Beasley wouldn't suspect you now. That's why he's arrested Mike; to get him to talk or to get you to talk. I'll bet you anything. And Mike won't defend himself because he wants to protect you. Vick— however you feel about Mike, you have to admit it's damned decent of him. You see"—he lowered his voice—"You see, I happen to know when his tire marks were made on the road there by the magazines they're building. I—well, I was with him. That day you went to see Colonel Galant. Thalia was strolling around camp and didn't want to see them and I did, so Michael took his car out along that road. The men were working, and we couldn't see much, so we came back. But the tire marks were made then; there wasn't any rain the next day, you know, to wash it away. And as for the motive Beasley's cooked up against him, that's all bunk. Mike wouldn't have killed Henry on the slim chance of later getting you to marry him. That's nuts. And besides, if they say Clistie was murdered because she knew who murdered Henry, then it wasn't Michael because she wanted you to marry Michael. Didn't she?"

"Yes." ("I'm glad things are turning out as they are. For your sake. After Wednesday . . ." Clistie had said on that last day of her life.)

"I'd better get along." They were in the hall. Agnew began to struggle into a raincoat he had over his arm. "Sorry, Vicky, I'm in a hurry." Tugging at his raincoat, he dashed out into the rain, hurrying along the driveway toward Judson's cottage and the garage.

Judson. She'd better find him and ask him what he meant by his message about the spade and then she would take the station wagon to Ponte Verde and make them let her see Michael.

No one saw her leave the house. Rain hung around the shrubs and trees like a heavy mist.

But Judson was not in his house and he was not in the greenhouse. The colored boy, Albert, was painting porch chairs in the shed back of the garage and had not seen him. "But Mist' Judson, he kind of mad," said Albert, painting industriously. "Fin' a brown patch of grass roun' that ol' millstone in the garden and blame me. Say I dig up the turf. I didn't touch no turf. He kind of mad. Ain' seen him, though. Want something, Miss Vicky?"

She went inside the garage and backed out the station wagon. Then, leaving it in the driveway, got out again. "I didn't dig up no turf," Albert had said. And Judson had blamed him for it.

It was, however, the simple association of the words dig and spade that led her through the wet and dripping garden, along the hedge and out onto the little promontory above the river with the sundial, and the old millstone set into the turf. There she and Michael had stood that quiet night, with the white moonlight and the sharp black shadows all around them. No one was there now.

But there was a patch—more than a patch of brown turf. Even under the reviving rain a rim of grass looked brown and dead. As if it had been lifted away from the millstone it encircled. She knelt down, the drone of the rain everywhere in her ears.

The millstone was sunken deep into the soil and gradually the soil and grass had been pushed further and further toward the center of it, and over its surface so that, now, only the center was bare. She didn't remember anything of it. She had only a vague idea that it had been brought home by her father from some trip—as he brought Italian chairs, and Oriental rugs and Dutch landscapes. Now it seemed to her that the close-grown turf had been sliced back, as one would slice

158

back an orange, and then replaced. The grass, exposed to the heat, no longer protected by a hard and compact layer of soil, had naturally turned brown.

She laid back a crumbling, soggy section of it, disclosing the stone below.

Perhaps twenty minutes later she sat back on her heels, and slowly wiped her muddy, wet hands on the wet grass beside her.

The words Cara Nome—quite clear and distinguishable, in spite of grass and soil and rain—were carved into the surface of the huge old millstone.

So there was some connection between Cara Nome and the house. The Steanes—herself. And Clistie had known it. Had Clistie dug away the turf Monday afternoon when she asked for a spade? Had she remembered, vaguely, perhaps, back in the past, before the words had been hidden by turf? Had she remembered and taken the spade and confirmed that memory? Or was it accident?

But then what had it meant to her?

After awhile she realized that, obviously, the first thing to do was ask Judson where he had found the spade, and what he had wanted to tell her about it. It was now important.

And then she must tell John.

Judson wasn't in the garden. He wasn't in the pump house; she looked there, uneasily aware of the drumming rain upon the slanting door. She walked back along the strip of grass beside the yew hedge which separated her from the garden and house on one side, and the pine woods, veiled and misty with rain, on the other.

The path that entered the pine woods was deserted. Spanish moss dripped from the trees, and it and the rain blended into shadowy, misty vistas. She wondered if by any chance Judson could have gone that way.

She stopped. She went into the pine woods only a little way. And then she saw Hollis, in a raincoat, hurrying along the path toward her. His eyes were as light and colorless as the rain. His face had no color at all, and he was breathing rather quickly. "Vicky!" he said. "You—surprised me! I thought I was alone."

"I was looking for Judson."

"Oh. Well, he's not around. I've just been for a—a walk. I couldn't sit there in the house and—and wait. Wait to be arrested; wait to be charged with murder. They're making a case against me, you know, Vicky. They've got to charge somebody with murder. They've arrested Michael. They'll arrest me too. But it won't stop the murders. It won't stop anything . . ." His voice was rising higher and thinner; the pupils in his eyes were hard, shiny black circles. She put her hand on his arm.

"Hollis, I've been thinking about Clistie, the night she was murdered." Hollis had seen her then; Agnew had said he had talked to her, and that they had quarreled, he thought.

"Well, what about Clistie? I didn't kill her, if that's what you want to know."

"Hollis—it's that stone. That millstone in the garden, remember? Near the sundial."

"Well?"

"It's got the words Cara Nome carved on it."

"Has it?"

"Do you—know anything about it?"

"About that?" he laughed shortly. "So Clistie asked you too?"

"Asked me what, Hollis?"

She must be very patient with him, she thought. His face was drawn, and he looked as if he hadn't slept for days.

"Asked you about a Cara Nome Company. She asked me, you know. Seemed to have got it into her head that I was trying to defraud somebody and that Henry knew it and I—well, pushed Henry into the river. But I didn't." He stopped and took hold of her arm suddenly and tightly and shook it. "I didn't. You believe me, don't you? I'm a coward—maybe. I hated Henry, yes. He—he had been after me about this Cara Nome Company too, the day before he died, but I didn't, I tell you, I didn't . . ."

"Hollis, wait. I don't understand what you're saying. Please tell me again." He was breathing heavily, like Bessie when she was excited. "What did Henry ask you? What did Clistie ask you?"

"Just what I've told you," he said. "Henry got hold of me the afternoon—the very afternoon before he died. He had some kind of letter about a Cara Nome Construction Company. And Clistie too; she'd got the letter from his room, the morning after he was killed. She said she went into his room before the coroner got there; to straighten it up, she said. You know Clistie; she was always nosey. Anyway, she found this letter. She wouldn't show it to me. But she as good as told me that all this time she'd been thinking that I killed Henry, and she kept the letter and wouldn't tell the police because she was sure they'd let you off and she was just as sure they'd convict me. She never liked me. I knew that; but we—the Steanes—were her life. That's what she said." His voice was not high and nervous now; it was very quick and low, as if the trees, as if the rain, as if the long gray wisps of Spanish moss touching his shoulder might hear. He said, "You believe

160

me, don't you, Vicky? That's right. I've got to have somebody believe me. Every time the telephone rings, every time a car drives up to the door, I think they're coming after me. *Me—Vicky . . .*"

"They aren't going to arrest you, Hollis," she said as soothingly as she could. "Hollis, tell me again. Slowly, so I—so I can understand."

He wrenched his arm away from her and rubbed his eyes with wet, nervous fingers. "I can't sleep."

She'd better get him to talk to John, she thought swiftly. She said, "Hollis, tell all this to John Campbell, will you? He'll . . ."

"Tell him! No—not anybody." He stopped suddenly and said in a more normal voice, "That Cara Nome, though, on the millstone—I do know about that. I remember seeing it when I was a kid, before the grass grew over it. It was your father's idea. He and your mother were trying to find a name for the house. Finally, one of them—they'd just been in Italy —suggested Cara Nome. They were sentimental, you know, in those days. Your father had brought that millstone from some of their travels; he had the name carved on it. But they never named the place. And your mother died . . . I expect mother remembers, or even Colonel Galant—but I don't know anything else about it. I—I'll walk this off, Victoria. We'll talk later. Just now—being here in the woods and thinking about Clistie and Joan . . . That's all, Vicky," he said suddenly, and jerked his arm away. She saw him disappear beyond the tall, yew hedge.

She'd better go straight to Michael, she decided, staring into the gray vistas of the pine woods.

Cara Nome, and a letter; and Clistie, and Cara Nome again, but this time, with a different—such a different significance.

Yes, she'd go to Ponte Verde. She'd not look for Judson now.

She glanced down the path in the direction Hollis had come from, hurrying from the gray wraiths of Spanish moss and rain, and saw the spade.

It was leaning nonchalantly against a tree, a little removed from the path, actually toward the river.

When she reached it, however, it was only a spade. Nothing unusual about it, nothing significant. Except that, against the tree, too, between it and the spade, as if it had been tossed there hurriedly, was a small wet bundle—gray, sodden, soiled, with pieces of leaves and grass clinging to it. It was so much the color of its background that it was visible only because Victoria looked closely. It was a gray-silk dress. She did not entirely unroll the sad, wet little bundle; she was sure it was Joan Green's dress.

She straightened up slowly. The path curved toward the river just there, and, to reach the spade, she had had to go still nearer the low bank. Standing there, holding the wet, crumpled silk, trying to think, she looked down at the water —almost at her feet, gurgling a little around the willows. A log floated there, caught in the willows sluggishly.

Only it wasn't a log; it was a brown leather jacket, sodden and muddy. It was Judson—his arm caught around the willows much as Henry's had been, and the gray leaves trailed in the muddy little eddies over his face.

The river was swollen with the rain, the brown thing caught there in the willows moved a little with the muddy current.

She moved backward. The pine woods had known it; they were shocked and still and gray along those shadowy, wraith-like arches. The rain knew it and made a dreary kind of dirge upon the leaves above her head.

She was running along the path, back toward the house. But suddenly she realized that Hollis was between her and the house. She skirted the garden, ducking behind the wet hedge. She reached the station wagon in the drive. Her hand was so steady on the ignition, on the starter, on the wheel that it was as if it acted independently of her own will. Yet she didn't really hear the roar of the engine.

She passed Judson's small, dark little cottage; she passed the gates; she turned into the highway and passed the bus stop where Joan Green came to keep that disastrous appointment.

She had almost reached Ponte Verde when it seemed to her that a car was following her.

22

The rain was heavy; she had turned on lights. The windshield wiper made quick swipes across her vision that cleared it for fractional instants at a time. The car behind her had turned on its lights, too. She could see them in the mirror above the windshield—glimmering distantly through the sheets of rain behind her, pale in the gray daylight, like two bright eyes following her.

Just outside Ponte Verde there was a turn which would take her to the main road going toward Camp Blakoe. Michael was at Ponte Verde; John was at Camp Blakoe. There was no time to consider. She glanced up into the mirror, the station wagon swaying along the slippery road; it seemed to her the following lights were closer.

Probably they were not following her at all; probably they would go on straight into Ponte Verde.

She swung around the corner, toward the direct road to Camp Blakoe.

It was a narrow road, just there, lined with liveoaks, streaming with rain; a mile further on it joined the highway that went to Camp Blakoe. She peered into the mirror trying to see the crossroads behind her that she had just passed, trying to see whether the car she had thought was following her turned or went straight into town. She didn't see Michael's long gray car swooping out of the rain directly in front of her until it was almost upon her; Michael was driving. Both of them tried to stop and glided past each other. Then she came to a full stop and rolled down the window. The long gray coupe was backing up, toward her. It stopped and Michael leaned out.

"Michael!"

"What's wrong? Where are you going? What's happened?"

"Michael, it's Judson. I just found him. In the river. His head . . . Oh, Michael, Hollis did it! There was the spade and Joan Green's dress; I've got it here. I was going to Camp Blakoe to tell them there. I couldn't go in the house. Oh, Michael . . ."

"I'll go with you. He must be crazy." A truck had come up behind him and was honking loudly. Rain streamed between them, cascading down the sides of the cars and along the windshields. He shouted above the rain and the honking of the truck, "I've got to pull up. Look—I'll follow you. Go ahead."

She started out slowly, keeping at a slow speed until she could see, in the mirror, that Michael's car had turned and was coming toward her. Then her foot went down on the gas throttle again. Michael must have been released from arrest; probably he was starting home, taking that road out of town when she met him. She remembered the car she had thought was following her and looked into the mirror. Michael had turned on dim lights too and they were close behind her, but in the rain she could see no one behind Michael's car. Probably the other car had gone on, as she thought it might, into Ponte Verde.

Michael was right, of course; Hollis really was crazy; it would be his defense; she thought of his face, drawn and white, his eyes, his jerky, almost incoherent words—everything he had said and done in the brief, dreadful encounter. She saw now that it had been dangerous. He had been running then from murder.

Michael's car drove up alongside, and he hailed her,

through the rain, rolling down the window. "There's a convoy on the main road," he shouted. "Better take the other one—I'll show you . . ."

He waved and drove on ahead through the outskirts of the little rain-drenched town, and out along a country road, narrow but deeply rutted, showing the passage of heavy trucks toward camp.

It was difficult driving; the ditches were already almost road level with muddy water. Michael's car plunged on ahead of her, swerving, righting itself; her windshield wiper stuck and after several futile attempts to free it she gave up. The streaming rain obscured her vision. Michael stopped to wait several times and then drew his car up to the edge of the road, jumped out of it, a raincoat over his head and ran to the station wagon.

"I'll drive," he said. "You'll go in the ditch. Get over. What's the matter with your windshield wiper?"

He too worked with it and gave it up and leaned forward to peer through the blinding rain. "Tell me about it," he said. "What makes you think it's Hollis?"

She told him, lifting her voice above the roar of the rain and the engine, the rattle of the old station wagon. She told him of meeting Hollis; she told him of Hollis' talk with Clistie the night Clistie was murdered and the reason for it; she told him of the spade and of Cara Nome and what, so far, they knew of it; she told him of Hollis' eyes and what he had said and how he had left her there in the pine woods—to go along in the direction from which he'd come and find what she had found.

She showed him, still rolled up in a wet, soiled little bundle the gray silk dress that Joan Green must have worn. He glanced at it, and then back at the slippery, winding road, the deep muddy ruts and the blinding rain ahead.

"Hollis didn't actually say he'd murdered Judson, did he?"

"No, but he—Michael, don't you understand?—I saw him running from the woods! I saw his face. . . ."

"I know. But all the same—you see, John Campbell one time threatened to kill Henry Frame. Thalia told me. . . ."

"Yes, but John . . ."

"Did she tell him she knew? Did Campbell admit it?"

"Yes. Thalia said she'd known all along. She didn't tell because—well, that isn't important. But there's no evidence against him, Michael."

He leaned forward over the wheel, watching the road. "There's a motive. That's been the main question—motive. Campbell himself has emphasized it constantly. Too constantly; he must have felt pretty safe when Thalia didn't tell.

164

He must have thought she didn't know. It would explain why he tried to get you charged with murder; if you, or anybody else was convicted, it would clear him. And why he dropped the case with the suicide verdict. He was in an ideal position. The State's Attorney, arrayed on the right side of the law, no question of his own implication in a murder it was his duty to investigate."

"Why would he warn me only last Monday?"

"I don't know, unless he knew that Clistie was on his trail. Perhaps he was planning a way out for himself. The earnest, conscientious former State's Attorney doing his duty, in spite of everything. Did he know I was coming that night?"

"No," she said and then remembered. "Yes. . . ."

"Perhaps I was to be a way out, too! Henry was murdered only a couple of days or so after I got here. If a murder was committed on the very night I arrived again, it might provide another valuable suspect."

"But the Cara Nome business, Michael? He could have known nothing of that."

"Do you know what his quarrel was with Henry? When it was? Anything about it?" He swerved around a turn, and righted the car. "There was something that brought them together. Perhaps that was it. Vicky," he was looking indecisively through the rain at the road and sparse black stumps of pines around them, "I must have missed the turn," he said. "Can you see the camp?"

The windshield was clouded with faint gray steam; he wiped a space with his hand; she peered through the window at her side. She could see nothing but wet, dreary stretches of half-cleared pine growth—sandy, wet, dotted with outcroppings of thick palmetto growth. There was no glimpse of any of the low buildings of the wide-flung camp.

"But this must be the general direction. Oh, yes," he said, "there's the lake off at the left. The road must follow it. We've missed the new road, but this will be all right."

The station wagon plunged rattling and careening ahead. The road had imperceptibly narrowed still further, had become only a rut through the desolate, deserted growth of pines and palmettos. At any rate, no car would follow them there.

"Agnew came and told Beasley this morning how my tire marks got on the new road the other day. On that basis Beasley had no reason to hold me. Beasley questioned me a long time last night and let me out this morning. Vicky, what do you suppose Clistie did with the letter? According to Hollis, she must still have had it Monday night. I wonder if she got hold of this Green girl after she talked to Hollis. Yes, that must be it. She knew the girl was in the office at camp and thought she might be able to find out who was back of the Cara Nome affair—that leads to Campbell again. Anyway, Clistie wouldn't ask Colonel Galant because he would do things too thoroughly. He'd not stop, no matter who was back of it, and Clistie must have been still worried for fear it was Hollis. And Joan Green liked him and wouldn't give him away. So Clistie—yes, she must have got the girl out to the house; met her at the gate, maybe; walked with her along that strip back of the yew hedge, perhaps—certainly somewhere out of sight, for I was there on the porch at the time and didn't see them. I thought once I heard somebody talking somewhere, it was distant and muffled. I didn't pay any attention to it. . . ."

"Yes, I heard that too. I was on the balcony."

"I know. I heard you. Well, anyway, the murderer must have got onto what was going on. There's plenty of places to hide in a place like that. He must have caught a glimpse of the girl in Clistie's dress; if Joan hid from him, say, in the pine woods and it was dark there and if she was then in Clistie's dress and he'd seen her only distantly, crossing that moonlighted strip of grass, perhaps, he might have followed and slipped up behind her and strangled her, quick—hard—thinking it was Clistie. Yes, that's it. . . ."

It conjured up a horrible picture against the rain ahead.

"And," said Michael, "when the girl was dead and he saw her face and realized his mistake, he—he took off your belt and got the girl in the river and came back to murder Clistie. And then Clistie, when you told her about the scream, must have thought of the girl. . . ."

"Yes," cried Victoria, remembering Clistie's pale, frightened face. "It's why she wouldn't call anybody to help her. It's why she wouldn't let me or Agnew go with her. She didn't want anyone to know."

"And then—well, then she must have gone down to the garden, maybe to the pine woods and looked for the girl. That would explain the mark of the slipper heel. It must have been made by Clistie. She—what would she do next? I suppose she would hide." He glanced at the gray bundle. "That's it, of course. She had to hide evidence of the girl's having been there. Clistie must have known then who murdered her."

"Then she must have thought it was Hollis. She wouldn't have protected anybody else."

"Unless—perhaps she saw the murderer. Perhaps she was terrified, trying to escape him. Perhaps she wanted to keep the dress—and the letter, Vicky, the letter!—from falling into his hands. The dress looks as if it had been buried. She had a spade that afternoon. She was in the garden when I got there, late, and I believe she came from the direction of the millstone. That's it; she must have left the spade there and remembered and buried the dress there, too. And left the spade again where, later, Judson found it—and the dress and the letter! I suppose she'd eluded Campbell—the murderer anyway—but then he knew he had to get her. He caught a glimpse of her, *or she saw him;* she ran along the yew hedge, perhaps, out of sight. And hid in the pump house. But he'd seen her and *knew she had seen him!* And Cara Nome, whatever it is, was a danger signal from the first!"

("Poison to somebody . . ." John had said that, too. But he couldn't have murdered.)

"That letter—yes, Vicky, it must be there. Shake out the dress. Look . . ."

Her fingers shrank from the clammy silk. She unrolled the dress and there were glimpses of white; white crumpled cuffs, a white crumpled collar—a newspaper clipping and a paper, folded like a letter.

"*Is* it the letter?" cried Michael.

The newspaper clipping was a printed list: a list of contractors. Reading unsteadily as the car bounced over the ruts, she cried, "It's the Cara Nome Company! In a list of contractors. It's marked with a pencil—it looks as if it had been cut from the Ponte Verde paper. . . ."

"What's the letter?"

There was no envelope; without examining the outside of the damp, wrinkled paper she opened it and read, with difficulty, for Michael was trying to see the letter and drive at the same time and the car jounced frantically. It was an official-looking letter; with the letter-head of the Secretary of State. It was addressed: Mr. Philomel Jonson, in care of the Steane Lumber Mills, in New York. Her eyes leaped that and went to the letter.

She read it aloud quickly: "Dear Mr. Jonson. We are herewith sending you, per your request, the copy of the charter of incorporation for the Cara Nome Construction Company. According to our records this original charter was dated June 9, 1918; the stockholders are the same as those of the Steane Lumber Mills. Since your own records have been destroyed by fire, we are glad to state further that this company is still in good standing, having fulfilled the legal requirements for this State, in that, every year, a report has been made of a meeting of present stockholders and the election of officers. Since you were fortunate in preserving the corporation seal, it will not be necessary to apply for a new one. Yours very truly . . ." She looked at the letter. "But there wasn't any fire! I don't understand. This sounds as if the Steane Mills owned the Cara Nome Company!"

"Probably they did. And do. It must have been a subsidiary company, formed years ago for some purpose or other; it was not uncommon. But, it hasn't done business, then, for a long time. Although Henry must have seen to it that it kept its charter, just in case he wanted to resurrect it sometime."

It was raining harder; Michael was leaning over the wheel, talking above the clatter of the rain.

"I suppose—why, yes, Vicky! I see exactly what may be the explanation of it. Somebody remembered it, perhaps found the old corporation seal somewhere and dusted it off and decided to turn a penny for himself. It would have to be somebody, of course, who somehow could deliver some lumber without paying anybody for it and then pocket the cash; using the Cara Nome name as a front. Simple, if it had worked. Apparently it didn't."

"You mean steal the lumber from the Steane Mills? Falsify the books as Henry did?"

"Not necessarily from the Steane Mills. Vicky, I wasn't going to tell you because—well, never mind why—but the quarrel Campbell had with Henry was originally over money. Thalia told me and asked me not to tell, but Henry got Campbell's father's money away from him. All of it. It seems that he (he was a doctor) knew of the Steane Mills, of course, and wanted to buy some stock; thought it would be a good investment. So he went to see Henry and just thrust the money at him. Henry had that effect on people; on us, on everybody, even your father. Before the old doctor died, he told Major Campbell—younger then and impetuous. He went to see Henry. What it simmered down to was that Henry flatly denied it and hadn't given the old doctor any sort of receipt. Campbell was wild; threatened to kill him; swore revenge; it seems the doctor was sick and needed the money. He died and—anyway that was the beginning of their quarrel. Well— we'll take the letter straight to Colonel Galant."

She folded the letter again without looking at it, staring instead into the gray sheets of rain.

And the car jolted to a sudden stop. Michael gave a groan. "Tire's flat—oh, for God's sake—in this rain—where's the tools? Vicky, I hate to ask you to move, but I've got to have a jack from under the seat. I hope the spare is all right."

Holding the dress and the letter, she stood in the rain while Michael jerked up the seat. She still couldn't see the camp, but the lake was just below them so they couldn't be far from it. The road would lead them there, although it wasn't much of a road, winding over hummocky ridges and around palmetto growth. The banks of the lake which lay within the camp had been cleared and leveled and planted. Here, outside the camp, the bank was sandy and steep, with palmettos growing thickly along its ridge.

Michael pulled out the jack and shoved the seat back. "Get in quick, Vicky," he said, "you'll be drenched. I'll change the tire."

He closed the other door as she got back into the station wagon. The rain drummed loudly upon the top of the station wagon and slashed against the windows. They were very near the lake, just above it, in fact. The bank sheered steeply down toward it, over the sandy ridge and, through a gap in the palmettos, she could see the gray water. It looked deep. She glanced to make sure that Michael had put on the brake.

He had, but he wasn't working at the tire yet. The car was quiet, except for the loud drumming of the rain. Her thoughts drifted off again. She was thinking about the maid who had entered the house, thinking that the appearance of the maid must mean something, must be important, when she realized that Michael wasn't changing the tire; was not, in fact, near the station wagon at all; was not anywhere.

She got out of the car and hurried around it; she called to Michael. There was nothing but streaming rain and tall, weird thickets of palmettos, and the ridge of palmettos outlining the bank of the lake. She walked around the car again and leaned into the driver's seat out of the rain.

As she did so she glanced up into the mirror and saw something that either had not been there before or she had not seen. That was the faint glimmer of two automobile lights, paled by the gray daylight, blurred by rain, on a ridge some distance, she thought, behind the station wagon, although it was difficult to tell because of the rain, and because the two lights were almost hidden by a clump of palmettos; she had caught only the smallest glimmer of light from them. Rain poured down between.

The following car, then, had found her again.

It had missed her at the crossroads, or had loitered along, after she met Michael, waiting its chance. As it waited now, half-hidden, there in the gray rain and thick palmettos, only that glimmer of light flashing in the little mirror had betrayed it.

He'd forgotten to turn it off. Or had been too hurried . . .

Hurried! But she must hurry—run, escape, do anything. Where was Michael? What had happened? Her mind raced,

169

stopped, raced again. If she got into the station wagon and drove as fast as she could go over that hummocky, narrow road, could she outdistance the car? Waiting there.

She could hide in the palmettos; she'd have to hide in the palmettos. That was what the Negroes did when the hurricanes came. For days they lived in the palmettos, huddling there, waiting . . . She kept the station wagon between her and the silent, waiting car. She had reached the nearest thicket of palmettos when she thought, gasping for breath, rain blinding her, that she had left the gray dress and the letter in the station wagon.

That was a mistake.

She couldn't go back, though. She tried to hold her breath and listen and there was only the rain. Had whoever was in that following car crept up to Michael as he bent over the tire —with the heavy jack perhaps there on the ground within reach of murderous and ready hands? She must try to reach camp. She must keep the ridge of palmettos between her and the car. The sand was thick and wet, the sparse grass was slippery; the rough palmettos scratched her hands and her face; she couldn't breathe properly. The rain was so heavy that the whole thicket seemed to tremble and sway. She stopped and listened again.

So this, she thought, suddenly and despairingly, was how murder happened. A silly, ludicrous and horrible game of hide and seek. Running through sand, slipping and grasping at palmettos that tore like ribbons through wet hands, listening, afraid that in the next thicket and in the next an ambush waited, pausing to push through the palmetto growth and try to see if one was followed. And how close that pursuer was! She listened again.

So she heard the rustle and the rasping of palmettos near her; she heard it and tried to escape the entangling harsh leaves, but not in time. A blinding crash neatly and instantly blotted everything out in pain and in blackness.

23

Fingers were on her wrist. Her head ached; she wasn't going to open her eyes. But Agnew's voice said waspishly, "I saw your eyelids move."

She opened her eyes.

Agnew was kneeling beside her. "You're all right," he said. His face was very white, but his voice was cross and nervous. "They said it might be a concussion. Have you got a concussion, Vicky?"

She was in the little library of the Colonel's house. She was on a sofa drawn up before the fire. She remembered then and started to get up, and Agnew—rather gently—pushed her down again. "You're not to talk," he said. "But you're not to feel sleepy, either. If you feel sleepy, it's a concussion. . . ."

"But what—*Agnew, what happened?*"

"It's all right, I tell you." He reached out and caught her foot and waggled it rather affectionately. "A hell of a business," he said glumly. "Anyway, it's about over now. Thalia and Beasley and Hollis and Michael and John Campbell are all over in Colonel Galant's office. I was there, too; but I came back to—came back here. Vicky, do you know what? I'm a *deus ex machina.*"

"*Agnew* . . ."

"If you talk, I'm to call the nurse and leave." He sprawled down on the hearth rug, his chin on his hands. "Of course, she didn't tell *me* not to talk. And, after all, when I supplied the motive . . . That's how I was a *deus ex* . . ."

"*Agnew, do they know about* . . . ?"

"Yes, yes! Everything! I . . ." He stopped, and said rather wistfully, "Of course I made my mistakes. I didn't know about Campbell and Henry. They'd had a terrific row. . . ."

"I know, I know. But *John* . . ."

"Shut up! Honest, Vicky, if you don't, I'll leave. But I don't think," he added broodingly, "that it would hurt you to know about the subsidiary company. It's not exciting. Except it began it all."

"I do know about it. There was a letter. . . ."

"Yes, they've got the letter. They think there are finger-prints on it, too. Showing who actually touched it after Judson was murdered. That's why he was murdered. They think it happened just after dinner last night. Only how did you . . . ? No, don't answer. You can talk later. But that letter was the big link, the important link; although any hint of Cara Nome was like a red flag. There was even the attack upon Colonel Galant, which luckily failed—although he never remembered what, if anything, he knew about it."

"It was the millstone; he must have seen it years ago when . . ."

"*Be still!* But the letter was the real dynamite. It was the final link; it showed Henry knew and had taken steps. It showed Clistie knew and had given it to Joan; it linked every-thing together. It was proof. Probably the murderer thought escape was still possible: bop you on the bean, dump you in the lake, the letter safe—well, anyway," he went on hurriedly,

171

"Colonel Galant had a wire from the Federal men this morning about the Cara Nome Company. It seems that they sent a copy of the corporation charter and a letter to the Steane Mills—because that was the real address of the Cara Nome Company, the address they had on file—instead of to the address that was given in the letter (they've got that on file, too) from this Philomel Jonson. . . ."

"I know about him too. Agnew, *what* happened? Where is John?"

"You like him, don't you, Vick?" His face was very sober. He looked at the fire and said, "If you'll be quiet, I'll tell you. I'll break it gently. . . ."

"You don't need to break it gently!" she said, exasperated and helpless. When Agnew got that look on his face there was never any use in arguing with him. She looked around for a telephone, and he saw her.

"Vicky, I mean it. Keep quiet."

Her head swam. She put it back on the cushions. "Oh, all right."

"Well, you see there were, really, about five or six lines of inquiry." He checked them on his fingers: "Why did Clistie act so suddenly—so sort of urgently? Who built up evidence against you and why? What about Clistie's dress on the girl? What of this Cara Nome business? And what was the motive? And you see, there's one answer for all of them."

"That's what John . . ."

"I'll take the Cara Nome business first; it was a subsidiary company; well, it seems that somebody wanted to make some money and found a way by which he hoped to get hold of some of our lumber, falsify the books, and then sell it to the government and keep the money. There was the old company seal, and with an available copy of the charter . . ."

"Agnew, I know about that. I told you. . . ."

"Shut up. Henry thought it was Hollis. Hollis denied it, and . . ."

"And after Henry was murdered the Cara Nome contract was canceled. But Clistie had the letter. . . ."

"And she was on the trail of Cara Nome. I wish you'd . . ." He stopped and looked at her sharply. "How'd you know so much? How . . . ? No, no! You're not to talk! Anyway, if you can bear to hear me out, Clistie had thought it was Hollis; but if it wasn't Hollis, she was going to act quickly—she had to, Vicky. Because of you . . ."

"Me?"

"Why, naturally. On account of your wedding. . . ."

The door opened and John Campbell came quickly into the

room. Agnew scrambled out of the way as John knelt beside her and took her hands.

"John," she whispered, "was it . . . ?"

"Sure," said Agnew. "There was just one answer to everything. Why did Clistie get so worked up about it all at once? Answer: because something new—some new element entered her calculations, something that made her work fast. There was only one new element. Who stacked up clues against you and why? Who could have known about Cara Nome and tried to make use of it? Who had a motive? All the same answer."

"Motive . . ."

John held her hands tighter. "Agnew told me what it was. After Agnew saw Beasley this morning he came on to me. The thing began with an attempted fraud by using the name of the old and forgotten Cara Nome Company."

"Never mind all that," said Agnew disgustedly. "She knows about it."

"But the point is," said John, "Henry, after Hollis denied it, guessed the true answer. There was nobody else; it meant exposure, finish, really; so Henry was killed. And the contract, out of fear, canceled. But then—then there was a really big prize, you see. Bigger than had been dreamed of, at first. Only at the last moment it slipped out of his hands— only a few hours after Clistie gave a hint that she knew something of the Cara Nome Company. Clistie was got rid of, and that girl, and—you see, Victoria, it was to be the same situation again, that had once before brought you into his arms. A duplication, a repeat; you were to be in danger again, harassed, clues and evidence against you—and you were to turn to him again. As you had done before."

"*Michael*," she whispered.

The fire crackled. John's hands were warm and tight. She said, finally, "He told me the truth, then. Everything. As it must have really happened that night. He was talking hard, talking so I wouldn't see or suspect, talking . . ."

"Tell us, Victoria."

They listened. It didn't take very long really.

"Why, then," said Agnew excitedly, "he must have met Clistie, really, *at the millstone*. And something he said, or did, or the way he looked made her suspect him. He was already here that afternoon when we got home. It was that afternoon while we were gone that she asked for the spade. Up to then, she had wanted Victoria to marry Michael; we know that. But something must have happened—something important. I think that Michael met her there at the millstone and somehow aroused her suspicion, so she began to think that if the murderer were not Hollis it must be Michael, and the point was she, had to find out right away. One of the reasons she had wanted Vicky to marry Michael was so that she would never marry Hollis. This is surmise," said Agnew, hesitated, then shook his head. "No, it's not surmise at all; the ingredients are there. It had to happen like that: the spade, his arrival, Cara Nome on the millstone which probably surprised Michael so he almost gave himself away, Clistie's sudden inquiry. That's on the letter, in Clistie's writing . . ."

"What's on the letter?"

Agnew's eyes glittered. "Ho, so there's something you don't know! You had it; it was on the outside. . . ."

"I didn't look there. Tell me. . . ."

"It was a few words in Clistie's writing. Evidently a memorandum for Joan Green. This: 'Name is Michael Bayne. If not Hollis am sure Bayne is back of it.' It was in ink," said John.

"That's why it was the link!" cried Agnew. "He might have got out of everything else. Oh, Vicky, he and Thalia were the only ones that really remembered you wore gold slippers. He —pretending to protect you—said you wore yellow slippers; Thalia said gold. Nobody else remembered. He thought they'd let you off, you know, as they did before. And he had an ace up his sleeve because Thalia had told him about John's quarrel with Henry. She told him after the jury's verdict of suicide, after he'd dug up proofs of Henry's embezzlement. The way your father left things, Vicky, invited embezzlement of one kind or another. But anyway—he seems to have believed that in a pinch he could use his ace—turn suspicion to John. But when it came to his life or your money, Vick . . ."

John interrupted; "I had quarreled with Henry, as I told you. Ages ago, when I was younger than I am now, and . . ."

"I know."

"Colonel Galant and Beasley knew all about it too," said Agnew. "John told them. He told the Judge of the Circuit Court too at the time of Henry's death; they all told him to forget it. They knew the old doctor, at least the Judge and Beasley knew him. And I guess they knew John. . . ."

"Thank you, Agnew," said John, cheerfully. "Now get out."

"Get out?" said Agnew in wounded surprise. "Why, look here! You haven't—why, there's lots yet—why . . ."

"Get out."

"Wait, now, John. Vicky, he asked Judson about the spade; told him, maybe, you'd sent him, got the letter and dress. Left them in the pine woods, intending to return when it was dark. Then he was arrested. Yes, that's it. Oh, and Vicky, it was, of all things, the old corporation seal that must have started it all. John got a wire just now. An old filing cabinet was sent from the New York office to the Seattle office. The seal was accidentally left in it. So he found it and thought, now how can I use this?"

"Yes. That's all though," said John. "So . . ."

"And the maid!" cried Agnew in triumph. "The dress! You see, Vicky, that was the same answer too. Because Clistie must have been scared. She must have met Joan Green, talked, and then wanted to go into the house to get the letter. Probably when Clistie telephoned Joan, she wasn't sure whether or not Joan would co-operate to help Hollis. After she talked to Joan she wanted to give her the letter, because Joan needed the definite information in it. Let me see," Agnew said, "yes, I think that's what happened, because the letter was so important that Clistie wouldn't have given it to the girl until she was sure that she still cared for Hollis and would help. Clistie, in her heart, was afraid of Michael, and she was afraid to pass him with the important letter in her hand, so she made the girl change dresses with her. Clistie was always close-mouthed and independent; probably she had not told Joan anything about Michael, but being frightened, while she was in the house she wrote the note to Joan on the outside of the letter. Then also she must have searched Michael's room. I'll bet she did! And I'll bet that's where she was when you looked in her room for her, Vicky. And Michael had already come upstairs, got into your room (he knew you were on the balcony), got the belt and waited till I'd gone into my room (I followed him right upstairs, you know) and then he went down again. He didn't go near his room; I'll bet anything; and Clistie was there searching!"

"How do you know?" said John, quite seriously.

"Well, I . . ." Agnew stopped in full flight and considered. "I *think* so," he said stubbornly. "And Vicky, the answer to how Clistie's dress happened to be on Joan Green is the same answer too. Because if Clistie went to the house, and was scared, she certainly wasn't afraid of *me*. But Michael was walking up and down between the garden and the house. Clistie had to pass him, somehow, to get into the house. And she was scared and the girl's dress was gray. Like a maid's uniform—white collar and cuffs. So they traded. And Clistie was the maid."

"Nobody could see that her slippers were blue in the moon-light," said John. "But that wasn't proof, and it wasn't a motive. The other maid was Michael—always an opportunist, too sure of himself because Henry's death had been so easy, Michael in . . ."

"In the white dress of Ernestine's, taking advantage of the maid story. We nearly lost you, you know—in the car, I mean. You shot past us hell-bent in the station wagon; we turned around and went after you, and lost you in Ponte Verde. Drove all over hell in the rain till we came up just as you must have seen us, but Michael didn't, and . . ."

"Run along, Agnew."

"But I provided the motive, didn't I, John? When I told you that Vicky'd told him, that night, she couldn't marry him and why."

"Yes," said John, "you did."

"If he could duplicate the situation, be the big hero again, save the girl from the jaws of the law—he thought you'd fall for it again, Vicky, and . . ."

"*Agnew*," said John. He jerked his black head toward the door.

"Oh—well . . ." Agnew got up slowly. He shambled toward the door. "Oh, all right," he said and went out.

A moment or two later he opened the door again, put his head inside and looked disappointed. Victoria was on the sofa; John was sitting on the rug looking into the fire, his head against her arm. Agnew said, "Well, gosh, no use in leaving you two alone!" He banged the door.

John said, "I do love you, Vicky. I think it's for life. I—well—how about it?" He waited a moment and then turned, kneeling, and put his arms around her.

Off in the distance a bugle sounded, clear and high. From the artillery range they could hear guns—very distant but clear, too, in the silence of the little room.

His arms tightened around her. Agnew opened the door again, took a long look, saluted smartly and withdrew.